D1505064

GRENDEL'S
GAME

GRENDEL'S GAME

ERIK MAURITZSON

THE PERMANENT PRESS
Sag Harbor, NY 11963

For information, address:
    The Permanent Press
    4170 Noyac Road
    Sag Harbor, NY 11963
    www.thepermanentpress.com

Library of Congress Cataloging-in-Publication Data

    Mauritzson, Erik—
        Grendel's game / Erik Mauritzson.
            pages ; cm
        ISBN 978-1-57962-398-2
            1. Detectives—Sweden—Fiction. 2. Serial murder
        investigation—Fiction. I. Title.

    PS3613.A88315G74 2015
    813'.6—dc23   2015013737

Printed in the United States of America

In memory of my uncle, Julius,
who taught me to love books.

1

A Departure

Saturday, October 8. Three days before the cannibal's letter arrived and his life changed forever, Walther Ekman was at Stockholm's Arlanda Airport. It was an unusually bright, cloudless fall afternoon. Beyond the tinted glass wall overlooking the runways, sunlight glinted on taxiing planes, their engines' noise muted by the thick glass.

Arlanda was a clone of other large international airports: an anonymously modern, noisy sprawl, crowded with a bustling mix of the world's nations. Rushing to make flights, some trailed wheeled luggage, others waited in long lines at ticket counters, their faces edged with impatience or boredom. Clusters of people had gathered near gate exits searching expectantly for arriving family and friends, or like Ekman, were there to see them off.

His parents were leaving for a month's visit with friends in sunny Malta, and he'd driven them to the airport from their apartment in Gamla Stan, the city's medieval center. Why spend three hours to come from Weltenborg when we can simply take a taxi, they'd protested. But Ekman insisted he wanted to see them off.

He felt guilty about not visiting for two months. Most of all he was afraid he might never see them again, although he knew this was irrational: Gustaf, 83, and Maj, 81, were in good health, and Malta was safe.

Ekman's wife, Ingbritt, had agreed with his parents that it made no sense and decided not to come. She was working on her tenth children's book and had a long scheduled meeting with a new illustrator that she told Ekman she couldn't afford to delay.

"Give them an extra hug from me," she'd said that morning as she took his coat from the hall closet. He'd bent down to kiss her good-bye, as he had every day for thirty-three years, his six foot five dwarfing her petite figure.

His mother's simple blue pantsuit contrasted with his father's jaunty outfit: Gustaf wore a tan linen jacket with white trousers, a bright red tie, and a Panama hat tilted at a rakish angle. He leaned on an ebony cane, but claimed it wasn't needed, it was simply decorative.

Ekman noticed that although he had a protective hand on Maj's elbow, his father was ogling two pretty young women walking by. Gustaf glanced over, saw his son watching, and winked, as if to say, "I'm still not too old to look." Maj had also noticed Gustaf's actions and gave Ekman a faint, resigned smile, her comment on his father's futile efforts to ward off the rapidly advancing years.

Ekman was fifty-six, but only felt his age occasionally. He wondered what it must be like to be truly old. Was a young man inside, bewildered to be peering out through rheumy eyes, still not resigned to mortality? His father seemed to be like this. Perhaps it was always this way.

The line at the security post was taking forever, so Ekman used his police credentials to speak with a supervisor, and shepherded his parents down the corridor to their gate. He kissed and hugged his mother, feeling her slender bones, grown frail as a bird's. Then, with his arm around the old man's thin shoulders, he kissed him on the cheek, something he hadn't done in many years, bringing a look of startled surprise to his father's face.

"Have a wonderful time. Call us when you arrive," Ekman said, as they turned and headed down the ramp to the waiting plane.

Looking at their receding figures, he had a persistent sense of inevitable loss. In his work he frequently confronted unexpected death. This was different. He knew these two people he'd loved since childhood would die; it was more certain with every passing day. But he wasn't ready to accept it.

Ekman would not have believed that in a few days his premonition of impending death would become a reality.

2

Grendel

Sunday, **October 16.** Grendel rubbed his gloved hands together and stamped his boots on the concrete floor to keep warm, his breath lingering in the chill air. Despite the numbing cold, he smiled with satisfaction as he looked around the refrigerated room.

Bathed in a white fluorescent glare, the meat locker's floor sloped toward a center drain; in the left rear corner, attached to a wall spigot, was a hose, coil on coil, ship style. A metal roll-down door took up a third of the right wall.

The ten-foot high, rough cement ceiling was fitted with connected steel trolley racks supported by I beams. Pulley chains attached to large hooks allowed heavy weights to be hoisted up to the racks where they could be shifted about easily.

Suspended from the hooks by coarse ropes wound tightly around them were bulky cocoons. Barely visible, swathed beneath thick plastic sheeting, were ashen faces with blind, staring eyes.

On a wooden butchering table against the left wall were kitchen shears next to an object shrouded in bubble wrap. Grendel picked it up and placed it on a bed of dry ice in a plastic-lined, white cardboard box. Covering it with tissue, he put a note on top, and pushed the lid *closed. He hummed a repetitive, off-key tune as he wrote an address on the lid, then wrapped twine tightly around the box. Stepping back, he admired his handiwork.*

"A gift to remember, boys," Grendel said with a smirk, nudging the body nearest him. It slowly swung back and forth on its hook.

3

Pawn Opening

Tuesday, October 11. This raw, overcast morning, the River Lagan ran gray-green in the weak light. There was a scent of dampness from mist, gradually clearing as a pale sun rose.

Weltenborg's riverfront was lined with stone warehouses recently converted to luxury apartments, some popular ethnic restaurants, and a few imposing mansions, their immaculate lawns sloping to the riverbank. Outside the city, the Lagan turned southwest, widening near a new industrial park, then cutting through brown, stubble fields. The river was almost hidden miles later in dense pine forests when it emptied into the narrow Kattegat strait separating southwestern Sweden from Denmark.

Stark white and aggressively angular, the county police headquarters overlooked Stortorget, the city's main square. A block of ancient, dilapidated buildings had been razed to make room for it, despite the loud protests of preservationists. Its five stories now loomed, incongruously, over the remaining weathered structures fronting the cobblestoned plaza.

The county councillors, by a narrow vote, had approved the demolition and controversial design. They'd insisted

Weltenborg needed "a fresher image, something to show we're in the twenty-first century."

Ekman, like many in the city, believed they'd lost their minds. He remembered with something like affection the run-down building four streets away: until last year, it had served for three decades as police headquarters. This new one was less crowded, more efficient, but far too austere, too sterile for his taste. He doubted he'd ever feel comfortable there.

The cannibal's letter arrived in his morning mail.

Ekman was curious about it because there was no return address. Slitting the envelope, he removed the pages:

My Dear Chief Superintendent Ekman:

"I am not an animal! I am a human being!"
The poignant words of the "Elephant Man," that
pitiable, grossly disfigured creature, echo in my
mind. Is it inappropriate for me to feel a strong
kinship with him, since I am not pitiable, dis-
eased, nor an animal? My deep sense of injustice is
exactly the same, and so with him I feel entitled to
say, "I am not a monster."

On the contrary, many of you find me hand-
some, charming, and robust, which I ascribe in
no small measure to the diet you find so distaste-
ful. Your revulsion is quite unreasonable, but I
acknowledge it's partly my fault, a failure to com-
municate. How can I persuade you to see things in
a more balanced light?

First, let me say with a certain pride, that each
of my food sources—I refuse to use the prejudicial
"victims"—has died an instantaneous death. They
do not linger, as most people do when dying.

I abhor the infliction of suffering. It is uncivilized, uncalled for, and appeals to the worst sadistic impulses, although, admittedly, anyone may experience a fleeting desire to inflict pain. I emphasize "fleeting." Our unfortunate history, however, is replete with whole societies reveling for centuries in torture and horrendous deaths. I find this profoundly repugnant.

Second, I never treat the young as food, even though their tender flesh is tempting. I push such thoughts into the dimmest recesses of my mind, although you do not.

You are, no doubt, taken aback by this observation; however, a moment's reflection will reveal its truth. The youth of food is prized, even advertised as inducement: "Get your baby back ribs, suckling pig, tender veal, kid, or squab," young this, and baby that. Their names fill cookbooks and menus. It doesn't bear thinking about.

You protest, how can you take the lives of sentient beings? It seems unnecessary to point out that if food is not vegetable, fruit, or insect, it is sentient, some of it very sentient indeed. Pigs, for example, are known for their high intelligence and emotional sensitivity, as are, to some extent, the apes, dogs, horses, sheep, cattle, goats, birds, deer, elk, moose, bear, raccoons, opossum, squirrels, rats, whales, porpoises, seals, and on and on, that fall into voracious human maws.

All these creatures respond to kindness, and all (perhaps fish and octopi, as well) can suffer, which, as Gandhi said, is much more relevant than whether they can reason as humans do or speak. These few comments should make clear that I am no more a monster than you, and perhaps less of one.

Third, and final observation. Even if you accept my arguments, you still blanch at including humans as acceptable food, though people have considered each other edible on numerous occasions: the Donner party comes to mind, as do tales of shipwrecked mariners, and Leningrad under siege. And there are many other instances, from New Guinea to South America to Jeffrey Dahmer.

But these, you argue, were extraordinary irregularities, done with repugnance under great distress, or reflect the bizarre religious practices of primitive peoples, or the pathology of a madman (which, by the way, I assure you I am not). They are not an everyday, shopping-at-the-super-market sort of thing, which is what you do.

This is a failure to understand my position. People have, from time to time, treated each other as food—and have considered nonhumans as so inferior and disposable they can be consumed without a pang of conscience. I have done the same and will continue to do so, not out of necessity, but like you, for the quite sensible pleasure of a varied and tasty diet. As someone once said, "Chacun à son goût." You just happen to be mine.

With deep appreciation,
Grendel

Ekman shook his head in disbelief. Either this was just a hoax or the writer was one twisted, arrogant bastard. But he was puzzled. He'd gotten publicity-seeking-crank confessions before to murders, kidnappings, rapes, robberies. They'd all been ongoing cases. This one was different: they had nothing involving cannibalism.

He put the letter down and, opening a desk drawer, removed a pair of white latex evidence gloves. He'd already handled the pages, but didn't want to make matters worse.

Pulling the gloves over his meaty hands, he slowly reread the three double-spaced pages on cheap computer paper. It was even more disturbing on a second reading.

Picking up the envelope, Ekman held it near his desk lamp, turning it from side to side: it was unremarkable and had little beyond the obvious to tell him. Postmarked yesterday in Weltenborg, legal size, it was addressed to him in bold, block letters with a black marker.

He replaced the envelope on his desk, removed the gloves, and heaved his 270 pounds out of the oversized brown swivel chair. Its worn leather fitted him perfectly after thirty years of hard use.

Rubbing his chin, he paced up and down his fourth floor corner office. The triple-paned, soundproof windows made the hurrying pedestrians and traffic below seem spectral.

4

~~~~~~

Ekman

That morning, Ekman had opened his eyes at five forty-five. Turning in bed, he saw that Ingbritt was up already. It was pitch dark outside as he shuffled in sheepskin slippers to the adjoining bathroom and fumbled for the light switch.

Staring back at him from the mirror were dark brown eyes set in a long, heavy face with deepening furrows from nose to mouth. His expression was somber. You look like you take yourself much too seriously, he thought; lighten up. He attempted a broad smile, but the mirror told him it looked strained and somewhat menacing. Shrugging, he gave it up as pointless.

Sharpening his straight razor on a leather strop, he shaved his graying beard closely so he wouldn't end the day with five o'clock shadow. A blistering needle-point shower brought him fully awake.

Going to the closet, he selected one of six vested suits: all were solid black worsted. Out of a large, mahogany bureau his parents had given them that had been in the family since his great-grandfather's time, came a folded, starched white shirt, a black tie and socks. From the shoe rack, he took a pair of soft, thick-soled black shoes that helped bear his increasing weight.

Ekman had once overheard colleagues joking that he was always prepared for a funeral. Twenty years ago, he'd dressed in black when Bernt Osterling was killed. His partner of ten years had died trying to stop a robbery while Ekman was on leave. Since then he'd always worn black on duty. It somehow eased the guilt he still felt at not having been there for Bernt. The work is serious, depressing, he told himself; it's never bright and cheerful, why dress as though it is?

As he came downstairs, he could hear pans being shifted on the range. The aroma of cooking sharpened his appetite. This morning there was creamed oatmeal, scrambled eggs, bacon, and toast slathered with lingonberry jam—all taken with several cups of strong black coffee. Ingbritt, worried about his weight, had once tried giving him just oatmeal with soy milk, "For your own good Walther," she'd said; but he'd rebelled. He believed he needed adequate fuel for the long day ahead and shouldn't skimp; calories be damned. Still, he felt guilty about ignoring his expanding waist.

Everything was served on white china that stood out against the blue linen tablecloth. He ate while browsing through two morning newspapers, first passing several sections to his wife.

Her gray-blue eyes peered at him through bifocals over the tops of their open papers. He seemed engrossed in an article. "Anything?" she inquired.

"The usual," Ekman replied, meaning the too familiar mix of local scandal, political conniving, and foreign catastrophe that constituted the daily news. Nevertheless, he read it all carefully, consigning the information to the back of his mind before turning to the editorial page.

The *Sydsvenska Nyheter* pilloried Magnus Amdahl, the deputy foreign minister, for trying to cover up involvement in a prostitution scandal similar to an infamous 1970s affair. The justice minster then, Lennart Geijer, had given his name to that one. Ekman thought it typical of sanctimonious politicians to pretend they were immune from human frailties when everyone knew they were among the most susceptible.

"And you?" he asked her.

"Halvorsen has published a new novel. The reviewer thinks it's boring."

"Is that likely?"

"Frequently," Ingbritt responded with a slight smile. She had a professional's detached view of the literary world.

"Will your day be interesting?" she asked.

"I hope to God not," he muttered, folding in half the paper he'd been reading and placing it on top of its similarly creased mate as he pulled himself out of the chair.

The drive in his black Volvo S80 took fifteen minutes down tree-lined Brunnvagen through light traffic. There's little, he thought, more ludicrous than a big man struggling to get out of a tiny car, so the luxury was worth the cost.

Ekman thought about the coming Sunday. He was looking forward to a long planned visit with their son, Erick, an orthopedic surgeon, and the two little granddaughters. It had been almost a month since he and Ingbritt had seen them, although they lived only an hour away on the coast in Halmstad. It had been even longer since they'd visited their daughter, Carla, in Malmö, and he missed the smiling face amd tousled blond hair of his young grandson, Johan.

It's the damned work, Ekman thought. The children have become adults mostly without my help, and the grandchildren barely know me. Thank God for Ingbritt; somehow she still loves me despite everything.

What he couldn't admit, even to himself, was that the real problem wasn't the work, it was his obsession with it.

Ekman pulled up at seven thirty as usual. He waved at the windowed booth housing the underground garage's guard, who raised the red-and-white-striped steel barrier. Parking his car in the center of his assigned space, he thought about taking the elevator to the fourth floor, but resisted the temptation. Ingbritt always urged him to walk up, and while he often ignored her advice, today he took the stairs. He arrived more than a little out of breath.

His thirty-two-year-old assistant, Inspector Enar Holm, was already at his desk in a cubicle outside Ekman's office. He looks more like twenty-two, Ekman thought. He was far too thin, a constant reproach to his own expanding girth. He noted with approval Holm's blue suit, crisp white shirt and sober tie, elegant on his tall, slender frame.

"*God morgen*, Chief. The DC wants to see you right away."

"I don't suppose he said what it was about?"

Holm shook his head.

Hanging up his coat and hat, Ekman sat down and glanced through the twelve-page draft policy directive from the National Police Board that Holm had placed on his desk. It set out updated instructions for detectives in charge of crime scenes. Inaccurate and tedious, Ekman thought: typical of bureaucrats with too little experience and too much time on their hands.

Putting it to one side, he got up and walked to the two windows looking out on the square just as the old-fashioned mantel clock on the bookcase chimed a quarter to eight. Taking the engraved gold watch inherited from his grandfather from his vest pocket, he clicked open the lid and checked the time. With a grunt of displeasure he went to the clock, opened its beveled glass door and adjusted the minute hand. He knew it was compulsive, but did it anyway.

Sitting down, he opened a desk drawer and took out the needlepoint cushion cover he was working on. Eight years ago, a drunken driver had totaled Ekman's car, confining him to a wheelchair with a broken leg in a hip-length cast. To help pass the time, Ingbritt had given him a needlepoint kit. He'd discovered that stitching while he thought through problems was relaxing and helped him concentrate. Now, his hands automatically began adding a scarlet thread to the half-completed, intricate floral pattern as he weighed several possibilities.

The most likely subject seemed the recent rise in home burglaries. The commissioner must be getting increasing flak about them, he thought. Yesterday's had been at County Councillor Westberg's, in daylight. He'd immediately assigned an inspector to deal with it.

The burglary had been mentioned on the local TV evening news. Politically, this must have been the final straw. He'd probably have to shift senior detectives from more important investigations.

He put the needlepoint back in the drawer, and heading for his meeting, gave the policy memo to Holm.

"They want our thoughts on this, strange as that seems. It should be revised: it's too detailed where it doesn't have to be, and not detailed enough where it needs to be. And try making it more interesting. I'll be with Malmer for who knows how long," he said with a grimace.

It was only a few minutes from his office to the elevator, then to the fifth floor, and down the beige carpeted hall to the deputy commissioner's office. Annika Dagard, secretary to the commissioner and his deputy, was at her desk between their offices. She lifted a stylishly coiffed gray head from the document she was reading, and smiled as he approached.

"He'll be with you in just a minute," she said, looking at a light on her telephone console that quickly went out. "There we are, go right in." It was exactly eight A.M.

5

Malmer

Seated behind his massive walnut desk, shaven-headed, grim-faced Olov Malmer looked intimidating, and meant to have that effect. His secret was in the tall, red leather armchair, raised so that his waist was level with the desktop; only his powerfully built torso was visible. Stunted, bandy legs that barely skimmed the floor beneath the desk made him a short five foot five. He tried to conceal his height from his colleagues, hiding his sensitivity behind a brusque manner. It proved very effective in keeping people at a distance.

"So, Walther, come in, come in, and sit down please," he said in a grating, high-pitched voice. He intensely disliked tall men standing over him.

Ekman's ample rear perched on one of the two hard, straight-backed wooden chairs in front of Malmer's desk. They weren't intended to be comfortable or prolong meetings.

Malmer looked directly at him for several moments without speaking. It was a trick he often employed to fluster subordinates. Ekman was used to this; imperturbable, he waited him out.

"We have a serious problem," Malmer said at last.

"Yes, I know. I'm dealing with Westberg's break-in. I've already assigned an inspector."

"That's not adequate. This can't be treated as a routine matter. What else will you do?"

"All right, I'll assign Alenius and Rosengren to the investigation," naming two senior inspectors. "If additional people are needed it will be disruptive, but it will be given priority."

"Consider this your most important task until it's solved. I expect daily reports," Malmer said.

"You'll have them every morning. Perhaps we'll get lucky and this will lead to solving the other burglaries."

"It will take more than luck, Walther. Hard work is what's needed. The commissioner and I expect quick results," he said, slapping an open hand on the desk to assert authority over Ekman.

"Of course," said Ekman, getting up to end the discussion and heading for the door.

One of these days, he fantasized, he'll push me too far and I won't be able to resist picking up that pompous little prick by the neck and banging his shiny skull against the ceiling. He understood why Malmer's stature led him to harass taller men; he knew he should empathize. But the mental image of Malmer's terrified expression when he lifted him out of his rigged chair brought a wide grin to Ekman's face as he closed the door behind him.

Arguing with Malmer about the real priorities of police work was always a mistake. He, and his friend the commissioner, political appointees who'd arrived a year ago, had shifted all daily responsibilities to him. They preferred to spend their time meeting with council members like Westberg, lunching with other influential people, and junketing to pointless police conferences around Sweden and Europe.

Ekman missed their predecessors whom he'd dealt with more or less amicably for fifteen years. They'd retired, one after the other, leaving him to establish some kind of working relationship with the bureaucratic Malmer and the amateur commissioner.

He had Holm arrange a meeting in two hours with the new inspectors he was going to put on the Westberg case. Ekman knew they'd resent it because a more junior officer had already been assigned, but it couldn't be helped. This was part of the job he intensely disliked . . . catering to political superiors.

6

The Choice

After rereading the cannibal's letter, Ekman walked to the windows, back to his desk, and then stood motionless again at the windows, looking out into the square for a few moments before sitting down. He reached into a drawer for his needlepoint and began stitching.

It may be just a practical joke by someone who wants me to run with it and end up looking ridiculous, he thought; there are plenty of people around here who'd laugh their heads off if I took the bait.

Perhaps it's a ploy by the animal rights people. They'd love to have the police treat the letter seriously, give it publicity, and get the public worked up.

If either possibility were right, the best course was to ignore it.

But what if that's not what it was about? How can we know whether to take it seriously? It would be irresponsible to just set it aside and there was a murder, or worse still, a series of murders. Suppose, after killing, the writer sent the letter to the media. How could we defend ourselves when we hadn't tried to prevent a murder we'd been warned about?

The fundamental problem was where to begin a possible murder investigation without any evidence of a crime, let alone a body.

If the letter was a real threat, the writer is a man. A woman wouldn't set out to be a cannibal; it just felt wrong to him. The letter's style was stilted; he was trying too hard to be cute. He was no doubt insane, but clever.

Ekman hesitated. He didn't want to, but had to get Malmer and the commissioner involved.

He replaced the needlepoint, and, pulling the gloves back on, took the envelope and letter to Holm. "Put on some gloves and place these in clear covers please, make three copies, and give them back to me. Package the originals for Malmquist at the forensics lab. Get a uniform to hand deliver it to him. I'll let him know it's on the way."

Ekman went back to his office and phoned Ludvig Malmquist, the director of the National Forensics Laboratory in Linköping. They'd worked together for more than a decade.

"It's been weeks since I heard from you, Walther, how are things?"

"The same. The family is fine. Malmer still enjoys being an obnoxious bastard far too much. And you and yours?"

"Olivia and the children are well thanks. At the lab we're overworked, short-staffed, and underpaid. The usual."

"Ludvig, I need your help with something special." Ekman knew he was using his friendship with Malmquist to jump a long queue of other jurisdictions with forensic specimens awaiting analysis.

"I was afraid you were leading up to that," Malmquist said in a flat voice. "What can I do for you?"

"I've gotten a letter from a maniac who's threatening a killing spree. I'm sending it by courier. Can you tell me anything about it by tomorrow evening?"

"You don't ask much do you?" He paused. "A maniac you say? Okay. We'll do what we can."

"My fingerprints are on the envelope and letter. The fingerprints of my assistant, Inspector Holm, are on the envelope only. They should be in your database."

"Well, that makes it so much easier, Walther," said Malmquist drily. "I'll do my best. I'll call you tomorrow. Late."

"I owe you one, Ludvig."

"Actually, Walther, I've lost track of how many you owe me, but never mind."

When Holm returned with the copies, Ekman said, "Call Malmer's office and tell Annika I need to see him again right away."

He looked up from his desk at Holm, "You've read it?"

"Yes."

"What do you think?"

He valued Holm's opinion. His intelligence and drive had made him an inspector in record time. More than that, Ekman had become fond of him; Holm was almost a second son.

"There's nothing you can do except treat this as a real threat."

"Good. It helps to know you agree. It may be a prank, someone looking for attention, but we can't disregard it."

"Don't tell me you've already broken the Westberg case?" Malmer asked.

"Something else has come up. You need to read this. It just arrived this morning," he said, handing him a copy of the letter.

"Sit down, for God's sake," said Malmer. Ekman sat while Malmer read.

"This is bizarre, preposterous. You're not suggesting we take this seriously?"

"It may be somebody's sick idea of a joke, but I don't think we have a choice. If it's real, something happens, and it came out that we ignored it after we were warned . . ." He trailed off.

Malmer hesitated. The fear of adverse publicity was his strongest motivation. He hated to rely on Ekman, but depended on his expertise.

"The letter's being sent to forensics. We may know more tomorrow. It could be a challenge, as well as a warning. The killing may already have begun. I have another copy for the commissioner," he said, giving it to Malmer. "I think he should be informed."

"I scarcely need you to tell me that. I'll speak with him right away."

"Tell him we can assume a few things."

"Such as?"

"The writer is an intelligent, literate man. The style of the letter isn't a woman's. Neither is the threatened cannibalism. Whoever he is he likes attention. He may send this to the media at some point, but I think not yet. He wants to challenge us first. We need to treat this as a real threat and spoil his fun before he starts, if he hasn't already."

"I'll take this to the commissioner now," Malmer said, but didn't stand. He avoided getting up when Ekman was in the room.

"Would you like me to come along?" Ekman knew Malmer would hate this, but couldn't resist needling him.

"I can handle this quite well alone, thank you," he said, his face reddening with irritation. "I'll get back to you."

"You've got Alenius and Rosengren waiting in your office," Holm said.

"I almost forgot."

"We've been working major crimes and now we're supposed to give a routine break-in priority?" protested Rosengren again. He's a short, fireplug of a man with side-combed, thinning red hair. His partner, Alenius, tall, gaunt, and taciturn, just nodded agreement.

"It's what needs to be done, so get on with it. Malmer wants daily morning reports. You don't have much time." Ekman gestured at the bookcase clock.

Defeated, Rosengren got up and looked at Alenius, who was leaning against the wall near the door.

"Okay, Chief. If that's the way it is . . ."

"That's the way it is. Don't either of you take it too hard. This isn't personal," said Ekman, standing. "On the contrary, the reason you guys have been picked is because you're the best and everyone knows it."

Rosengren half smiled at this as they left. Alenius remained expressionless. As they walked out, Holm stuck his head in, "Malmer wants to see you again."

7

The Team

"**I**'ve just spoken with the commissioner," Malmer said. "He thinks there could be public hysteria if this letter gets out. We need to keep a lid on it until we have something to say, and then can report progress. After all, as far as we know, no crime has been committed. There may be no need for anyone to be alarmed. Probably nothing has happened. But still, the commissioner wants you to quietly, I repeat *quietly*, handle this as a potential major problem before it becomes one. I agree with him."

"We're not starting from zero." Ekman had been thinking about what the letter writer must be like and had reached some tentative conclusions.

Malmer raised thick, dark eyebrows, prominent under his shining dome.

"Whoever he is, he probably doesn't have a serious criminal history. If he had a record that would lead us to him, he wouldn't have sent the letter. It would make it too easy for us. He's also probably under fifty, or we'd have become aware of him. He may have been treated for mental illness, but not confined to a mental hospital. Again, that would make it too easy.

"He's sent us this virtual declaration of war because he feels he can play hide-and-seek with us. He believes he's a genius and we're imbeciles. We'll no doubt hear more from him. I think this publicity-hunting lunatic, sooner or later will go to the media. And he's told us point-blank there have been, or will be, victims."

"So how would you proceed?" asked Malmer.

Ekman had thought of a strategy. He'd been the youngest chief superintendent in Sweden when he was appointed twenty years before. By now he could have been a DC, or even a county commissioner, but Ekman couldn't tolerate the constant need for political maneuvering that occupied higher ranks. It was bad enough at his level.

"We need to get a team into high gear right away, so if he goes public, we can say we're already on it and didn't want to precipitate a panic. First, we look at unsolved missing-person cases for the last three years. Second, we consult a psychiatrist to build a profile.

"This should be done simultaneously. I have to warn you the search will eat up manpower. We'll be working overtime, too, and this will impact our budget. If this is a hoax, or a publicity stunt by the animal rights people, I think they'll come out of the woodwork soon enough to claim credit."

"I'll have to speak with the commissioner again about your budget and overtime. Be careful you don't go too much over. And while you're dealing with this," Malmer added, pointing to the copy of the letter on his desk, "don't forget about Westberg."

Ekman got to his feet and put a hand on his back, aching from sitting in that damned chair too long.

"We should be able to give you and the commissioner more information soon."

"I expect you'll have something. Is that understood?"

Holm was on the phone. Ekman tapped on his desk to get his attention and gestured toward his office. Holm raised two fingers, and continued talking.

When he came in, Ekman said, "We need to look at missing persons, starting with the newest cases, going back, let's say, three years, focusing first on people over sixteen and under sixty." He paused. "They're probably the tastiest."

Holm got it and grinned. That was one of the things Ekman liked about him.

"I'll get started now."

"Enar, no one expects you to do this alone. We've got authorization from on high for a crew and overtime. We have to work fast. This takes priority over whatever they're doing. Draw up a list of six candidates. I'll pick three, plus the two of us, and we'll meet first thing tomorrow."

In an hour, Holm returned. He'd not only listed six detectives, but what each was working on, and who could take over their cases.

Looking at the list, Ekman said, "You've picked the same people I'd have. Therefore this must be right." He glanced up at Holm who smiled and left.

Ekman now regretted assigning Rosengren and Alenius to the Westberg case, but it couldn't be helped, he'd already committed himself to Malmer.

Going out of his office ten minutes later, he handed Holm the list. "I've checked three names. Let's plan on the five of us getting together in my conference room at eight tomorrow."

Holm picked up the phone to make the first call.

8

~~~~~~~~~~~~

The Opponent

Ekman looked through his battered address book and found the phone number for Jarl Karlsson, a psychiatrist and longtime friend. Perhaps, he thought, it was time to keep all the numbers on the new smartphone he'd been issued. But modern technology was more trouble than it was worth; he'd have Enar set it up for him.

Two years before, Jarl had proven invaluable in solving the brutal murder of a nine-year-old boy. His profile had helped Ekman narrow the field of suspects to the innocent-seeming killer, a grandfather and music teacher.

This was one of the many cases that had increased Ekman's visibility as a criminal investigator. It was publicity he didn't want, and tried hard to avoid.

"Jarl, it's Walther. How are you?"

"Just fine, Walther. I'd be delighted if this were a social call, but should I assume it's not?"

"You're right, unfortunately. Can I come by today? It's urgent." There was a pause while Karlsson checked his schedule.

"Six this evening is the best I can do I'm afraid. Use the front entrance."

Karlsson had an office in a small addition to his house with a separate, side entrance for patients. Ekman would be meeting him in the main house.

"Thanks, Jarl. See you then."

He called Ingbritt to tell her he'd be working late. Over the years, she'd become inured to his frequent late hours.

"Shall I hold dinner for you?"

"Set something aside for me, but you go ahead and eat. I should be home by nine."

An hour later, looking at the clock, he saw it was almost one and decided to have lunch at a popular Chinese restaurant a few blocks from headquarters. He disliked eating alone, but apart from occasional lunches with Enar, found himself doing it most of the time. Somehow Ekman had grown socially distant from his colleagues; they never got together for a drink after work. Perhaps it was his senior rank, or simply the person he'd become over the years. It was a fact of life he sometimes regretted, but had become used to and made no attempt to change.

As he walked along busy Brannkyrkagatan, the sky was a deepening gray that promised rain, and if it became just a little colder, snow. The restaurant was almost full, but he managed to get a small table near the windows.

After some hesitation, thinking guiltily about his weight, he gave in and ordered half a Peking duck, his favorite Chinese dish. Folding a thin crepe around the sliced meat and scallions, he munched contentedly while looking at passersby. There were Africans and possibly Middle Easterners among them. Some of these foreign-looking people were probably Swedish citizens.

Diversity in Sweden had moved well beyond the international mix of Stockholm, bringing with it cultural changes with which he wasn't entirely comfortable. He knew Gustaf, proud of their family's Swedish heritage, didn't approve of this new world. Just as he hadn't when Ekman had decided not to follow in his footsteps and gave up a boring corporate law practice to join the police.

Past time to drop your father's worn-out prejudices, Ekman, he said to himself. Adjust to the present, or become old and irrelevant. Whoever these people were, they were in his city and he was personally responsible for their safety. Over his years on the force this sense of obligation had come to weigh more heavily on him as violent crime increased.

He'd looked at studies that tried to identify the causes of the increase, but they seemed inconclusive. Perhaps we just have better data, he thought, and nothing has really changed. Yeats's words, "Things fall apart; the centre cannot hold; Mere anarchy is loosed upon the world," kept running through his mind. He was trying to make the center hold as best he could, while the world shifted rapidly around him.

Karlsson had a large, rambling house in the country in the exclusive Arboga district, on the opposite side of Weltenborg from Ekman's home. It was thirty minutes down Fahlbergvagen from police headquarters. The house was on a side street, hidden at the end of a long, curving gravel drive, and sheltered by a copse of tall beech trees. The setting sun filtered through the bare branches as Ekman pulled up in front.

At his ring, the door soon opened on Karlsson's smiling, creased face. He was only a few years older than Ekman, but already looked elderly, with sparse white hair, and stooped shoulders. His clear, light brown eyes, however, were those of a much younger man.

"Come in, come in, Walther," he said, reaching out to shake Ekman's hand. "It's good to see you."

Taking Ekman's coat and hat and putting them in a closet by the door, Karlsson asked, "And how are Ingbritt and the family?"

They moved down the wide center hall toward his cluttered, book-lined study on the left.

"Everyone's fine. And Teresia?" he asked, referring to Karlsson's wife. They had no children.

"Very well, thanks. She's at a church meeting this evening and will be sorry to have missed you. Can I get you a drink?" he asked, busying himself at a little bar against the right wall, as Ekman sat down.

"Perhaps a small Renat." He liked vodka the traditional way, straight and ice cold. Because of his size, he knew from long experience that his blood alcohol level wouldn't rise much from a short drink and the effect would be gone by the time he had to drive home.

"I'll have the same," said Karlsson, pouring two glasses from the bottle he'd taken from an under-the-counter refrigerator.

After they'd settled in armchairs across from each other with drinks in their hands, Karlsson asked, "So what can I help you with, Walther?"

Ekman reached into his inside jacket pocket and, taking out a folded copy of the letter, handed it to Karlsson.

"This came for me in the morning mail, posted yesterday in town. It had no return address. The original is at the forensics lab."

Placing his drink on a small side table, Karlsson put on a pair of gold, wire-rimmed glasses. When he finished reading, he looked up at Ekman.

"Strange, and very interesting. You've quite a problem here, Walther."

"What do you think, Jarl? Is this just a hoax or something much worse?"

"It could be an elaborate joke, and it reads like an animal rights satire. If it's their idea of a prank, it could backfire on them by diverting police from real crimes. In any case, you'll soon know whether this is a publicity stunt, but I don't think it is. You're right to treat this seriously. I think this was written by a very disturbed person."

"What type of maniac are we dealing with?"

"Let's not call him a 'maniac.' It oversimplifies. We need to take a nuanced view to try and understand him."

"So you agree it's a man?"

"Yes," Karlsson nodded. "It's unlikely this is a woman pretending to be a man. Notice how he compares himself to the 'Elephant Man'; a woman wouldn't have made that allusion."

Ekman told him his theories about the writer's age, literacy, and lack of a record.

"Yes, I think you're right about all that. Certainly, he's intelligent. It seems to me he's not going to have a record that would make him easy to find. Let's also assume for now he's somewhere between twenty-five and fifty."

"Is there anything else you can say?"

"Oh, there's quite a bit more. The letter is revealing. You're dealing with a 'hollow man,' a psychopath. He feels his emptiness and wants to fill this inner void with some humanity . . . literally." Karlsson gave Ekman a thin smile.

"He sets himself apart from other humans. He's cleverer than anyone, including the famous Chief Superintendent Ekman."

"What would he seem like to the casual observer?"

"Or even to those who think they're close to him. Of course, no one is. He's probably single, although he may have casual intimate relationships with women . . . or men. He's isolated inside, always focused only on his own needs. But on the surface, as he's told you, he's 'charming, handsome,' very likable, and may have friends who think the world of him. This is often typical of the psychopath. He wears what some psychiatrists call 'the mask of sanity.'"

"But he has rules about killing . . . no children . . . and how painlessly he does it, or will do it. If he can be believed," said Ekman.

"He may be trying to throw you off. Psychopaths are typically deceptive and manipulative. So it might be best not to exclude children as possible victims. But perhaps he's telling the truth, because everyone, even a psychopath, will attempt to justify his actions, no matter how terrible. It's part of his rationale for what he's compelled to do by inner drives he doesn't understand and can't control.

"He may boast of not killing children, but again, notice he says he's tempted. As far as painless killing goes, he gives no thought . . . it totally escapes him . . . that there will be an enormous burden of psychological pain for others. He doesn't think about the grief of the families and friends of his victims.

"He justifies his actions as no more immoral than those of any person of normal appetites. Walther, haven't you found that evil often boasts of superior moral virtue? He said he considers himself less a monster than you."

"Many people think the same," Ekman said, grinning.

"His letter to you makes this personal in other ways. This is someone who presents himself as a misunderstood Grendel. He's singled you out. That, of course, makes you his Beowulf, though I can't say you look the part." There was a faint smile on his face.

"He wants to humiliate you personally, not just the police. You've become the opposition. He's not simply warning you, but issuing a direct challenge." He paused for a moment.

"At the very end of the letter, he says 'You' are to his taste. That 'You' could mean people generally, but it could also mean 'You, Walther Ekman.'" Karlsson looked at his friend. "You'd make wonderfully hearty meals for several weeks," he said, straight-facedly.

"You're not serious?" said Ekman, taken aback.

"Unfortunately, I'm quite serious, Walther. This could become extremely personal. You know where to begin looking for him?"

"We're going to check missing-person cases for the last few years for leads. Any suggestions?"

"You're right to think he's already killed. His letter is evidence of a later stage of his disease. He's committed perfect crimes and has never been found out. Now he wants his genius known. More than that, he wants to see if he can be caught. Maybe he even wants to be caught, so he can bask in the notoriety. And he's decided you're the one most likely to catch him."

"It feels right. The person you've described has killed before, and is rubbing our . . . my . . . face in it, because we haven't had any idea what's been happening. He's had to tell us point-blank to wake us up."

"You said the letter was posted in town, but he may have done this on purpose to trick you. This person lives to deceive and is very experienced, very good at it. He could be anywhere. Perhaps Stockholm, Malmö, or Göteborg. The anonymity of a large city would suit him, and also offer a wider choice of victims. You'll have a hard time finding him at the outset. I hate to say this, but you may have to wait for him to act. When he does, he may get careless . . . perhaps on purpose . . . just to see if you can recognize the trail he's left you."

"It's all a game to him."

"Yes, and he's invited you to play, Walther. But I've no doubt you'll win."

"I wish I felt your confidence, Jarl."

"This is an awful business and will probably get worse. What a fearful waste of human life and energy," Karlsson said, his face drawn.

"I know it's getting late, but would you please write all this up and e-mail it to me tonight so I can have it for an early morning meeting? And attach an invoice. Don't shake your head no. You've earned it," Ekman said, as they stood. He gripped Karlsson's hand.

"When we get him, your help will be remembered, publicly."

"Actually, I'd prefer if we kept my involvement strictly confidential. My patients might get a bit nervous," Karlsson said with a brief grin, handing the letter back.

Walking Ekman to the door, he helped him on with his coat.

"Let me know if I can be of any further help. Good luck. And be careful." His face was serious as the door closed.

On the drive home, taking the E4 bypass part of the way to save time, Ekman went over their conversation. He felt more confident now that he had a clearer picture of his opponent. The ball is in my court; let's see if we can send it back at him.

His jaw had set so tight without his realizing it that his teeth had begun to ache. Relax Ekman, he said to himself, you've done this many times before. But not with such a maniac, or should I say, "very disturbed person."

It was eight forty when Ekman got home. The light from the tall front windows of the stone house he'd grown up in, and his parents had given him and Ingbritt, was welcoming and warm in the chilly night. It was the place he felt most comfortable and had always loved; he couldn't imagine living anywhere else. He pressed the garage door opener and drove into the brightly lit, oversized space. Ingbritt's smaller, blue Volvo S40 was on the right.

Coming through the connecting door to the house and peering into the kitchen, he saw the table set with two places. Ingbritt had waited dinner for him anyway.

"You should have eaten," he protested as he entered the kitchen, giving her a kiss.

"I wanted to have dinner with you. It's too lonely eating by myself."

He washed up in the half bath off the hall, and going back into the cheerful, yellow curtained kitchen, sat down at the white birch table.

Ingbritt served an appetizer of sweet, pickled herring with dark bread, while Ekman poured a Renat for each of them from the bottle he kept in the freezer.

"*Skål,*" he said, as their glasses clinked. Neither spoke for a few minutes.

"Well," Ingbritt broke the silence, "aren't you going to tell me why you're late?"

Ekman paused and chewed before answering.

"We're beginning a rather strange case. It may even involve cannibalism, believe it or not. I'd rather not talk about it now, over dinner," he said, grinning.

Ingbritt frowned. He usually liked to share details of his cases.

Seeing her expression, he said, "Maybe later, when there's more to tell. For now there's just a weird letter and a lot of blind conjectures. No real facts." He didn't want to alarm her about a possible personal threat.

"What's the main course? It smells wonderful," he said, changing the subject.

She went to the oven and brought out one of his favorite dishes she'd been keeping warm: pork with brown beans, and a side of mashed rutabaga.

"This deserves a good accompaniment," he said, and going to the refrigerator, took out two bottles of Dugges Ale.

Ingbritt didn't press Ekman for details, at least for now.

After dinner, Ekman said good night as he hugged her. "I'll be up in a little while."

"Don't stay up too late, Walther. You know how cranky you get without enough sleep," she said, as she headed to the stairs.

Low bookcases lined two of the deep ochre, white-trimmed walls of his study hung with his framed needlepoint covers and a collection of antique maps. Ekman paced up and down the bright Persian rug covering the wide-planked, oak floor.

He mentally summarized the conversation with Karlsson. So, Jarl thinks this madman views me as his Beowulf. This is all very grim, but that's really funny. He smiled tightly. If he sees me that way, he's the only one in the world who does. The legendary Grendel was sword-proof, but if it comes to that, let's hope this one isn't bullet-proof.

He went to the heavy, metal gun safe required by law that was bolted to the left wall, and taking out his key case, unlocked it. On the top shelf, above the rack supporting his father's rifle and two shotguns, was a steel box he carried to his desk. Opening it, he took out his pistol, a Sig Sauer P239 Tactical. Ekman hadn't worn a gun in more than five years, although it was mandated. He qualified annually, however, and prided himself on being an excellent shot.

He weighed the gun in his hands and then going back to the safe removed a leather belt-clip holster. Checking the pistol's well-oiled slide, he took the eight-round, 9-millimeter magazine from the box, snapped it into place, and making sure the safety was on, slipped the gun into the holster.

He relocked the safe, and not wanting Ingbritt to see him in the morning with the pistol, he went out to the garage. Opening the car's glove compartment, he put the gun inside and locked the car. Before heading to bed, he checked the doors to make certain they were secure.

That night Ekman didn't fall asleep right away, as he usually did. He turned from side to side, his mind churning as he went over all that had happened. It was midnight before he drifted into a troubled sleep.

9

The Search Begins

*W*ednesday, October 12. An early blast of Arctic air had left three inches of snow during the night. It promised a hard winter. The snow had stopped falling, and was covered with a glistening ice crust. Ekman could hear the wind, still rising and falling, when he woke.

Looking out through the kitchen windows at the snow glinting in the early morning sun, Ingbritt said, "It's beautiful, isn't it, Walther?" turning to pour him more coffee.

"Not if you have to drive in it," he grumbled. "I'd better leave early."

Stepping out of the garage, he inhaled deeply. The air was cold and crisp. It smelled clean. He grinned in sheer animal pleasure at it.

A silver Volvo sedan was parked three houses up the street from Ekman's. Its windows were filmed over, but a space had been cleared in the windshield. Grendel sat huddled in a heavy parka, watching as Ekman's car pulled out. He started the engine, and slowly pulled away from the curb, keeping six car lengths behind. Soon, very soon, Ekman would have that self-satisfied grin wiped from his fat face forever. He could hardly wait.

The road had already been plowed by the time Ekman left, fifteen minutes earlier than usual, and the drive in presented no problems. When he pulled into his space at seven fifteen, he took the gun out of the glove compartment and slipped it into his coat pocket. Upstairs, he was surprised to find Holm hadn't come in yet. He was usually the first to arrive.

Ekman put the gun in a desk drawer, locked it, and booting up the computer, checked his e-mail for the profile Karlsson had promised. It was there and ran to ten pages of analysis. Jarl had included classic case histories of similar, violent psychopaths.

He printed out a copy. A cover note with the profile said an invoice would follow. Ekman grunted. He guessed he'd never see one, but would pester Karlsson until he gave up and presented a bill.

Knocking first, Holm came in. "Sorry I'm late. Some minor car trouble."

"Enar, here's Karlsson's profile of our man. Please run off extra copies and also make more of the letter," he said, handing them to Holm. "I'll distribute them at the meeting. Don't say anything to the team before then."

At eight, when Ekman opened the side door to his conference room, he found the four others already there.

"God morgen. Thanks for being so prompt," he said, taking his seat at the head of the rectangular table and placing the packages of handouts in front of him. Everyone knew if they weren't on time, the chief would give the offender one of his famous scowls. It was worth avoiding.

Ekman looked around the table. Holm was seated on his right. Next to him was Alrik Rapp, forty, the senior inspector of the group, his bullet head covered by close-cropped, bristling gray hair: most people's image of a tough cop.

On Ekman's left was Mats Bergfalk, thirty-four, trim and fit, a handsome, blond-haired man who had transferred in from Stockholm six months earlier. He was wearing a burgundy jacket with an open-collared, bright lime shirt, the type of work clothes Ekman couldn't stand. Bergfalk had a somewhat feminine manner that made Ekman suspect he was gay. He tried not to let it prejudice him because Mats was quite competent, even if he also seemed color blind.

The only woman in the group, Gerdi Vinter, sat next to Mats. Just over thirty, she was a recently promoted inspector, grudgingly acknowledged by her male colleagues as unusually capable. She was short, with a plain, round face emphasized by black hair pulled back tightly and a refusal to wear makeup.

"I know you're all wondering why I asked you to meet," Ekman began. "We're starting a rather strange investigation. You're the most qualified detectives we have, and that's why you're here." He paused, looking around the table at each of them. "We'll be working as a team. I'll coordinate and Enar will assist me. It will require a great deal of research and it will be tedious, but I know each of you will persist. In the end I think we'll find the answers we need."

He handed the packages to the three new team members, gave one to Holm and kept the rest for himself.

"Please first read the letter on top. I received it yesterday. It came in a plain envelope addressed to me. The originals are at forensics. Under the letter is a proposed psychological profile of the writer."

For the next fifteen minutes everyone, including Ekman, read the documents. When the last person, Rapp, looked up, Ekman went on.

"Tell me what your impressions are, and please be frank. No comments are out of line now, or in the future." Ekman meant it. His experience working with a team had proven to him that the group was more insightful than any single person, himself included.

Rapp spoke first, his deep baritone edged with doubt. "Chief, maybe this letter is for real. You've already gone to a lot of trouble over it. But I'm not so sure this isn't just a joke."

"That was also my first reaction," replied Ekman.

Bergfalk interjected, "Alrik may be right, but can we take the chance?"

"That was my second reaction," said Ekman.

Holm added, "Since I saw the letter yesterday, I've gone over this in my mind many times, and like the chief, I think we have to treat this as serious."

Ekman turned to Gerdi Vinter who had been staring at the ceiling, drumming a finger on the table. "What do you think, Gerdi?"

"I'm not sure. The letter, taken with the profile, which is very well reasoned, sounds . . . how shall I put it . . . too pat. It feels to me like a prank by someone who may be an animal rights activist. But I don't think it's the work of an organization. They might at first think it would be fun to have us running around in circles, going nowhere, but in the end it would become bad PR, too risky for them."

"So, what would you do?" Ekman asked in a neutral voice.

"I'd take this in stages. First, I'd look at recent missing-person cases for evidence they might be related to the letter's threat, let's say over the last few years. If nothing appears likely, I'd stop, and wait to see if there's a second letter that might give us more to go on."

"Why do you think there'll be another letter?"

"Because whoever sent this one is looking for attention and will try to get even more by sending a second one."

Ekman nodded in agreement. She'd confirmed his feeling that she was quite astute.

"I don't think we should just take it for granted that he's got no criminal or mental hospital record. The profile indicates he probably doesn't, but we need to make sure," Rapp said.

"You're right. Karlsson was agreeing with my assumption, but we can't assume anything," said Ekman.

"If he's for real, where would he live?" asked Bergfalk.

"He may have an apartment," Holm responded. "But I don't think this sort of crime would have been committed there. Too messy, too much risk in moving bodies."

"I think you're right," said Bergfalk. "Also, the smell would give him away. He'd need a really big refrigerator," he added with a crooked grin at Ekman.

"So, he may be well-off enough to own his own house, or at least a weekend cabin," said Rapp.

"These are all good ideas that should help us narrow down suspects. When, of course, we have suspects," said Ekman. No one smiled. "Do the rest of you want to proceed as Gerdi suggests?"

Rapp and Bergfalk nodded agreement.

"Enar?"

"I agree we should focus on unsolved missing-person cases."

Holm and Vinter echoed Ekman's thinking.

The others exchanged glances, and Rapp said, "That seems the way to go, Chief."

"Very well then, we're agreed. Alrik and Mats, I'd like you to look at criminal and mental hospital records going back three years. If access is refused, call me. Gerdi, you and Enar take unsolved missing persons using that time frame. We'll meet here again tomorrow, same time."

Ekman stood up, "I'll need to brief Prosecutor Edvards-son. Let me know right away if you turn up anything. Of course, all of this is confidential. Others may wonder what's going on and ask you, but it's not to be discussed with anyone outside the team. And you need to safeguard the documents. Keep them locked up. Understood?"

Ekman thought the meeting had been successful. The steps he'd outlined to Malmer were moving forward. The three-year time frame made the most sense. There was little point in going further back.

Ekman called Edvardsson, who'd been appointed ten months earlier in January. Their relationship was pro-fessional, but cordial. Because a prosecutor had ultimate responsibility and could take over a police investigation at any time, he wanted to make sure she always felt con-fident enough to let him proceed.

"God morgen, Malin, it's Walther Ekman. If you have some free time today, I'd like to come over and brief you on a new case. Yes, eleven would be fine. See you then."

Holm came in as he hung up. "Here's the first report from Rosengren and Alenius," he said, handing it to Ekman.

"Thanks. Sit down, Enar. Let me take a minute to go over this. You've already read it?"

Holm nodded.

Although the report was signed by both inspectors, Ekman knew it had been written by Alenius. He rec-ognized his style: matter-of-fact and concise. Rosengren tended to wander before reaching the points he was trying to get across.

The Westberg break-in had occurred Monday, some-time between two and three in the afternoon. Westberg had been at his insurance office, and his wife was out shopping. She'd left at two and returned about an hour later. She only noticed the rear door had been forced after first going upstairs and not finding some jewelry she knew she'd left on her dresser. A family photo had also been taken from the living room.

A crime scene team had photographed the broken doorjamb, and several pictures were attached to the report. A crowbar or tire iron appeared to have been used. They'd dusted for fingerprints, but could immediately identify only those of the couple, whose prints they'd taken for elimination purposes. Hair and fibers had been vacuumed and preserved for a possible future match once a suspect was found.

The Westberg house was in one of the best residential neighborhoods in the city. It sat toward the back of a two-thousand-square-meter lot, shielded from its neighbors on three sides by tall yew hedges. They'd found a break in the rear hedge where the intruder forced a path after coming through a small patch of woods behind the property. The ground was hard and left no footprints.

They believed this was a carefully planned burglary. The thief hadn't just randomly picked the Westberg place, and he'd been patient. He had to watch the house to know when it was vacant and then had to act quickly. He'd probably been in a vehicle parked where he could see the house. Alenius and Rosengren planned to canvass neighbors and ask about an unfamiliar car or van on the street. The report concluded that after that they would begin to question "the usual suspects."

"They also need to compare this break-in with the recent others to see if a pattern emerges," said Holm.

"Exactly. That's really the next stage. Let them know that's where I think they should head after they canvass the neighborhood. A pattern might indicate the most likely suspects."

"I'll tell them," said Holm, as he got up.

"And Enar, send the report up to Malmer, and put a note on it from me about what we propose to do next."

10

~~~~~~~~~~

Edvardsson

Ekman saw he had more than half an hour before his meeting with Edvardsson. He decided to first take a break and get an espresso. Putting his hat and coat on, he glanced at the drawer containing his gun, but decided not to take it. Edvardsson's office was just four blocks away in the courthouse. He picked up a handout package, putting the rest in a desk drawer, and following the advice he'd given, locked it.

The papers were stowed in an expensive-looking black leather briefcase with polished brass fittings and *W. F. E.*, for Walther Forstan Ekman, embossed in gold on the lower right corner. It was that year's birthday present from Erick.

It had become a brilliant day, almost cloudless, with a slight, fresh breeze. Last night's snow was rapidly vanishing from the sidewalk, and traffic had turned it to gray slush in the roads. Ekman was glad he'd chosen short, waterproof boots that morning. In Kopmangatan, just off the central square, was a small coffee shop he sometimes patronized.

He exchanged "god morgen" with the owner, a rotund, middle-aged woman with a pretty face, named Karin. Ekman didn't know her last name. He was the only

~ 52 ~

late-morning customer and ordered a double espresso and biscuit.

He wondered about how Edvardsson would react to their new case. She was usually very cooperative, but because they had no evidence of a crime, she could be reluctant to let them go ahead. He might have to persuade her.

Looking at the clock on the wall, he saw it was time to go. He got up, collected his briefcase, and walked over to where Karin, in her long white apron, stood behind the counter at the espresso machine, and left thirty-five kronor.

"Thanks, Chief Superintendent," she said with a smile.

Ekman was surprised. He hadn't realized she even knew he was a police officer, let alone his rank. He nodded without saying anything and headed down the street. This was in some ways still a small town where word got around. Perhaps she'd seen his photo in a newspaper or on television. More likely, she'd asked one of her customers, a uniformed officer, if he knew who was the big man dressed in black. His size had always made him stand out in any crowd, but he'd now become personally recognizable, and that was something he hadn't appreciated before.

He turned onto Biblioteksgatan, walking past the large, stone library building, before entering Fridhemsplan. Across the wide square was the handsome, four-story, Beaux Arts courthouse designed by Isak Gustaf Clason in the late 1890s. It was the finest building in the city. A far cry, Ekman thought, from the modern monstrosity he worked in.

The police officer at the metal detector knew him and saluted as Ekman, walking around the security post, waved a vague salute back, and headed toward the ornate, gilded elevator. Creaking, it rose slowly to the third floor.

Edvardsson's office on the east corner of the building was a short way down the white marble-floored corridor.

Opening the door, he saw that the receptionist was a pretty, slender brunette he hadn't met before.

"God morgen, I'm Walther Ekman," he said. "Fru Edvardsson is expecting me. You're new here."

"God morgen, Herr Ekman," she replied, getting up from her desk, and with a friendly smile, extending her hand. "I'm Ide Sundquist. Fru Edvardsson hired me last week. Her other receptionist moved to Malmö. I'll tell her you're here, but first let me take your hat and coat."

After hanging Ekman's things on a corner rack, she buzzed Edvardsson who immediately came out of the inner office.

"God morgen, Walther, it's good to see you," she said, with a warm smile. Malin Edvardsson seemed an unlikely person to have a well-founded reputation as one of the most able and aggressive prosecutors in the country. She was a small, wizened woman of fifty in a simple black dress with a starched, white lace collar. She had a slightly hunched back. The handshake she offered Ekman was firm and dry, her fingers gnarled by arthritis.

"Please come in," Edvardsson said, leading the way into her office. "Why don't we sit on the couch over here? It's more comfortable." She tended to conduct business informally, rather than from behind her large desk. Her attitude was at the opposite end of the spectrum from Malmer's.

Before closing the door, she said, "Can I get you something, some coffee?"

"No thanks, I'm fine," said Ekman, sitting down.

She joined him on the couch and turned toward him. "So, Walther, what is it you wanted to see me about?"

Ekman responded by taking the papers he'd brought out of the briefcase at his feet and handing them to her.

"This letter came yesterday, addressed to me," he said. "I've obtained a possible profile of the writer and have put together a team. Malmer and the commissioner have, of course, been briefed. Please read these and let me know what you think."

Edvardsson put on her horn-rimmed reading glasses and they sat there in silence as she read.

Ekman looked around the office, noting the framed letters of commendation, a floor-to-ceiling bookcase filled with sets of law books on the facing wall, and a few family photos arranged on a credenza behind the desk. The corner office had large, sunlit windows overlooking a small park.

"Well, Walther," she said, putting the papers in her lap. "You're taking this very seriously."

"Yes, I am. Do you think I'm wrong?"

"Not wrong, exactly, but perhaps . . ." she hesitated, looking for the right word, "overreacting."

"I've worried about that too, Malin, but I thought it was better than waiting for something awful to happen. I could never forgive myself if there was a tragedy that could have been averted."

"That's important, although you realize you're using resources that might be better employed where a crime has actually been committed. I'm just saying there are costs, as well as potential benefits, to the path you're taking."

"Do you think I should stop?" Ekman asked, knowing the prosecutor could halt the investigation right now.

"No, I value your instincts on this, but I think we should agree on a time frame. If nothing else turns up at the end of that, it might be best to put this on hold."

"That seems reasonable, Malin. What would you suggest?"

"Let's say, one week from yesterday, if nothing else happens? Of course, if you find evidence of a crime, the time limit is dropped."

"That would make it the eighteenth. Like you, I don't want this to drag on, eating up manpower. But I also don't want to ignore it."

"So," Edvardsson said, "we're agreed. Now fill me in on what your team will be doing."

Ekman sketched out the tasks they'd started that morning.

"All of that seems eminently sensible to me," she said. "I couldn't add anything. Let me know in a couple of days how things are going, okay?"

Standing up, she took Ekman's papers and leading him to the door, opened it and said, "Ide, please put these in my locked cabinet," handing the papers to the receptionist before turning to say good-bye to Ekman.

On the way out, Ekman picked up his hat and coat and also said good-bye to Froken Sundquist who smiled brightly in reply, then turned, and started filing the papers away.

11

A Robbery

Heading across the square, Ekman had a strange, momentary feeling he was being watched, but looking around saw only the usual pedestrians, cars, and a few motor bikes. Nothing caught his attention.

He thought he'd take a shortcut back to his office, and turned into a narrow alley on the west of the plaza. The buildings on each side cast an unexpected gloom as he trudged along.

After going half a block, he heard the revved motor of a scooter coming up fast behind him. He stepped closer to the wall on his right to let it pass. It was the wrong decision.

There was a rider behind the driver. As the bike came abreast of him, it slowed for an instant. The rider reached out with a knife, cut the strap of Ekman's brief-case where it hung on his left shoulder and grabbed its handle as they roared away.

Ekman stood there in shock for an instant, then reached into his coat pocket for his gun. He remembered he'd left it in his desk just as the scooter banked sharply and vanished around the next corner. It had happened so fast he hadn't been able to get the license number.

It was the first time in a long career of putting criminals away that he'd become a victim himself. Like so many others, he was enraged at the violation, and at the same time had a humiliating feeling of powerlessness.

Ekman thanked God he hadn't taken his gun. He was so angry that in the heat of the moment he might have lost control and shot at them. He was appalled that he was capable of reacting so violently. Ekman had always practiced rigid self-control. In all his time as a police officer, he'd never had to fire his weapon at anyone.

With only a lightning glimpse of the helmeted driver and rider, it was hard to tell, but from their slender body builds he felt they were quite young. Despite the tension of the moment he half-smiled to himself imagining Malmer's horrified reaction to what might have been tomorrow's headline, *"Chief Superintendent Kills Boys Over Stolen Briefcase."*

Still somewhat shaken, he thought, what are you going to do about this Ekman, file an official report you've been robbed? Not very likely. He'd become a laughing stock, even though there was nothing he could have done to prevent it except, of course, to have stepped to his left. Too late now.

But the robbery couldn't just be ignored. He probably wasn't their first victim, and wouldn't be their last. They had to be stopped before someone was hurt, as well as robbed. And besides, he missed his briefcase. Maybe it could be recovered.

If this had to happen, he was glad it was after he'd left the papers with Edvardsson. The briefcase had been empty.

Back at the office, he asked Holm to come in. "Please close the door, Enar," he said.

He told Holm about his conversation with Edvardsson and observed, "We're going to have to work even faster, now that there's a deadline.

"There's something else," Ekman added, and told Holm about the robbery.

"That's incredible," Holm exploded, incensed that his boss had been victimized. "In broad daylight, near the courthouse! It's outrageous."

"I couldn't agree with you more," said Ekman with a wry smile. "They've got to be stopped before someone is hurt. People could easily be dragged if they hung on to their bag. I'd like you to find out whether there's been an increase in bag snatching using this method, and what's being done about it. I don't remember it being mentioned in the daily incident reports."

"I'll do it right away. I'm sorry you went through this," Holm said.

"Enar, for now, this is just between us."

"I understand, Chief. We'll find them, have no doubt."

"Thanks, Enar. I appreciate your treating this as confidential."

Looking at the clock, Ekman saw it was past his usual lunchtime. The strain of the robbery had made him forget he'd intended to have lunch before coming back to the office, but now he didn't feel like going out again.

I guess it's time to go back to the cafeteria and see if the food has gotten any better, he thought. He hadn't eaten there in months, preferring the superior food, available alcohol, and above all, quiet, of outside restaurants.

The cafeteria was thinly occupied with uniformed officers. He nodded to one of them he had worked with recently, but chose a table in the corner overlooking the enclosed courtyard with its small stand of birch trees and some wooden benches. Going to the counter he ordered an open-faced shrimp sandwich and double espresso. He took a few bites of the sandwich, but the robbery had taken away his appetite and he pushed the plate aside, staring into the courtyard. He felt despondent. Perhaps that's how crime victims always feel, he thought. It's the powerlessness that's humiliating and depressing. Shoving back his chair, he headed up to his office.

Ekman found a message waiting for him. Malmquist had just phoned. Ekman called him immediately.

"Ludvig, thanks for calling. What have you got?"

"Unfortunately, not a hell of a lot. The paper is available everywhere and the printer used is a popular Canon model. There are no unidentified fingerprints. The ones we found match file prints for you, Holm, and the mail people. The sender probably wore gloves, which may indicate his prints could be on file. The good news, however, is that by carefully lifting the envelope flap we were able to extract some fragments of DNA. He either made a mistake, probably using saliva on his gloved finger, or doesn't care about DNA because we don't have his on file and he thinks he'll never be caught."

"But is there enough for a match?"

"Yes, perhaps. We ran it through the DNA database, but all we got was confirmation the sender is male. That could be because the sample was inadequate or there was just nothing to match it against. In my opinion, it was probably the latter."

"That would be my guess, as well. This is someone we have no DNA record of."

"When you have a suspect we can try again."

"Ludvig, you've been a great help, as always."

"In a negative sort of way." Malmquist paused. "If you want my unsolicited opinion, you're right to pursue this. I don't believe he's just a crackpot. I think he's dangerous. Possibly, already a killer."

"That's what I've been afraid of. I hope we'll know more soon. I've got a team working on it."

"Good luck. And Walther, if I can be of any more help, don't hesitate."

"Thanks, Ludvig," said Ekman, ending the call.

Paper had piled up in his in-basket as usual and Ekman, looking at it, sighed. It had been an eventful day. He was feeling worn and had no patience for routine paperwork; instead he took out his needlepoint to try and relax. He was relieved when Holm knocked and came in.

"I've checked on the bag snatching," Holm said. "There've only been occasional reports in the recent past, nothing lately, and no motor scooters have been involved." He'd often seen Ekman stitching while they spoke.

"So, I guess I was their first, but not their last. Please keep an eye open for similar incidents, Enar."

"Sure, Chief. Is there anything else you'd like me to do about it?"

"Right now, I think we'll just have to wait and see what develops. How are the missing-person cases going?"

"Gerdi and I have been making good progress. From their background, almost all the unsolved cases we've seen seem to have been properly handled as likely family or business problems: husbands and wives running out on each other, teens taking off, and people escaping creditors. Most of these are still being worked because a trail is active. There are a few unresolved disappearances, however, that don't fit the usual pattern and aren't easily explained. We should have more for you by tomorrow's meeting."

"Sounds interesting. I'll let you get on with it," Ekman said, getting up as Holm left.

12

Confession

The stress of the robbery had made Ekman more tired than he'd realized and he decided to head home early. First, he wanted to stop at the stall in the square and get some flowers for Ingbritt. He'd have to tell her about the robbery, and somehow hoped the flowers would ease a difficult conversation.

Unlocking the drawer where he'd put his gun, he took it out of the holster, which he left, and slipped the gun into his overcoat pocket. Although he wasn't expecting anything more to happen, that afternoon's incident had made him cautious. He also hadn't forgotten what Karlsson had said about the letter writer's apparent fixation on him.

Holm wasn't at his desk, so Ekman left him a note saying he could be reached at home. He took the stairs and went out the front entrance into the square.

Near the large nineteenth-century bronze fountain in the middle of the plaza was a flower stall with a bright green-and-white-striped awning. He chose a huge bunch of blue irises, which the vendor wrapped in sheets of green tissue paper. Handing her 265 kronor, he was surprised how expensive they were, but figured they must have been flown in from somewhere south.

Heading back across the square to headquarters, for the second time that day he felt as though he were being watched, but looking around, saw nothing that caught his attention. He walked the short distance to the garage entrance, and nodding to the security officer—who eyed the flowers, obviously curious—Ekman went down the ramp to his car.

It was four P.M. He hadn't told Ingbritt he'd be home early. When he pulled into the garage he saw her car wasn't there. He thought about calling her on her mobile, but decided she'd be back shortly.

Ekman hung his coat in the closet, leaving his gun in the pocket. What would Ingbritt do with the flowers? Going into the kitchen, he found a suitable vase in a cabinet, and taking it to the sink, filled it with warm water. Unwrapping the flowers and cutting their stems with kitchen shears, he placed them in the vase, arranging them as he'd seen her do. He put it in the center of the table and examined his effort. It was satisfactory.

Pleased with himself, he took out the Renat, and poured himself a drink. He felt he deserved one; it had been an extraordinary day, his first as a crime victim.

Taking the glass to his study, he settled into his big, dark-green leather recliner, reaching to the side table for the book he'd last been reading two days ago. It was an impressive biography of Peter the Great, who had, by sheer force of personality, dragged a still medieval Russia, kicking and screaming, into eighteenth-century Western Europe. His mortal enemy, Sweden's Charles XII, was another megalomaniac with unbounded ambition. Both had built their achievements, thought Ekman, at tremendous cost in human suffering.

Like Grendel, Peter and Charles believed they were above any law. Today, they could be labeled war criminals,

Ekman mused, hauled before the International Criminal Court for crimes against humanity. Perhaps things had gotten somewhat better. At least our perception of right and wrong had become a little clearer, although constant wars seemed to be the human lot. Maybe we're the victims of our genes and nothing can be done about it. He hoped he was wrong and that people willing a less violent world could somehow make it happen.

At that moment he heard first the garage door, and then the door to the hall, open and close.

"Ingbritt," he called, "I'm in here." There was no answer.

For an instant, Ekman became irrationally anxious, until he heard her cheerful, "Thank you for the flowers, Walther. They're beautiful."

Today's incident has made me edgy, he thought, as he pulled himself out of the recliner, and went into the kitchen.

"You're home early," she said. "Is anything wrong?"

"I'm just a little tired," he replied. "Although," he paused, "there is something else."

"Sit down and tell me what's happened," she said, concerned.

He told her about the robbery.

Her face went white.

"Walther, how awful for you," she said, as she came over and kissed him, putting an arm around his shoulders.

"Well, after the first moments, it wasn't so bad. It could have been a lot worse. I could have been injured, or I could have done something stupid if I'd had a gun and shot them. It actually crossed my mind. Apart from Holm, no one knows, and I intend to leave it that way. Otherwise, I'd look foolish, even though I couldn't do anything about it."

"Thank God you weren't hurt. It was only a briefcase that can be replaced."

"So, now that I've told you all about it, let's put it out of our minds. You were shopping?"

She opened the grocery tote she'd brought in and took out two large ribeye steaks, a bag of fingerling potatoes, a head of cabbage, and a bottle of French cabernet.

"That looks wonderful. While you're pulling that together, I'll open the wine and let it breathe."

After they'd eaten and cleaned up the kitchen together, he went back to his study to read. But he couldn't stay focused on his book and took up the needlepoint he kept at home. He worked on it for ten minutes and then put it aside.

The day's events kept running through his mind. They were at the beginning of the strangest case he'd ever had, and right now everything seemed disjointed. He knew from experience that this was temporary. Persistence would eventually make things clearer, he hoped.

13

A Challenge

Thursday, October 13. A steady drizzle was blowing against the windshield and made him keep the wipers and headlights on. The sky was light gray with dull, scudding clouds. Few cars were on the road. Ekman had compulsively made up for leaving work early yesterday by arriving just before seven.

No one else in his area was in yet. Entering his office, he saw a large, flat white box in the middle of his desk. As he hung up his coat, he became aware of the weight of the gun still in his pocket.

Ekman went over and looked at a message slip on top of the box. It was from the night duty sergeant: the package had been delivered just after eleven P.M.

It was addressed to him in now-familiar bold black letters. A thin white cord wrapped tightly around it held the cover in place.

Ekman reached into a drawer for evidence gloves and took out a pair of scissors. The string was tied in front and he carefully cut it away from the knot, to preserve any unusual characteristics. Lifting the cover, he set it to one side. Inside was an object wrapped in layers of white gift paper. Slowly unfolding them, he saw his stolen briefcase. It had his initials in the corner. There was a sheet of paper on top.

My Dear Chief Superintendent Ekman:
I am returning your briefcase with sincer-est apologies. I trust the torn shoulder strap can be repaired or replaced without too much inconvenience.
It should never have been taken. Let me assure you it was done not only entirely without my authorization, but against my express instruction that you were just to be observed.
You need not trouble yourself about the thieves. They have been severely chastised and will not bother you (or anyone else) again.
With highest regard, I have the distinct honor to remain,
Esteemed sir, your most humble, most obedient servant,
Grendel

Ekman put the note back on top of the briefcase, and pulling off his gloves, sat down heavily in his chair. The nerve of the bastard. The sheer, fucking nerve, and with an old-fashioned flourish at the end of that damned note. And those poor, stupid kids on the scooter. His anger at them had changed to pity. They're dead, he guessed, unless Grendel was just trying to mislead him. But he didn't think so. I wonder what Karlsson will make of all this.

He picked up the phone and called the front desk.

"This is Ekman. Is last night's duty sergeant still here?"

"Yes, sir. He's just about to leave. Let me get him."

The sergeant came on the line. "It's Lindberg, Chief. What can I do for you?"

"Please come up and see me before you leave."

"I'll be right there, Chief."

A few minutes later, Lindberg knocked and came in. He was a pleasant-looking man in his early thirties. An unruly cowlick of light brown hair contrasted with his sharply pressed uniform. He stood at attention and saluted.

"Please sit down, Lindberg. I know you're going off duty and won't hold you up too long. I just have a few questions."

"Yes, sir."

Pointing to the box on his desk, Ekman asked, "Did you take delivery of this yourself?"

"Yes, sir. It was hand-delivered at 11:05 P.M."

"Who brought it?"

"It was a woman."

"Please describe her."

"She was young, nice looking, late twenties I'd say, fairly tall, around five eight, slender build, long blonde hair. She had on a tan raincoat, a broad-brimmed matching hat, and brown gloves. She was wearing tinted glasses so I can't tell you the color of her eyes."

"Did she say anything?"

"No, I thought that was a little strange. She just put the box on my desk, pointed at your name, smiled, and left."

"Is there anything else you can tell me? Any other impression she made?"

"Not really, sir. Just that she seemed friendly enough."

"I assume the video monitor was recording?"

"Yes, sir. Always."

"Okay. Thank you, Lindberg. You've been very helpful. Just ask the desk sergeant to have the images from shortly before eleven to a few minutes after she left sent to my computer. Also, I'll need the exterior camera's recording for the same period." This was at least one useful advantage of a building with advanced technology, he thought.

"Yes, sir. Will do." Lindberg paused, a worried frown flitted across his face. "I hope I didn't do anything wrong by accepting the package, sir."

"Not at all, Lindberg. Don't be concerned about it."

The sergeant got up, saluted again, and left, closing the door behind him.

Rising, Ekman paced about the room for the next few minutes. The case had fundamentally changed; it was no longer just a theory that what was happening might be personal. He stared out the window. The rain had picked up and was coming down in sheets out of a darkened sky, drifting hard across the square, leaving small pools of water on the slick, glistening cobblestones.

Back at his desk he booted up his computer and searched for the images he wanted. There was the woman carrying the box past the heavy glass entrance door and approaching the front desk. She looked exactly as Lindberg had described. He's taking the box from her. She points at it, smiles, turns, and waves as she walks out. It was all over in less than thirty seconds.

Ekman next looked at the exterior shots. The woman could be seen approaching on foot. When she left, she took the same route until she was out of the camera's range around the corner. He'd hoped there'd be a car and perhaps a glimpse of a license plate, but no such luck. He felt frustrated.

There was a knock at the door and Holm stuck his head in. "Are you busy, Chief?"

"Come in, Enar. We've been sent a surprise package," Ekman said, pointing to the box. "Take a look, but first use these," he said, giving Holm a fresh pair of gloves from his drawer.

Putting them on, Holm peered into the box, and involuntarily sucked in his breath.

"It's your briefcase, isn't it?"

"Yes, it's been thoughtfully returned," Ekman said in a flat voice. "Now read the note that came with it."

Holm picked it up, and when he finished reading put it back in the box. He looked over at Ekman. "He's a wiseass bastard. And it sounds like he's done something to those guys on the scooter, probably killed them."

"My thinking too. I've already talked to the desk sergeant who took delivery," Ekman said, describing his conversation with Lindberg and the videos he'd seen.

"It seems our dear friend has an accomplice," he added.

Holm thought for a moment. "This makes the robbery part of the case now. We're not going to be able to keep it to ourselves anymore."

"Exactly. Of course, we'll bring the others on the team up to date." He sighed, "And then, I'm going to have to brief Malmer on what's happened. I thought yesterday was bad. Today promises to be worse. Please make copies of the note, then put it back in the box and prepare a package for Malmquist. Again, by courier."

Holm went out, taking the box with him. While he was gone, Ekman phoned Malmquist.

"Ludvig, it's Walther. I'm sending you another rush job." He described the robbery and the surprising return of the briefcase.

"The only fingerprints on this one that I know about are my sergeant, Lindberg's. The person who delivered the box was wearing gloves, but may have gotten careless earlier. I was careful about the knot on the wrapping cord, if that's any help."

"All right, Walther. This is getting stranger by the day. I'll do everything I can with it. After we're done tomorrow, I'll send back your briefcase, although you'll want to keep it in your evidence room until this is resolved."

"Thanks, Ludvig. As always."

"I know: you owe me another one. Good luck."

14

The Missing

It was almost eight. Ekman and Holm went into the conference room. Holm sat down, and Ekman, picking up the phone on a table against the wall, called the front desk.

"This is Ekman again. Please have those images you just sent me also put on the projector in my conference room. Thanks."

The hall door opened and the other team members filed in. They took the same places as yesterday.

"Let's get started," said Ekman, sitting down and putting the copies of the note in front of him. "We've a lot of ground to cover." Turning to them, he asked, "Alrik and Mats, what have you got for us?"

"I've got a friend in central hospital records, so we didn't need help getting the information," Rapp said with a grin. "There are no cases involving cannibalism. We've worked fast, but I think we've been thorough." Bergfalk nodded his agreement.

"Okay. Negative findings are helpful too. Gerdi, what about you and Enar?"

She looked at Holm before she began, as Enar smiled encouragement. "Chief, we've covered the unsolved missing-persons national database going back three years and it looks like almost all involve people running away from obvious bad family, personal, or business situations. A number are still being traced and there may be results on some of them very soon. But there are four cases that can't be easily explained." She turned toward Holm, and he continued.

"They stand out because there are no apparent problems that might have led someone to try to run from them. Of course, as we dig deeper, we may find things that could have caused people to take off. Right now, however, there's nothing clear, so we're treating these as suspicious. We'll look at the complete case files. If they seem promising, we'll talk to the officers who've been working the cases, and then reinterview family, friends, and business associates."

"That sounds right," Ekman said. "Now, give us an example of what brought these cases to the surface."

Gerdi replied, "A guy named Gustaffson, an engineer, midthirties, single, popular, with a good job, just vanished a month ago in Åseda. He's the most recent one. He had no apparent family or financial problems. He was walking home to his apartment around five fifteen, but never made it. Gustaffson's usual path between office and home was retraced, and he hadn't stopped anywhere. He simply disappeared."

"And the other cases are similar?"

"Yes," said Holm. "There seem to be no reasons for the vanishing acts."

"I meant beyond that. Same sex, same age, and general location?"

"Yes and no," said Holm. "Three men, one woman, midthirties to midforties, but different occupations and family circumstances. They lived in an area ranging over one hundred kilometers in every direction from here."

"So, we're going to have to cover a good swath of southern Sweden?"

"Yes, Chief. It looks that way."

"Remember when you go into other jurisdictions, don't forget to check in first with the local station. But be vague. Just say it's in connection with another case we're working. If there are any problems, have them call me," Ekman said, glancing around the table. "We're looking for any pattern in possible victims, circumstances, location—anything that would give us some handle on our dear friend and help us anticipate his next move."

"Alrik and Mats," said Ekman, turning to them, "I'd like you to help Gerdi and Enar on the four cases they've turned up.

"Now, let me bring you up to date."

Ekman told them about his conversation with Edvardsson and the deadline that had been agreed to. "So we all need to move as fast as possible, without becoming sloppy, if we're going to justify pursuing this guy. We've only got five days left to come up with something."

Then Ekman described the robbery. The others sat there in stunned silence. "The silver lining, if you can call it that, is it may qualify to lift the deadline."

He told them about the unexpected return of the briefcase, and as he did so, passed out copies of the note.

"Jesus, Chief," Bergfalk said after reading the note, "this is really weird. Maybe he likes it that way. He's good at throwing us off balance, isn't he?"

"Yes, and we're dealing with an increasingly dangerous character. I'll be speaking with Karlsson again. He may want to adjust the profile."

Ekman repeated his conversation with Lindberg. Then, getting up, he lowered the projection screen on the wall behind his chair, and going over to the opposite end of the conference table, turned on the computer-driven projector there.

"If you'll look at the screen, I'll show you what happened. Enar would you please work this thing," he said, pointing to the projector. "I can turn it on, but the rest is beyond me."

Holm got up, and soon they were all watching the woman entering, delivering the package, leaving, and walking away.

"Well," said Ekman. "What do you make of that?"

Rapp said, "He's got a helper. That's going to make things harder for us."

"Why is that?" asked Bergfalk.

"Because it gives him more flexibility in whatever he does," responded Rapp. He wasn't just a tough cop, he was surprisingly sharp.

Ekman nodded in agreement. "Anything else?"

"We shouldn't assume she's an actual accomplice," said Holm. "She could be helping him without knowing what's going on. Maybe he told her it was a joke he was playing on a friend."

"Also, we shouldn't even assume it's a woman," added Vinter. "I can't be sure, but it could be a man in disguise. The hat, glasses, gloves, and long coat look like a disguise to me. The hair could be a wig."

"Let's play those videos again," said Ekman. "Can you slow it down for us, Enar?"

The images came up on the screen in slow motion. "Well, Gerdi, what do you think? Woman or man?"

"I just can't be sure, Chief. Even if it's a disguise, and I really think it is, it could be either a man or a woman. The face looks feminine enough, but that could be clever makeup. The movements aren't exaggeratedly female, the way a man pretending to be a woman might act. Maybe it really is a woman. I'm just suggesting we shouldn't assume it."

"No, you're absolutely right to bring it up. We can't take anything for granted. And I agree with you, even if it's a woman, she's wearing a disguise."

"It sure looks like a woman to me, Chief," said Bergfalk. "And good looking, too."

"Perhaps that's why Lindberg didn't question her," said Holm. "He may have been a little flustered by her and so didn't press her for information. The voice might have been a sure giveaway, and that's why she didn't say anything."

"Good point, Enar. Her not speaking may mean Gerdi's suspicion that it's a man is right," said Ekman.

He summed up, "It seems to me there aren't just two, but actually three possibilities. First, we may be looking at a disguised female helper; second, a male accomplice; or third, our friend himself. Even so, we may have something we can use. He's trying too hard to be cute. Sending the briefcase back that way may have been his first mistake."

Ekman looked around the table. "Is there something else?" No one spoke.

"Okay, then. Don't be discouraged that we don't have a clear path yet. We're just starting and I believe we've already made progress. We'll meet again tomorrow, same time."

Seated at his desk, Ekman rubbed his heavy chin. I've given them a pep talk, he thought, but do I really believe it? Grendel is still a very dim figure. Maybe Jarl can help bring him into focus. He picked up the phone and called Karlsson.

"Jarl, it's Walther. There've been some further developments and I could use your help again. Do you have time to meet for lunch? Good. How about that little Italian place we've been to before? Yes, the one off Fahlbergvagen, about halfway between your house and town. Let's say around twelve. Thanks, Jarl. See you then. And by the way, the meter is ticking, and I'll be looking for a bill."

Ekman mulled over what they really had. It wasn't much. A fingerprint on the briefcase or the box it came in might give them a break, if it could be matched. There wasn't anything he could do except wait and see.

The missing-person cases they were focusing on now might turn up something. These could prove their best chance of tracking Grendel, if he was involved. Ekman reminded himself that even if a crime had been committed in these disappearances, they couldn't assume their dear friend "the maniac" was the perpetrator. It could as easily be someone else, or several others.

Well, he sighed, it's still early. What they needed to give them more time to work the case was proof of a serious crime connected to the letter writer. So far, apart from a petty robbery, they had nothing.

Holm knocked and came in. "Here's the second report from Alenius and Rosengren, Chief." He handed it to Ekman, and sat down.

Alenius again obviously had prepared the report. He and Rosengren had interviewed everyone in Westberg's neighborhood about any strange vehicles on the street before the robbery. No one had seen anything. Then they'd gone through reports of recent break-ins, looking for a pattern.

All were done in daylight when the owners were out, which wasn't unusual. In the Westberg break-in, an expensive sound system had been left. But in the three other burglaries they'd looked at, every portable thing of value had been taken. And unlike the Westberg case, no family photo had vanished. Their next step was the same as they'd done with Westberg, interview neighbors about a strange vehicle in the vicinity on the day of the burglaries.

When Ekman finished he looked up at Holm, "Well, Enar, what do you make of all this?"

"It's too bad no one saw a car at Westberg's. There had to have been a vehicle watching the place. Just our luck no one noticed. The stolen picture there seems to be the unusual item separating it from the other cases."

"Yes. The photo. The question, of course, is why it was taken. Perhaps as a souvenir of the crime? Well, until we solve the break-in we can only guess. Send the report up to Malmer. Maybe he'll have an answer for us," Ekman concluded with a twisted smile.

15

A Walk in the Rain

He'd have to bring Edvardsson up to date and decided it would be best to do it in person. He called to make sure she'd be free.

"I'll be over in fifteen minutes," he told the receptionist.

Looking outside, he saw rain coming down steadily, but not in torrents. He thought about driving, but parking around the courthouse was scarce, even with a police permit on the dash.

Ekman got his hat and coat, and considering the gun in his pocket, took it out. He held it in his hand for a moment. Do I want to continue carrying it? he asked himself. The answer was clearly yes. Best to do it the right way. He went to his desk drawer and, removing the holster, attached it to his belt on his left side, slipping the pistol in with the butt facing right. Ekman favored a cross-body draw on the practice range, but hoped he'd never have to use it. He grabbed his umbrella as he left.

Outside it was chillier than he'd expected and he was tempted to go back and get his car. Though the walk will do me good, he thought, and started out. Few pedestrians were about. He kept an eye out for anything suspicious, but saw nothing. At least there were no scooters on a day like this. He would have liked to stop for coffee, but there was no time now. Perhaps on the way back.

The security officer at the courthouse was the same one as yesterday's. Ekman returned his salute and, going around the metal detector, took the ancient elevator to Edvardsson's office.

Ide Sundquist got up from her desk as he came in.

"God morgen, Herr Ekman," she said, coming forward to take his dripping coat, hat, and umbrella.

"Thanks, Froken Sundquist. Watch out you don't get wet from those things," he said with a smile as she hung up his coat.

"Please go right in, she's expecting you." As he turned, she stared at Ekman's back for a long moment, and then ran damp hands along her tailored brown woolen slacks before sitting down at her computer.

He knocked and went into Edvardsson's office. She was seated behind her desk, but seeing him, got up and came forward to shake his hand.

"God morgen, Walther." Noticing his wet shoes, she said, "You walked? I hope you didn't get too wet."

"God morgen, Malin. I needed the exercise. Walking is about all I get."

She moved to the couch and he joined her. "So, what has happened since yesterday? Anything interesting?" she asked.

"You could call it that," Ekman responded, telling her about the robbery and the return of the briefcase.

"How terrible for you! Walther, you weren't hurt were you?" Genuine concern showed in her face and voice.

"No, not at all. The only injury was to my sense of being personally exempt from crime. Maybe it's a good thing, in a strange way. I've suddenly become much more empathetic with victims."

"I don't think we'll recommend this as part of the training for new officers," she said with a slight smile.

"I'm so glad nothing happened to you," she said, taking his hand for a moment. He was surprised and moved by the gesture.

"As far as the case went, I'm afraid we don't know much. But at least this is certain: our letter writer was having me watched, and didn't like the robbery any more than I did," he said, and handed her a copy of the brief-case note.

Edvardsson read it. "How strange. And this note feels sinister."

"That's what my team and I think too."

"He implies he's done something to the robbers. Do you think he really has?"

"Yes, I'm afraid so."

"Yet there's nothing to prove he's actually done anything criminal, either to them, or by carrying through his cannibalism threat."

"Malin, I don't want to say we're eager to discover crimes; God forbid. It's just that I have a police officer's instinct that evidence of major crime is out there. It will surface if we dig deeper."

"I agree with you, Walther. In view of the robbery, I'm going to forget about the deadline. You take this as far as you can. We need to make sure nothing awful has been going on," she concluded, getting up.

"Thanks, Malin. You've made our job a lot easier, but you can be sure we'll work as fast as possible."

"And Walther," she said, as he turned to leave. "Be careful." She was the second person in two days to say that to him, and it resonated. The unaccustomed weight of the gun on his hip made the warning difficult to forget.

Ekman collected his things in the outer office. The receptionist was away from her desk.

The rain had stopped for the moment, but from the look of the sky, promised to start again. Heading across the square, he was watchful, but saw nothing. Ekman decided not to tempt fate by taking the alley shortcut, and kept to the main streets.

Passing the coffee shop, he again thought about stopping. His lunch date with Karlsson was coming up, so instead he just went on directly to headquarters.

Grendel was seated in the coffee shop, his back turned from the window. He sipped at his cup and watched Ekman as he went by. He was easily noticeable. Grendel followed him with his eyes until Ekman turned the corner. Grendel's face was expressionless, but hatred of Ekman seethed inside; it was always on his mind, gnawing away at him. He considered speeding things up, but pushed the thought aside. Everything was moving exactly as he'd planned. Now was not the time to alter anything. He would have to be patient just a little longer.

16

An Italian Lunch

Back in his office, with his coat still on, Ekman looked to see if there were any important messages, but only saw that someone had added still more paper to his overflowing in-box. He would somehow have to find the time to at least look through it. But not right now. He unlocked his drawer and put a copy of the most recent letter in his pocket. Holm wasn't at his desk, so he left a note telling him he was going to lunch and took the elevator to the garage.

The restaurant where he was meeting Karlsson was twenty minutes away. Il Positano was a popular place, a favorite of his and Ingbritt's. It was bright, cheerful, and had a friendly staff. The Northern Italian food was, they both thought, quite authentic. It compared favorably with what they'd eaten during last year's vacation at Sirmione on Lake Garda. Besides, it was much less expensive.

Pulling into the large, gravel parking lot just before noon, he saw only three other cars. It was the middle of the week and, Ekman guessed, an off day. The rain hadn't returned yet.

Karlsson was already there, sitting at a table for two toward the back, away from the few other customers. He got up as Ekman came over and reached out to shake his hand.

"Walther, it's good to see you again so soon. Or is that a bad omen?"

Ekman hung his hat and coat on a nearby wall hook. "You're right, it's not a good sign, at least as far as the case goes."

Pulling out a chair, he sat down. "Let's order first, and then I can fill you in. What looks tempting to you?" he asked, glancing through the menu.

A young waiter came over. "May I suggest the grilled branzino, gentlemen. It's not on the menu. We just got it in fresh today. It's served with mushroom risotto."

"That sounds tasty," said Karlsson. "I'll have that, with a small salad, some bread, and a glass of pinot grigio." Looking at Ekman, he added, "I'm a little hungry, today."

"I'll have the same," Ekman told the waiter. "And make that a half bottle and two glasses," he said, smiling at Karlsson.

The waiter left, and Ekman told Karlsson what had happened since their last meeting.

"And here's the note that came with the briefcase," he said, handing it across.

Karlsson put on his glasses and read. When he finished he looked over at Ekman.

"So, what do you think, Jarl?"

"He's 'upping the ante,' as they say. Addressing the note to you by name, he's telling you first that you're watched, that he's in charge of what happens, and is in strict control. He's saying he's ruthless about that control; he doesn't tolerate unauthorized initiatives, and punishes associates who deviate. Second, his flowery language flaunts his literacy. He wants you to know he's familiar with eighteenth-century letters. Finally, his expression of 'esteem' underlines his actual contempt for you. He considers you ineffectual. He believes you're at his mercy and can't do anything about it. He's laughing at you and wants you to know it."

"Okay, I get the insult. That's what he thinks he's doing. What does this tell us about him?"

"We know he's a megalomaniac psychopath, controlled by his delusions. He's becoming more excited by his feeling of power over you, over his associates, and over the world at large. But this is a false sense. It conceals a profound fear of powerlessness. His deep need to show he's in charge tells us something about his childhood.

"I'll be Freudian for a minute, and say that one, or even both, his parents were so overwhelming they almost destroyed his ego. My guess is that it was his father, which helps explain why he's very focused on you. You represent the paternal authority he's still afraid of. I think he's growing more dangerous. He's resisting that authority, boasting about his own punitive power."

"So the pace of his game is picking up, Jarl?"

"Yes, I believe so," replied Karlsson, as their food arrived. The waiter poured the wine and they concentrated on their lunch.

"This is really good," said Ekman between mouthfuls. "You picked the right thing to order. The fish is perfect and so is the risotto."

"My sense about food is unerring," said Karlsson with a smile. "But my sense of what's going on with Grendel may not be so accurate."

"I don't agree. It feels exactly on the mark."

They finished their meal, and Ekman poured them a final sip of wine.

"Where do you see your investigation going?" Karlsson asked.

"Frankly, right now we're struggling, looking at unusual missing-person cases, and hoping a lead will appear. I've sent the briefcase to forensics and perhaps they'll turn up something."

"You might have to wait for his next move."

"Possibly, but I'd much rather not. If we have to wait, someone else may be harmed, and that's got to be prevented."

"There's one other possibility you might want to consider."

"What's that?"

"An enemy. Over your years in the police, you may have helped convict someone who saw you as the authority figure, the father he hated. Now he may be looking for revenge. You wouldn't have recognized him as a psychopath, he's too concealed and devious."

Ekman paused and considered. "I can't think of any enemy, other than Malmer, of course," he said with a wry smile. "No one comes to mind right now, but I'll give it serious thought."

The waiter brought the check and Ekman grabbed it. "No, Jarl, this is mine. Don't protest, because I want you to write up your analysis and e-mail it to me today, if you can. This time, please, with a bill."

They left the restaurant and shook hands in the parking lot.

"You've given me a better sense of who we're up against."

"You're very welcome, it makes me feel useful," said Karlsson, smiling. "And thanks again for the fine lunch."

17

Past Enemies

On the drive back, Ekman mulled over their conversation. Perhaps somewhere in his past was the lead they'd been stumbling around looking for. He'd need to go back over some old cases that might jog his memory.

The theory that Grendel didn't have a criminal record was just his initial gut feeling. Now he'd look at major crimes where he'd been responsible for a conviction, and the guy had been released in the last three years. Ekman was actually pleased. He liked nothing better than digging into a case himself. It was much more satisfying than just directing the hunt.

Turning on his computer, Ekman scrolled to the database he kept of important cases he'd personally solved. It could be searched by a list of defendants convicted and their sentences. Five were premeditated murders where the life sentences had been converted on appeal to set periods. In two of these, the defendants had been released within the last three years. Ekman made a note of their names. Try as he might, he had only a vague recollection of the cases, which had occurred almost twenty years ago. He'd have to go back and review them to see whether either of these criminals was a good candidate to be Grendel.

After scanning the other important cases . . . a rape, robbery, fraud, kidnapping . . . Ekman now had a complete list of eight names. They would have to be gone over carefully before he could eliminate them as the "enemy" Karlsson had suggested.

The bookcase clock struck four and he reflexively checked it against his pocket watch: they matched.

He'd been avoiding it, but he'd have to brief Malmer. Ekman couldn't help momentarily considering how wonderful it would be if Malmer turned out to be Grendel, but dismissed this with a shake of his head as wishful thinking. Malmer wasn't that crazy, or that smart, just obnoxious. Ekman called Annika to see if he was available. Unfortunately, he was.

Sitting uncomfortably on one of those miserable wooden chairs, Ekman briefed Malmer on the team's progress. Malmer said nothing, just nodded. Then Ekman told him about the robbery, the return of the briefcase, and the team's work plans.

"But you never reported the robbery?"

"No. I didn't see much point in it. I checked on recent bag snatching, however, and there was nothing."

"Walther, as a senior police officer, you had a particular responsibility to report a crime," Malmer said. "This was a failure of duty and will be noted as such," he added, with unconcealed satisfaction.

"As you wish," Ekman responded. There was no use arguing with Malmer, who was always looking for something, however petty, to hold against him. It was aggravating, if nothing else. Malmer couldn't fire, or even discipline him; Ekman was much too senior, with too well-known a record of accomplishment, and had several influential friends on the National Police Board. Besides, he and Malmer both knew that Malmer and his friend the commissioner would be lost without him.

"You've spoken with Edvardsson already?"

"Yes. It was important to consult her as soon as possible."

"In the future, you will report to me first before you speak to that bitch. May I remind you, you work for me, not her," said Malmer. He'd had several confrontations with the prosecutor and had always come away the loser. Their enmity made Ekman's job harder since he had to coordinate with Edvardsson. Besides he respected her, and despised Malmer. I'll talk with her whenever I need to, he thought, and Malmer be damned.

"I'm expecting a revised profile from Karlsson later today, and I'll send it up," said Ekman, standing.

"Just a minute. We're not finished yet. From the reports I've seen, the Westberg investigation is going too slowly. I want you to get more involved. Check out the scene yourself and talk to Westberg, and anyone else who has anything to do with it."

"I have every confidence in Alenius and Rosengren; they're very experienced. But I'll take the time to go there myself, if you insist."

"I do," said Malmer, looking down and sorting through some papers on his desk. Ekman had been dismissed.

Motioning to Holm to follow him to his office, Ekman slumped into his chair.

"Malmer wants me to look into the Westberg case myself. Rosengren and Alenius aren't going to be happy about it. I'm going to have to talk with them. You'd better set up a meeting for tomorrow."

"You're right about them being pissed, but maybe you'll pick up on something they missed."

"Would you also please call Westberg. I'd like to see him after I talk with Alenius and Rosengren."

Handing Holm the list of eight names he'd prepared, Ekman said, "I wanted to check out these old cases myself, but now that I have to deal with the Westberg break-in, I won't have the time. Could you get started on them? What I'm looking for is someone from the past who's out of prison, might hold a grudge against me, and could possibly be Grendel. See who looks good to you." He glanced up at Holm and smiled. "I have implicit faith in your judgment."

"I'll get right on it, Chief."

"Thanks, Enar. How are the missing-person cases going?"

"So far, nothing has shaken loose. Maybe we'll have better news for you tomorrow."

As Holm headed out the door, the phone rang. It was Malmquist.

"Walther, we're not finished with the package you sent, but you should know that although the cord is office supply cotton twine available everywhere, you were right to save the knot."

"What did you find?"

"It's a bowline, unusual for most people, but common among sailors. I thought it might help narrow your suspect list."

"It may very well do that, Ludvig, when we have one," Ekman said. "But the quick call is appreciated. Thanks."

"I may have more for you tomorrow."

Ekman checked his e-mail and found Karlsson's six-page analysis of the second letter from Grendel. It summarized and elaborated on their luncheon conversation. This time it came with a bill for twelve thousand kronor, covering everything Karlsson had worked on so far. He printed out the report and the invoice, scrawling "Approved for payment" on the bill, initialing and dating it.

Holm came back in. "I've set up a meeting with Alen-ius and Rosengren at ten, and with Westberg at eleven at his office. It's on Yakullsgatan," he said, handing Ekman a slip of paper with the address and phone number.

"Thanks, Enar. And here's Karlsson's bill. Please send it to accounting," he said, passing it to Holm.

"Karlsson has developed an addition to the profile, based on Grendel's last letter," Ekman said, giving it to Holm. "Sit down and look it over."

Holm looked up when he finished reading. "We're getting a deeper understanding of this character every time he writes. It should help us catch him."

"Yes, and it should make him easier to manipulate in interrogation, if we ever get someone to interrogate," responded Ekman.

"We'll need copies of Karlsson's report for tomorrow's meeting."

"Will do," said Holm, rising and heading for the door.

"And Enar, if I'm pushing you too hard, let me know. Really."

"It's not a problem, Chief." If it ever was, of course, he'd never say anything, Ekman thought.

18

Concerns

Turning to his stacked in-box, Ekman began sorting through it. Most were routine reports sent to him for his information. He flipped through them, but there was nothing of importance. Initialing them, he put them in his out-basket. There were, however, several personnel matters he had to deal with, and these he set to one side. They involved performance reports and promotion recommendations he'd have to act on soon. All of this was the bureaucratic drudgery he longed to get rid of, but there was only so much he could pass to Holm. Some things were his unavoidable responsibility.

Ekman sighed, and reached into the drawer for his needlepoint. As his hands stitched, he went back and forth over the Grendel case, searching for things he'd ignored which could give them at least a toehold. They were doing all they could with the little they had, he concluded. Be patient, Ekman, he said to himself; but he was always impatient when he felt frustrated by a case.

During dinner that evening, Ekman had said nothing about the day's events.

"What's been happening with that case, Walther? Do I have to pry it out of you?"

"I had lunch with Jarl Karlsson today," he said. "At Il Positano. It was quite good. We both had the branzino."

"And?"

Ekman thought about what he could tell her, leaving out anything about the personal focus that Karlsson had emphasized.

"And . . . he's been very helpful, giving us a better understanding of this new case. Also," he added, almost as an afterthought, "there's no need to get me a new briefcase. It was returned."

"How did that happen?" she asked.

"It seems the person who wrote that strange letter I told you about retrieved the briefcase from the robbers," Ekman said, between bites on a veal chop.

"He knew the robbers? That's quite a coincidence, Walther. What's the rest of the story?" She wouldn't let him get away with not telling her more. Now he regretted even mentioning the briefcase.

"It seems he was having them watch me, God knows why," Ekman said, "and they took matters into their own hands by robbing me. So he retrieved the briefcase and sent it back with an apology." He omitted what may have happened to the robbers.

"Walther, I don't like the sound of this at all. You said the other day that letter had something to do with cannibalism, and now the writer is having you watched?"

She was putting it together much too fast, Ekman thought.

"This guy's just a run-of-the-mill weirdo, a crank. Apart from the robbery, which he didn't plan, nothing's happened. Certainly nothing for you to worry about," he said, helping himself to another serving of garlic mashed potatoes.

"Nevertheless, I am worried. There's no telling what a disturbed person may do." There's that psychobabble phrase again, Ekman thought, why don't we just say "crazy" and be done with it.

"Ingbritt, I'm not concerned, and you shouldn't be either."

"Walther Ekman, you can't fool me. You've started carrying a gun. Yes, I saw you trying to hide it from me when you came in this evening. You took it off and shoved it in your overcoat pocket."

"All right," Ekman said holding up his hands, "I confess. I thought it prudent to wear it after the robbery and didn't want to alarm you. But that's all." He thought he sounded convincing, but hated lying to her.

"You'll tell me if something more happens won't you, Walther? I don't want to have to pry things out of you. When I do, it just makes me anxious," she said in a soft voice.

Ekman got up and hugged her. "There's nothing for you to worry about, darling," he said, hoping it was true, as he kissed the top of her head.

19

Captured Pieces

Friday, October 14. Yesterday's rain-laden clouds had been replaced by a brilliant blue sky. There was still a strong breeze moving the bare treetops. It was getting colder. With the sun shining, it was a day to be cheerful, but Ekman didn't feel that way. On the drive in, he mulled over the meetings ahead of him. None of them promised to be easy.

When he got to the office, Holm wasn't in his cubicle, but had already placed the handouts for this morning's meeting on Ekman's desk. I should think about promoting him soon, thought Ekman, except he's become too valuable to lose. He immediately reproached himself for selfishness.

Feeling the need for more coffee, Ekman took the stairs down to the cafeteria. When he got there he realized the others might also like something and asked the counterman for a large pot of coffee and a basket of sweet rolls to be delivered every morning. Taking a double espresso with him, he headed back to his office.

When the cafeteria worker arrived with his order, Ekman asked her to put it on the side table in his conference room.

Holm stuck his head in the door to say good morning.

"Enar, god morgen, thanks for getting the handouts ready. I've had some coffee and sweet rolls put out in the conference room. Please help yourself."

"Thanks, Chief, that's good of you," Holm replied. Coming back with a cup of coffee and a roll, he sat in a guest chair.

"So, how have the missing-person cases been going?"

"Well, we each took one, and I haven't spoken with the others about their cases. But I can tell you about mine if you like."

Ekman looked at the clock. "It's almost time for the meeting, why don't we save it for then so you don't have to repeat yourself," he said, getting up.

As they settled into their seats at the conference table, the others came in.

"Thanks for the refreshments, Chief," said Rapp, as he spotted them and, going over, took two pastries.

"You're very welcome. Everybody please help yourselves and then we'll get started."

Ekman was pleased that with one exception everyone was properly dressed, but winced at Bergfalk's open-necked, shimmering orange shirt with a gold jacket.

Once they were all seated, Ekman looked at Holm.

"Enar, why don't you begin?"

Holm took out face photos from a file folder and passed them around. "Mine is a male, thirty-seven, named Bertil Henriksson, a land surveyor, who lived in Jönköping."

Ekman looked at him with raised eyebrows.

"Yes, Chief, I did check in first with the locals. They were very helpful and I didn't have to give details about why we were interested."

Holm continued, "He went missing three months ago for no apparent reason. He was due in his office at nine, but never made it. He lived alone in an apartment that was twenty minutes away and always walked. Henriksson was seen leaving his building that morning and going down the block, and that was the last anyone saw of him.

"He had no financial problems, and apparently no personal ones either. I went over the case file with the investigating officer, and then went to Henriksson's office and spoke with his colleagues. The guy was well-liked, did a good job, and had no enemies, as far as anyone knew.

"After that I interviewed his closest relative, his mother. Everyone, especially his mother, is still really shaken by his disappearance. She told me he'd had several girlfriends, but hadn't been involved with anyone for several months when he vanished. I also spoke by phone with the last girl he'd dated. They'd seen each other for half a year and then just drifted apart, but were still friendly."

Holm looked around the table. "I'm sorry to say that's all I've got. I think it was thoroughly investigated at the time. There don't seem to be any leads left unexplored."

"Thanks, Enar," Ekman said. Turning to the rest of them he asked, "Did anyone hear anything that rang a bell with you?"

"It sounds similar to the Gustaffson case we spoke about yesterday. What struck me was that both men vanished while walking to or from work," said Vinter.

"Good point," said Ekman.

"That happened in my case, too," Rapp exclaimed. "It was a year ago last February in Falköping. The guy, Rudy Bohren, a thirty-six-year-old store manager, was going home after working late, and never made it."

"I can't say quite the same," said Bergfalk. "The woman in mine, forty-five, lived with her sister. She disappeared two years ago from her apartment in Växjö one night after saying she was just going out for a breath of air. There was no apparent reason for her to just disappear. She had a good job, family, and friends. She'd made firm plans for the next day and was supposed to go on vacation with some girlfriends the following week. The investigator questioned everyone, and followed up all possible leads. Like Enar, I think they did a thorough job and I couldn't improve on it."

"So, let's say for now the missing woman is an outlier who doesn't fit the disappearance pattern, and we focus on the three similar cases involving men who vanished while walking to or from work. Is there anything else we can say?" asked Ekman.

"People don't just vanish into thin air," interjected Rapp. "Someone had to intervene. And since in at least two cases it happened in daylight, no one is likely to have just knocked them down and dragged them away. I think they were picked up by a car or some other vehicle."

"Alrik, you've put your finger on it," said Ekman. "Now the question is why would they get into a car? Was it someone they knew? Also, it occurs to me, what was the weather like? Did walking unexpectedly become a problem and make it more likely they would accept a lift, even from a stranger? Another possibility, of course, is they were forced in at gunpoint. The most basic question, however, is why were they singled out in the first place? If we can find the answer to that, everything else may fall into place.

"Enar, why don't you check the local weather on the dates the three men disappeared. And Alrik, Gerdi, and Mats, I'd like you to draw up lists of each man's educational background, business associates, friends and relatives. See if any common names leap out at you.

"Does this sound like the way to proceed?" Ekman asked. They all nodded agreement.

"We've got to remember we started out looking for some connection with Grendel, thinking he might be a serial killer. But these disappearances may have nothing to do with Grendel. We could be on the track of a killer, nonetheless. So don't feel your work may be for nothing.

Even though it's possible these disappearances are uncon-nected, I don't really think so. They're too similar for it to be just coincidence. I believe we're onto something. What do you think?" Ekman looked around the table.

"I agree with you, Chief," said Vinter. "I have to admit I was skeptical at first, but what we've found so far makes me feel there's a real problem out there, whether or not it has anything to do with this Grendel."

Rapp, Bergfalk and Holm chimed in their agreement.

"Good, we've gotten a sharper focus. Now let me bring you up to date," he said, handing out Karlsson's latest addition to the profile.

They sat silently for the next five minutes, reading.

"All I can say, Chief, is that Karlsson's right, this guy's got some sort of fixation on you," said Bergfalk. "Maybe you should take this very personally."

"Because we still don't really know whether we're deal-ing with a killer or just a nut who's focused on you, you should take precautions, Chief. Whether Grendel planned it or not, that robbery was directed at you." Rapp's voice showed his concern.

"Thanks, Alrik. I'm being extra careful these days." Changing the uncomfortable subject, he went on, "I think it would be helpful to set up a situation room." Ekman pointed to the corkboard on a side wall and the large whiteboard next to it.

"Enar, I'd like you to get a detailed map of southern Sweden and put it up on the corkboard. Then take photos of the three missing men and put them around it. Show the distances and driving times among the locations.

"The rest of you, please put your lists on the whiteboard. We'll need three columns with the men's photos, names, ages, dates of birth and disappearance, and all the other information you've gathered."

Ekman looked around the table. "Okay, you've got your assignments. I know tomorrow's Saturday, but let's make this a short weekend and meet again tomorrow."

Vinter and Holm looked glum. He guessed he was ruining some weekend plans.

"On the bright side," Ekman added, "you'll all be on overtime pay. We'll take a break on Sunday."

20

~~~~~~~

Westberg

At his desk, Ekman mulled over the meeting. His vision of the Grendel case was still clouded, but he felt they were making progress. That is, if there really was a connection with the missing men. He only hoped they weren't going too slowly.

Ekman frowned at the stack of papers remaining in his in-box, the personnel items. He'd made a considerable dent yesterday on the routine paperwork and the out-basket showed his progress. Now came the hard stuff.

He reached for the top item, an annual performance review for Rapp. Looking over the self-assessment section, he thought Alrik had been much too modest. He would have rated him higher. Rapp had been an inspector for more than eight years and was past due for promotion.

If he also wanted to promote Holm soon, to be fair, he'd first have to recognize Senior Inspector Rapp's very real accomplishments. These were the sorts of administrative considerations he disliked, but it was his responsibility, and there was no escaping the difficult choices. He wrote out a promotion recommendation for Rapp to chief inspector.

Knocking, Holm reminded him, "Alenius and Rosengren are here, Chief." Startled, Ekman realized it was already ten o'clock.

"Please sit down," said Ekman. "How is the Westberg case going?"

"I hate to say it, but there's been no real progress, Chief," said Rosengren, always the spokesperson for the duo.

"We've run out of leads. We've looked at other recent burglaries and there's no pattern we can see. Some were daylight, some weren't. Nobody saw anything. Also, we've run down all the local break-in artists and checked their alibis against the burglary time frames without results. It's all here in the report," he said, handing it to Ekman. "We know Westberg and the DC aren't going to be happy."

"Thanks for all your work," said Ekman. "It's no reflection on what you've both done, but Malmer wants me to get involved. I'm meeting Westberg in a little while to brief him." Their faces tightened.

"This is one of those high-profile cases that needs some window dressing. It's political, that's why Malmer is pushing it hard. I don't think I'm going to find anything you missed. This is just PR, okay?"

"We understand, Chief," said Rosengren, getting up. "Right, Alenius?" Always taciturn, he just nodded his agreement.

Ekman knew they were unhappy, but there was nothing more he could do about it.

Asking Holm to come in, Ekman handed him their report. "Send a copy to Malmer with a note telling him I'm meeting with Westberg this morning. Thanks, Enar."

Instead of driving, Ekman thought he would walk to Westberg's office, but before he left went back into the conference room. Pouring a cup of coffee, he reached for a sweet roll, stopping himself just before his hand touched it. Fat, Ekman, he thought, you're getting way too fat, and with an effort, turned aside, sipping his coffee.

Westberg's office on Yakullsgatan was ten blocks away. Ekman was looking forward to the walk on a sun-filled day like this, but not the conversation with Westberg. Despite their best efforts, Alenius and Rosengren hadn't come up with anything solid and Ekman very much doubted he could do any better. He would try to put things in a positive light, but the councillor had a reputation for being difficult and wouldn't be satisfied. It promised to be an unpleasant conversation.

Ekman walked along Dalagatan thinking about what lay ahead. Rounding the corner on Sturegatan, he passed an antiques shop and was stopped by the window display. An easel had been placed on a red-and-blue-patterned Persian rug, and on it was a gilt-framed panoramic view of old Stockholm. Peering at it, Ekman could just make out the legend at the bottom: "1648," the end of the Thirty Years War.

It was likely an original etching and he wondered whether he could afford it. He made a mental note of the address. If it was still available, maybe he could come back another day. Right now, he didn't have the time.

Turning from the window, for an instant Ekman caught the slight moving reflection of a person across the street, just vanishing around the corner. He suddenly realized that while he'd been looking at the picture, the dimly reflected figure—he couldn't be sure if it was a man or a woman—had been staring at him. He briefly considered following, but then thinking it was pointless, shrugged, and continued on his way.

Three blocks farther down, Yakullsgatan cut across Sturegatan. Going right, climbing up a hill, Ekman saw the ten-story building he was looking for near the top. In the elegant, marble-floored lobby, he checked the directory and found Westberg's name, with the words "Commercial Insurance" after it, listed on the tenth floor.

The elevator rose smoothly and when the door opened he found himself facing a large, modern console desk with a receptionist. Westberg's firm took up the entire top story. Going across the thick brown carpet, Ekman announced himself to the frowning, middle-aged woman behind the desk.

"Yes, Herr Ekman, Herr Westberg's expecting you. His office is at the end of the corridor on the left," she said, picking up the phone to call him.

Ekman knocked and, opening the door, entered a huge corner office with floor-to-ceiling windows on two sides. Eugen Westberg was coming around his glass and steel desk to meet him. He was a big man, almost as tall as Ekman, about sixty, with brushed back, thinning brown-gray hair, and a carefully trimmed gray moustache.

"Herr Ekman," he said in a booming voice, extending his hand, "it's good to meet you. I've heard so much about you. All very complimentary, of course. Thank you so much for taking the time to talk with me," he continued with every appearance of earnestness. Ekman could see why he was successful as a politician, as well as a businessman.

"I'm pleased to do it, Councillor," responded Ekman, as Westberg led him to two armchairs with a window view.

"Can I get you some coffee?" Westberg raised a phone to call.

"That would be great." Sipping coffee together might make this easier. Ekman looked around the office.

"You have a wonderful view of the city."

"Yes, it's enjoyable, even on a bad day, let alone one like this," Westberg smiled.

"Have you always had your office here?"

"No, we moved in a year ago. Before that we were in a sort of hole-in-the-wall place on the other side of town. But business has been good over the last few years."

There was a knock, a side door opened, and a young man came in carrying a tray with coffee and biscuits. He set it down on the table between their chairs.

"Thanks, Frans," said Westberg, as the man smiled, poured and left.

After they'd drunk some coffee, Ekman began, "I wanted to personally bring you up to date on the investigation. I know the break-in must have been very upsetting for you and your family."

"Yes, for my wife especially, since she was the one who discovered it."

"The men I assigned, Alenius and Rosengren, are two of my most experienced investigators. They've been very thorough, looking not only at your burglary, but others to see if there's some common pattern. They've also questioned potential suspects and checked their alibis."

"But . . ." said Westberg, leaving the sentence unfinished.

"Yes, I'm afraid they've been unable to get any further with the investigation. However, I'm going to go over the case in detail myself, starting with a visit to your home, if that's all right with you."

"Yes, certainly, Herr Ekman. I know you have many other things to do and I appreciate your taking the time to look into this yourself."

This is going to be easier than I thought, Ekman said to himself. He was premature.

"Like you, I want some clear answers," said Westberg in a harder voice. "When do you think you'll have them?"

"That's difficult to say. I don't want to promise something I can't deliver. I want to assure you, however, that whatever can be done to find the burglar will be done. This is not being treated in a casual manner."

"I appreciate that. I know you're giving this unusual attention," Westberg said, getting up. The interview was over.

Ekman shook his hand. "I'll let you know as soon as we come up with anything."

"Thanks for taking a personal interest," said West-berg in a flat tone, walking him to the door.

Ekman was relieved Westberg hadn't been more hos-tile. He'd look at the crime scene as he'd promised, but thought that at this late date he wouldn't discover any-thing new. He was going through the motions primarily to get Malmer off his back.

At his office, he decided there was no point in prolong-ing things, and called Westberg's house. A woman, he presumed the wife, answered.

"Is this Fru Westberg? This is Walther Ekman. Your husband may have told you that I'd like to come by. Yes, in an hour would be fine. I'll see you then."

Malmquist called back sooner than he'd expected.

"We've finished with the package you sent, Walther, and apart from the distinctive knot we discussed yes-terday, there really isn't much to say, I'm afraid. There were no unidentified fingerprints on the package itself. Yours were on the briefcase, along with some unusable smudged prints.

"However, the white gift box was a type made over the last three years only for the Åhléns department stores. From a few fibers we're still tracing, it seems to have contained a garment made of good quality, brown merino wool. The tissue might also have come from that store, but looked new and could have been bought anywhere. The address on the box was done using a standard black marker of the same type used on the letter envelope, and in the same handwriting. The note itself was prob-ably copied on the Canon printer, using a cheap grade of paper. And that's it."

"Ludvig, don't feel discouraged. I really appreciate the fast work."

"Are there any other leads?"

"We're looking into some missing-person cases, but so far, don't have anything."

"Walther, I should say the same thing to you, 'Don't feel discouraged.' Just remember it's still quite early: it's Friday, and this got started on Tuesday. I'd say you've already covered a lot of ground quickly. It will just take more time to find him, unless he slips up."

"You're realistic, my friend, and you're right. I'm too impatient and the frustration level is rising."

"Call me if you need anything."

"Thanks, as always, Ludvig."

21

House Call

Ekman thought it was too far and would take too much time to walk to Westberg's house. Besides, he felt he'd had more than enough exercise for the day. He took the elevator to the garage.

In light traffic, it took him fifteen minutes. Westberg's home was on a street off Eddavagen, in a quiet neighborhood of large, expensive homes. Pulling into the semicircular driveway, Ekman could see the house was insulated from its neighbors by high hedges on both sides. From Alenius's report, he knew the curtain of hedges extended around the back.

Fru Westberg was a short, thin, fair-haired woman in her late fifties, carefully made-up. She wore a dark blue dress with a diamond and gold brooch at her shoulder and a string of pearls around her neck. She looked as though she were about to go to a formal luncheon.

"Please come in Herr Ekman," she said without warmth. She hung his coat and hat in the guest closet and ushered him into the bright, high-ceilinged living room on the right, two steps down from the hallway level. It was painted white with sleek, upholstered furniture and thick carpeting, all in white. A huge abstract painting in brilliant reds and yellows dominated one wall. She pointed toward a long couch and they sat down facing each other at opposite ends.

"Fru Westberg, as I told your husband, I've taken personal charge of the investigation and thought it would be helpful to examine the scene," he said, gesturing with his arm as he indicated the house in general. "I hope you don't mind the intrusion and some of the repetitious questions I may need to ask. This shouldn't take very long."

"We do appreciate your getting involved, Herr Ekman." Her voice made clear that she didn't mean it. "As you can imagine, this was particularly upsetting for me, having our home invaded like that." She smoothed down a few strands that had somehow escaped her stiff hairdo.

"I can certainly understand your feelings," said Ekman, remembering his recent personal encounter with crime. "Perhaps we can start by your walking me through what happened when you came home that day."

She repeated what he'd already read in the reports, and then led him up a wide, white carpeted staircase to the bedroom she shared with her husband.

Pointing to a white and gold Louis XVI dressing table, she said, "This is where I first noticed something wrong. I'd left out a gold mesh bracelet and a ruby and gold ring I'd taken from the safe in the morning, thinking I might wear them. They were gone."

He looked around the room. It was very neat. Missing jewelry would have been apparent.

"Do you have a housekeeper, Fru Westberg?" he asked.

"Yes, of course. But she didn't come in that day. She's trustworthy and has been with us five years. She's quite above suspicion," she replied.

"Certainly, certainly, but she may have seen something on a previous day. Perhaps someone lurking around the house or neighborhood. So we'll need her name, address, and phone number. Just routine," Ekman said in a mollifying voice, taking out a small, black leather notebook and pen.

He was surprised Alenius and Rosengren had missed this. Probably because they'd been pissed at the assignment, they'd gotten sloppy. It was unprofessional, and he'd soon let them know how he felt about it.

"Her name is Hulda Fransson. My address book is in the study. I'll get you the other information before you leave."

She took him back downstairs to the commercial-sized kitchen's rear door. "I came down next, thinking maybe I'd somehow left the jewelry on the kitchen counter, and saw the doorframe was splintered and the lock broken."

Ekman bent over to look, but the damage had already been repaired. He opened the door and stepped out onto a wide, flagstone patio. A stiff breeze had come up. He saw the line of hedge at the rear of the property and could just make out where it had been disturbed.

"I'll be walking around the outside for a while after our visit, Fru Westberg," he said, closing the door. "I assume you have a lawn service?"

"Yes. Haksson Brothers. They have an office downtown, I can give you the address."

"I may want to speak with them, as well."

Leading him back into the living room, she pointed to a glass-topped side table. "Our family portrait was there, in a silver frame. I noticed it missing when I came in here that day. Why was it taken?" she asked, her voice quivering with indignation.

"That's something we'll try to find out, Fru Westberg. It may be significant, because it's unusual. Who was in the photo?"

"My husband, myself, and our son, Rodger."

"Does your son live nearby?"

"Yes, he has a condo in town, not far from his law office," she replied, with unconcealed pride.

Ekman took out his notebook. "That's Rodger West-berg, and for our records could I please have his home and business addresses and phone numbers?"

"I don't see why he needs to be involved."

"Again, Fru Westberg, it's part of normal police routine to be thorough and speak with everyone who might be able to shed any light on the burglary."

"I don't know how he could do that."

"He may have seen some small detail that could be helpful, perhaps something he'd noticed before the burglary, without his even realizing it." He could find her son without her help, but wanted her cooperation.

"All right, I'll give you the information if you think it might help somehow," she gave in, with an exasperated shake of her head.

"Is there anything else you noticed on the day of the robbery, anything at all that stood out?"

"No, there's nothing else I can think of."

"Please call me if something comes to mind," he said, handing her his business card. "And if you could get me that information, I'll look around outside."

She went into a room across the hall, and coming back, gave him a piece of paper with the addresses and phone numbers of the housekeeper, the yard company, and her son.

"Good-bye, Fru Westberg," Ekman said, as she got his coat and hat from the closet. "Thank you for your time and help. I hope to have something more to tell you in a while."

"I certainly hope so," she said, closing the door firmly.

Ekman had been surprised at her reluctance to provide information about her son. *I wonder if she thinks he might be involved somehow. Even though he's a lawyer, perhaps he's short of money and owes some shady characters. His parents may not have wanted to lend him* any, so he arranged a break-in to pay off his debt. Ekman thought it was a very remote possibility, but still needed to be followed up.

Crossing the well-tended front lawn, he walked around the house to the break in the hedge at the back and could see the heavily wooded lot on the other side. Ekman circled the house and walked down the concrete drive to the street. He had a clear line of sight in both directions. A vehicle parked where someone could watch the Westberg place would have been obvious.

How was it done? he mused. The house had to have been observed before the break-in. Straight across the street, about half a kilometer away, was a forested hillside. Ekman, on a hunch, decided to drive over.

Parking on the street closest to the base of the hill, he got out and looked for some way to get to the top. Almost hidden beneath undergrowth was a narrow dirt path. He struggled up the fairly steep incline, almost losing his foothold, stopping several times to catch his breath. You're out of shape, Ekman, he thought, grossly out of shape.

From the crest of the hill he had an unobstructed view in the distance of the front of the Westberg house. Looking around, he noticed an area where weeds had been broken and flattened, as though something heavy had pressed them down.

Someone lay here, he thought, and he began searching the ground around the depressed area. No cigarette butts; too bad so many people have given up smoking, it would have helped. Almost invisible against the dark earth, hidden under a bush, were two, circular black plastic discs with raised edges. Ekman bent down and carefully picked them up with his handkerchief. He racked his brain. Where had he seen these before? Of course, of course, they were covers for binocular lenses. He folded them in his handkerchief, and put it in his coat pocket.

Now he knew how it had been done. Someone lay here and waited, perhaps for hours, watching the house until the occupants left. Were the other burglarized houses cased in the same way? Their general surroundings needed to be examined for possible observation sites. The more he thought about how much Alenius and Rosengren had missed, and the time and exertion they'd caused him, the more aggravated he became.

In his car, he took out his mobile and called Holm. "Enar, I'll be back in fifteen minutes. Get hold of Alenius and Rosengren and have them in my office in half an hour. Thanks." Perhaps I'll have calmed down by then, Ekman thought.

Stopping first in the cafeteria for an espresso to take with him, twenty minutes later Ekman was seated in his office, waiting with grim anticipation for the interview. He hadn't calmed down much.

22

Mr. Nice Guy

"Are you wondering why I wanted to see you?" he asked them.

"Not really, Chief," said Rosengren. "We guessed it was something about the Westberg case," he added, looking at the silent Alenius for confirmation.

"You're right about that. It's one of the very few things both of you have gotten right in this case."

"What do you mean, Chief?" said Alenius, speaking up for the first time.

"What I mean," said Ekman, his voice loaded with sarcasm, "is that this was the sloppiest, most inexcusably careless investigation I've ever seen from you two, or any other inspector here, for that matter. You didn't like the assignment and so you went through the bare motions. In the process, you got me called on the carpet by Malmer, and left me to do the heavy lifting. It's not appreciated and won't be tolerated."

"But, Chief . . ." protested Rosengren.

"Don't try and bullshit me, either of you. You know damned well I'm right. Your conduct was uncalled for, unprofessional, and totally unacceptable. Do I make myself perfectly clear?"

"Yes, Chief," said a subdued Alenius, glancing at Rosengren. "I guess, we were in too much of a hurry to drop the case and get back to what we thought was more important work."

"Unless I've suddenly forgotten something, I'm the one who decides what's important work around here. Am I right?" he asked, in a too quiet voice.

"Absolutely, Chief. It will never happen again," said a downcast Rosengren.

"If it does, you'll find yourselves back in the uniformed division," declared Ekman, his anger dissipating. "Now, let me tell you what I found," he said, summarizing his conversation with Fru Westberg and his discovery on the hilltop.

"You're both back on this case and will stay on it until we find out what's going on. Here's the information on the housekeeper, the yard service, and Westberg's son. You'll interview them thoroughly, but gently, especially the son. And then you'll go back over the other break-ins, step by step. I want a report on my desk by this evening on what you've done. Got it?"

"Yes, Chief," they each responded in a despondent voice.

"I'm sending the lens covers to forensics and I'll let you know what they come up with. Now get the hell out of here and try to live up to your past reputations."

Ekman was satisfied that to redeem themselves they'd do the most thorough investigation he'd ever seen.

"You shouldn't have told me to call if I needed anything, Ludvig."

"You've gotten something more on that guy?"

"No, I'm afraid not. It's another case. There've been a series of break-ins we're trying to get a handle on and I've found a couple of binocular lens covers that may give us a lead. Apparently the burglar was casing a house and lost them. This one's high profile and political or I wouldn't ask for special treatment."

"What are friends for anyway, right? Send them over and we'll see if we can get anything."

"This must be at least the thirty-third favor."

"You must mean the hundred thirty-third."

"Thanks, Ludvig. I really mean it. When I see you next, a lunch in the best restaurant is on me."

"You can't bribe a public official so easily. It's going to have to be dinner."

"You've got it."

Holm was at his desk on the phone. Ekman waited until he'd hung up and then opened the handkerchief to show him the lens covers.

"Enar, put some gloves on, please, and then slip these into a plastic bag. Photograph them and send them by courier to Malmquist. He's expecting them. When you've finished, I'll tell you all about it." Ekman always brought Holm in on what was happening. As his assistant, Enar should know everything he was working on, Ekman thought. He'd never had any reason to distrust him or doubt his discretion.

When Holm came back, Ekman told him about the latest developments in the Westberg case, and how he'd reamed out Rosengren and Alenius after he found they'd let him down.

"I'll bet they'll never try anything like that again, Chief."

"I believe you're right, or I wouldn't have put them back on the case."

"Sometimes you're too easygoing, Chief, and some people think they can take advantage. Those two, and a few others around here, need a wake-up call."

"Too easygoing? Really, Enar? I've never thought of myself that way."

"Maybe you should."

"Okay, okay," Ekman laughed, "no more mister nice guy." He'd always believed he was sometimes too harsh. It was surprising others might have a different view.

He suddenly realized he was quite hungry. "Are you free for a late lunch, Enar?"

"Sure, Chief. Just give me few minutes to finish something I'm working on. Where do you want to go? The cafeteria?"

"Not there. How about the little place across the square?" It was a favorite of his.

23

~~~~~~~~~~~~

Knight Down

The wind had died and the sun was still very bright. Ekman put on his sunglasses as they came out of headquarters and strolled around the perimeter of the busy plaza filled with pedestrians and traffic.

Sitting near a window where they could look out on the square, Ekman and Holm consulted the day's menu written on the large chalkboard hanging on the front wall.

"I think I'll have my usual," said Ekman.

"The herring?" asked Holm, remembering their last visit the previous week.

"Yes. And a bottle of Dugges."

"I'll just have a salad and sparkling water. I need to watch my weight." There was a fleeting, hurt look on Ekman's face.

"Maybe I'll have that ale after all," Holm said.

When the waitress had taken their order, Ekman asked, "Have you had a chance to look at that list of names I gave you?"

"Yes, I've been able to eliminate three so far. Two have died and another has moved to Canada. I should be finished with a first cut at the others later tomorrow."

"I think it's a long shot that Grendel is some kind of enemy of mine from the past, but it's still worth pursuing. Thanks for taking it on."

"Glad to do it, Chief."

Ekman devoured the assorted open-faced herring sandwiches on brown bread. He liked the smoked ones and those in mustard sauce best. He thought about having a second ale, but they both needed to get back to work. Besides, he didn't want Holm to think he was ignoring his weight problem.

Ekman settled in at his computer and began typing. Malmer was going to have to be brought up to date and he wanted to do it in writing. The phone rang. It was Rosengren.

"Chief, we can't find Rodger Westberg."

"What do you mean you can't find him?" Ekman asked, in an exasperated voice.

"We called him at home to set up an interview, but when no one answered, figured he was at work. We called his mobile, but got no response, so we called his law office. They haven't seen him in two days, he never called in, and didn't answer their calls. They were getting really worried and were just about to call us.

"So we went over to his place, thinking he might be sick or something. When he didn't answer, we thought maybe he'd passed out, so we got the manager to let us in. No one was there. The place was tidy. We checked the bedroom closet. Maybe he went on a trip without telling anybody, but no clothes seemed to be missing and his suitcase was still there. We thought you should know right away because it's Westberg's son." He paused. "And we'd heard around the shop that you've got a crew looking into missing-person cases."

"Okay, you did right calling me. Don't do anything more on this until you hear from me. You and Alenius plan on coming in tomorrow and meeting with me and the others working missing persons. At eight, in my conference room."

"We'll be there, Chief."

Ekman sat there for a few minutes digesting the news. Suddenly, the Westberg case had the possibility of becoming more than one in a string of burglaries. It might be linked to the other missing-person cases they'd been working on, hoping to get a lead they could follow to Grendel. But Ekman didn't want to jump to conclusions. There could be many other explanations for the younger Westberg's disappearance.

He debated with himself whether to tell Malmer about his suspicions. Although Malmer was obnoxious, he wasn't stupid. He knew Ekman was looking into missing-person cases and would make the connection quickly enough. It was best to bring it right out in the open before he did.

"Is he in, Annika? I need to see him right away. He's busy? He'll want to see me anyway. Tell him it's about the Westberg case."

On his way out, Ekman said to Holm, "Rodger Westberg's suddenly gone missing. No one knows where. I'm on my way to see Malmer."

Holm's head jerked up. "This will really complicate things."

"Yes. And will put even more pressure on us," said Ekman, hurrying to the elevator.

A few minutes later he was sitting in Malmer's office.

"What's all this about Westberg? You interrupted me in the middle of a conference call with Stockholm, so this better be important."

"It is. As you asked, I became personally involved in the Westberg case, interviewing the couple, and going over the crime scene. Fru Westberg gave me the names of several others to speak with. I also discovered where someone had been watching the house from a nearby hill and found some binocular lens covers there. They've been sent to forensics. Alenius and Rosengren are assisting me, and Rosengren called me a few minutes ago. The information he gave me is why I needed to see you."

"Yes, yes," said Malmer. "You still haven't told me anything so important you needed to interrupt me."

"I wanted you to know the background of what's happened. Rosengren just told me Rodger Westberg has disappeared."

"What do you mean 'disappeared'?"

"Exactly that. He's been missing from work, and it seems his apartment, for two days. He doesn't answer his phone. His office was about to call us when Alenius and Rosengren turned up to interview him about the break-in. I thought you should know about this before I speak with the Westbergs again today. You'll no doubt hear from Herr Westberg after I do."

Malmer was silent for a moment. "This is awful. I'll have to speak with the commissioner."

"Yes, he needs to be informed. But there's more. We've been looking into unusual missing-person cases in connection with the Grendel matter. The Westberg disappearance may, I stress *may*, be related."

"You're implying that a madman, a possible cannibal for God's sake, has grabbed Westberg's son? How am I supposed to break that news to him?" Malmer's face paled. Ekman guessed he was racing through all the horrendous political and media ramifications.

"We don't know Grendel is involved at all, or for that matter, even in any of the other missing-person cases. So I would never mention this to the Westbergs. My team has been meeting every day since the first letter came and we'll be at it again tomorrow morning to review all those cases, including Westberg's. I propose to tell his parents that their son's disappearance is now our first priority. When you speak with him, Olov, you can assure him we're doing everything possible, and will continue to do so."

"Yes, that's the approach to take. Say nothing about that lunatic. They'll only get hysterical. And besides, as you say, there may be no connection at all." Malmer seemed somewhat relieved.

"Westberg may just have gone away suddenly and for some reason chosen to stay out of touch," said Ekman in a reassuring voice. "Or he's shacked-up with a new girlfriend, or had a nervous breakdown. Those are the good alternatives. The bad ones are an assault with serious injury, kidnapping, or murder. When I speak with Westberg's parents, I'll try and get information about the better possibilities. While I'm doing that, Alenius and Rosengren will be checking hospitals for anyone with his description. He could be unconscious and without identification if he was robbed. They'll also check the morgue. Then they'll interview people at his office for leads."

"Those seem like the right steps. Let's pray this turns out to be nothing serious," said Malmer, his fingers tapping on his desk. He was clearly shaken by the sudden turn of events. He had even abandoned his usual readiness to blame Ekman for anything that went wrong.

"I'll keep you updated as this develops," said Ekman, getting out of that damned chair. His back had already begun to ache.

Calling Rosengren, Ekman told him to get a photo and physical description of Rodger Westberg from his office, and then begin checking hospitals for anyone resembling him who was admitted in the last two days. If there was some question about a possible identification, he was to take over a photo. After the hospitals, he was to call the county morgue.

"And while you're doing this, tell Alenius to start interviewing everyone at Westberg's office, asking about his appointments for the last week, any unusual behavior, or what they know about his personal life. As soon as either of you learn anything significant, call me."

"Got it, Chief. We're on it," Rosengren said, glad to show Ekman they were now working the case with enthusiasm.

24

The Westbergs

Ekman called Eugen Westberg. "Herr Westberg, something important has come up and I need to speak with you and your wife right away. Can I meet you at your house in half an hour? No, I'd rather not discuss this on the phone. And yes, I realize I'm asking you and Fru Westberg to drop everything to meet with me. I wouldn't ask this unless it was absolutely necessary. When we speak, I think you'll agree this was the right thing to do. Okay, I'll see you then."

Pulling into Westberg's drive, he saw a large, black Jaguar sedan parked in front. He guessed this was Westberg's. They'd been waiting for him; the door opened as he approached.

"Well, Herr Ekman, this had better be good. My wife is upset and the rest of my day is ruined," said Westberg, as Ekman entered.

He ignored the remark. "Can we sit down?" he replied, as Westberg led the way into the living room. His wife was already there, standing beside the mantel of the floor-to-ceiling white brick fireplace.

The couple sat on the couch while Ekman occupied a facing armchair.

"I apologize for this abrupt interview," he began. "Would you please tell me if either of you has spoken with your son in the last two days?"

"No, we haven't, have we Eugen?" asked his wife. Westberg shook his head. "But has something happened to Rodger?" Her voice was anxious.

"Your son, I'm sorry to have to tell you, appears to be missing. My officers went to his office to do a routine interview with him about the break-in and were told he hasn't been in for two days. They next went to his apartment, thinking he might be seriously ill. He wasn't there and everything appeared to be in order. No one has been able to reach him by phone."

"My wife and I spoke with him separately as recently as last week," said Westberg, his hands clasped together. "This is incredible."

"Do either of you know of any business or personal problems your son had lately?"

"No, nothing. Everything was fine," said Westberg.

"Did he mention a new girlfriend perhaps?"

"He's been seeing just one girl for quite some time, well over a year. As far as I know, they're still seeing each other," said Fru Westberg.

"We'll need to speak with her. Do you have her name and address?"

"Her name is Stina Lindfors. She's an accountant. I don't know her address." The dismissive tone told Ekman that Stina Lindfors was not one of Fru Westberg's favorite people. Her husband seemed about to interrupt, but stopped himself.

"I take it, you've met her?"

"Yes. Rodger asked us to invite her here for dinner. He's very serious about her, I'm afraid."

"Forgive me for saying this, Fru Westberg, but I get the impression you don't like her. Is there some particular reason?"

"There's just something about her that seems artificial, put on. Perhaps I'm prejudiced," she said, in a tone that indicated she didn't think so.

"My wife thinks she's just not right for our son," interrupted Westberg. "But many mothers no doubt feel that way about losing an only son." He turned to his wife. "It's time Rodger settled down, and if he thinks this is the right woman for him, we shouldn't stand in the way."

"Eugen, that's not it at all. You make it sound as though I'm possessive, when I'm not." Her tight face showed how angry she'd become.

"Rodger is taken with Stina and I don't blame him," said Westberg to Ekman. "She's not only very good looking and quite stylish, she's charming and intelligent. It's a good match." He turned again to his wife. "We need to accept Rodger's choice."

His wife didn't respond. She just gave him a stony glare.

Herr Westberg will have a difficult time tonight, thought Ekman. Aloud he said, "I see," in a neutral tone. "We'll locate her and arrange an interview," he said, jotting Lindfors's name in his notebook.

"What else are you going to do?" Westberg's voice had become harsh.

"Herr Westberg, we've already begun an intensive investigation. We're talking to anyone who might have information and we'll be tracing your son's movements. This is now our top priority and an entire team of investigators will be working on it. I want to give you my personal assurance we won't stop until we find him."

"That's all well and good. And I'm sure you're sincere. But I know how these things go. Other cases can come up that push this inquiry aside. I'm going to have to speak with Herr Malmer, and the commissioner, to make sure that doesn't happen. I hope you understand my concern.

It's no reflection on you or your officers," Westberg concluded, almost apologetically.

"I understand, Herr Westberg," replied Ekman, getting up. "Please satisfy yourself that everything possible is being done."

Fru Westberg came over to him. "He's our only child, Herr Ekman. Please find him, please," she said, her voice quivering. Her arrogant persona had vanished, and for that moment he saw the vulnerable woman she tried hard to conceal.

"We'll do all we can, Fru Westberg," Ekman said.

They both shook hands with him.

"You were right, Herr Ekman, I apologize for being so sharp before," said Westberg, walking him to the door. "Thank you for giving us this terrible news yourself."

25

Breaking the News

In his car, Ekman called Holm to have him check out local accounting firms for a Stina Lindfors. Then he phoned Edvardsson on her direct line.

"Malin, it's Walther. I hope you can give me a few minutes. Yes, there's been a significant development. Thanks. I'll see you in half an hour."

At the courthouse, he was in luck. There was a vacant space in the usually packed parking area strictly reserved for official police vehicles. He pulled down the sun visor with its police identification and went in.

"That's my personal car in the reserved area," Ekman said to the officer at the front door, who knew him. "Please keep an eye on it, in case someone wants it towed despite the ID."

"Sure, Chief," the officer said, touching his cap.

Going into Edvardsson's outer office, he saw the receptionist at work on her computer. She halfway rose as he came in.

"Please don't get up, Froken Sundquist. She's expecting me," Ekman said, as he went to the inner door, knocked, and entered.

"So, Walther," Edvardsson said after they were seated again on the couch, "I've been dying of curiosity since you called. What's happened?"

Ekman brought her up to date on the investigation, and then told her about Rodger Westberg's disappearance.

"Do you think Westberg and the other missing-person cases are related? Could they involve Grendel?" she asked, her eyes narrowing.

"Maybe. It's still too early to say anything definite, but yes, it's a possibility. I wanted you to know immediately about Westberg because this is so high profile and may have to become public knowledge." Ekman was thinking they'd have to go to the media to publicize Westberg's disappearance if nothing else turned up soon.

"You're quite right." Her face became serious and thoughtful, the professional prosecutor.

"We're going to have to become more formal now. I'll need a detailed report on your investigation by tomorrow morning. A national search for Westberg could be the next step."

"Unless a link to Grendel is established, even if we go public, I would want to keep that aspect confidential. Do you agree?"

"Absolutely. That's the last thing we want to happen. It would lead to disclosure of the letters. You can imagine the general reaction, and the media circus that would follow."

"Okay," said Ekman, getting up. "We're on the same page. And I know Malmer and the commissioner are as well."

"Walther, I hope our instincts are wrong. It would be too dreadful," Edvardsson said, as she walked to the door with him, reverting to what Ekman thought of as her real, as contrasted to her professional, self.

"I'm afraid, it's the sometimes nightmare world we live in Malin," he said, frowning.

Ide Sundquist came over as he was leaving. "Is something the matter, Herr Ekman? Forgive me for saying so, but you look upset."

"Thanks for your concern, Froken Sundquist. I hadn't realized it showed," he said, smiling at her.

"Now that's better," she said with a slight laugh. "Remember, things can always be much worse."

"You're absolutely right. I'll try not to forget that," he said, and shook her hand.

His car was where he'd left it, but some officious parking police attendant had put a note under his wiper telling him his police ID wasn't sufficient to allow him to park in a space reserved at the courthouse for official police vehicles. Aggravated, and cursing bureaucracy under his breath, he tore up the note, but put the pieces in his pocket. He felt it would be unseemly to just throw them in the gutter.

Ekman had left his mobile in the car, and checking it now, found a text message from Holm. He'd located Westberg's girlfriend. She worked at an accounting firm on Rydsgatan. Holm, thorough as usual, had included her office, home and mobile phone numbers, and her home address. He'd also obtained her driver's license photo. Ekman saw that to describe her as attractive was an understatement. When someone looked good in a license photo, then they must be very good looking indeed.

Ekman called Alenius. "How are you doing with the office interviews?"

"Nothing so far, Chief, but I'm taking a lot of notes for review and follow-up."

"Good. Try and find out how Westberg usually got to his office. Did he drive, take the tram, or walk? Also, I've gotten information about his girlfriend," he said, giving Alenius what Holm had sent.

"After you finish at his office, call her and set up an interview for today. Check with Rosengren and see if he's finished with his assignments. I'd like both of you to be there. If you find out anything out of the ordinary, call me. Otherwise, I'll see you at tomorrow's meeting."

"Okay, Chief. We'll take care of everything." The laconic detective for once sounded enthusiastic.

26

Lindfors

Rosengren had agreed to meet Alenius at five P.M. to interview Lindfors. The two inspectors drove together from headquarters to a modern office building at 170 Rydsgatan, twenty minutes away. Lindfors worked at Hackzell & Klinge, Authorized Accountants, on the third floor.

When the receptionist announced them, a tall, slender, blonde-haired woman who appeared to be in her midtwenties, dressed in a ruffled white silk blouse and dark brown woolen skirt, came out to the lobby to meet them.

"Froken Lindfors, I'm Inspector Alenius," he said, showing her his identification, "and this is Inspector Rosengren. We just need a few minutes of your time."

"Can you tell me what this is about?" she said, looking at them with widely spaced, almond-shaped gray eyes set in an oval face with full, sensual lips.

"Can we talk in private?" asked Rosengren.

"Of course," Lindfors responded, leading them down a side corridor to her small office and sitting down at her desk. The window behind her looked out on the wall of the building next door.

"Please sit down, gentlemen. Have I done something to warrant this visit?" she asked with an immaculate white smile.

Alenius and Rosengren were momentarily dazzled. "Not at all, Froken Lindfors," Alenius said. "We're doing a routine police inquiry and your name came up."

"In what connection?"

"Do you know a man named Rodger Westberg?" asked Rosengren, watching her face closely.

"Yes, he's my boyfriend. Actually, much more than that, more like my fiancé, because we've been talking about getting married. We've been together for the last fourteen months. Has something happened to him?" she asked, twisting a large gold and ruby ring on her right hand.

"Why do you think something has happened to him, Froken Lindfors?" inquired Alenius.

"When two police inspectors suddenly appear asking about Rodger, it's a natural conclusion, isn't it?"

"Or, it could be that he might have done something wrong," said Rosengren.

"Rodger? Not in a million years. He's the most honest, law-abiding person I've ever known," she said with a slight smile.

"Froken Lindfors, when was the last time you saw Advokat Westberg?" Alenius asked.

"Now I know something's happened," she said, biting her lower lip and looking at each of them in turn.

"Please, just answer the question," said Rosengren.

"It was last Saturday. We went out to dinner and then came back to my apartment. He stayed the night," she said without embarrassment.

"Then the last time you saw him was Sunday morning?" asked Rosengren.

"Yes. Now can you tell me what this is all about?" She'd become angry.

"One last question, Froken Lindfors," said Alenius. "Have you spoken to him since Sunday?"

"We spoke on Tuesday afternoon. I wanted us to get together that evening, but he said he was snowed under with a case coming to trial and just couldn't. We plan to meet tomorrow."

Rosengren thought that if he had a girlfriend who looked like Lindfors, he'd never turn her down. Work be damned.

"Froken Lindfors, we're very sorry to tell you that Rodger Westberg has been missing since sometime after you last spoke with him," said Alenius.

"Oh, no. That can't be."

"I'm afraid it's true. He's been missing since Wednesday morning at the latest. He hasn't been to his office or apartment, and isn't answering his mobile. We'd appreciate anything you can tell us that would help us find him."

"But there's no reason for him to have disappeared." Her chin was trembling and she was on the verge of tears.

"You love him?" Alenius asked in a soft voice.

"Yes," she said.

Rosengren wondered whether her feelings were genuine. She might just be putting on a great performance. Of the two, he, not Alenius, was the hardened cynic.

"He loves me. He would never, never, just vanish and not say anything to me." She stared at them with absolute certainty, daring them to contradict her.

"Do you know of any problems he had?" asked Rosengren.

"There weren't any problems. He had no health issues, business was good, and he never worried about money. Besides his successful law practice, and his family's wealth, of course, he had a large trust fund from his grandfather."

"Do you know any friends of his?" asked Alenius.

"A few. We went out to dinner with two other couples occasionally."

"Please give us their names. You can understand we have to look into all his relationships. It's just part of our normal procedure. We'd appreciate it if you didn't tell them we'll be calling on them."

"Certainly. I'll do anything I can to help." She paused. "This is so unbelievable."

"We're very sorry to give you such news, Froken Lindfors. If you could give us those names, we won't trouble you further."

Lindfors turned on her mobile and began jotting down names and phone numbers. She gave the list to Alenius.

"I hope this helps," she said.

"Please call me if anything that could possibly be useful, even the smallest detail, comes to mind," said Alenius, handing her his card.

As they left, they turned and saw her standing in the middle of her office, looking after them with a tense, frozen expression.

Outside the building, Alenius asked Rosengren, "What do you think?"

"She seemed really broken up about Westberg. But it could be an act."

"My impression too. She said he had no personal problems and wasn't concerned about money. Apparently there's a lot of it, and she's well aware of that: his busy law firm, his family's money, and then that large trust fund. He sounds like a very lucky, well-off guy, especially with a girlfriend like that. But let's find out more about his finances anyway."

"And hers," said Rosengren, ever the cynic.

27

At Home

When Ekman got back, Holm was away from his desk. He went into his office and closed the door, first putting a "Do Not Disturb" sign on the handle. He needed some quiet time to start drafting the memorandum Edvardsson had asked for. Ekman set it up chronologically, summarizing events, day by day, since everything had begun on Tuesday. He was seven pages in when he stopped with Westberg's disappearance and his meeting with the parents. He planned to finish the memo by including the results of tomorrow's meeting and the proposed next steps in the investigation.

Ekman was startled when the bookcase clock struck six thirty. It made him realize how tired he was. It had been an emotional, exhausting day; he was more than ready to head home.

Ingbritt gave him a warm, deep kiss when he came into the kitchen.

"What was that for?" he asked, grinning.

"Nothing special," she said, smiling. "I just felt like it."

"Hmm, and what else do you feel like?"

"Yes, that too," she replied in an embarrassed voice. Even after thirty-three years of marriage she was still shy about sex. Ekman thought of this as part of her charm, part of why he loved her.

"We'll have dinner and then go right to bed," he said. "No late night for me, at least downstairs." He laughed when she started to blush, and lightly smacked her rear.

Their dinner of roast chicken, mashed potatoes, and wilted spinach, with a bottle of chilled French chardonnay, was soon finished. He told her about Rodger Westberg's disappearance earlier in the week, and his own misgivings about the possible outcome. Her face darkened; she was becoming upset. He changed the subject by asking her how her writing was going.

They skipped dessert, and leaving the dishes in the sink, headed upstairs. He led the way, holding her hand.

28

The Game Develops

Saturday, October 15. It was an overcast morning, with rain coming down in torrents, when Ekman left at six forty. He wanted to get in early before this morning's meeting to review what he'd written yesterday evening. It was almost seven when he got to his office to find Holm already at work.

"God morgen, Chief," Holm said in a brisk, cheery voice, getting up.

"It's far too early to tell, Enar," responded Ekman with a smile. "But god morgen to you anyway."

"The others will be in soon to set up for the meeting."

"Good. That'll save time. I've asked Alenius and Rosengren to join us. Because Rodger Westberg's disappeared, I'm adding them to the team."

"I've made copies of Lindfors's photo for everyone. The package is on your desk."

"Thanks, Enar."

In his office, Ekman looked with pursed lips at the eight-by-ten enlargement. Picking up the phone he called the front desk.

"This is Ekman. Would Sergeant Lindberg happen to be on duty this weekend? He's in? Good. Have him come up, please."

When Lindberg arrived he saluted, and Ekman handed him the photo.

"Could this be the woman who delivered the package we discussed?"

Lindberg examined the picture intently. "She could be, Chief. There's a real similarity. She's pretty and blonde, like the woman I saw, but I just can't be certain."

"But it's possible?"

"Yes, Chief."

"Thanks, Lindberg. You've been very helpful." Lindberg gave him another snappy salute, wheeled on his heel, and left.

Lindberg must have enjoyed time in the military, thought Ekman. He overdoes it a bit, but I wish all the uniforms were more like him.

He began reviewing yesterday's memo, making changes as he went through it. By the time he'd finished, Holm knocked on the door to tell him the others were there and ready to start.

Ekman saw that one wall of the conference room was covered with the information he'd asked for. Alenius was seated beside Alrik Rapp, across the table from Rosengren, who was next to Gerdi Vinter.

Everyone was in business casual attire, except for Bergfalk who was wearing just a black tee shirt with a glittering, sequined rock band emblem hanging over faded jeans. Ekman was in his usual three-piece black suit. He couldn't conceive of appearing at work dressed informally, although he allowed a Saturday exemption to colleagues who felt differently.

"God morgen, everyone," said Ekman. "Thank you for coming in so early on a gloomy Saturday." He saw they'd already helped themselves to the coffee and pastries on the sideboard, and going over, got some himself, and sat down at the head of the table.

"I've asked Alenius and Rosengren to join our team because Rodger Westberg has suddenly vanished, as I'm sure they've already told you." He looked around and they all nodded. "The Westberg matter is now no longer about a break-in. The case now resembles our three other unusual disappearances."

"Alenius, why don't you bring us up to date," Ekman asked. Alenius described finding out at Westberg's office that he was missing, and his visit to Westberg's apartment.

"Then, as you wanted Chief, I asked his office staff how he got to work. Mostly, he walked. His apartment is less than fifteen minutes from the office. There are four people working for him—two paralegals, and two admin supports. I questioned each of them privately about Westberg—what kind of boss he is, what they know about his private life, any recent problems, and so on. Everyone likes him and is very upset about his disappearance. There don't seem to be any problems. They each mentioned the girlfriend, Stina Lindfors. She'd been in at least once a week over the last year or so. He was gone on her, and they said it looked like the real thing."

"Thanks. Rosengren?"

"I checked all the hospitals and the morgue. One hospital thought they might have him because someone like him had been found unconscious on the street. He'd been robbed, so there was no ID. But when I got there with the photo, they said it wasn't him. Also, the guy had come to and identified himself. Then I checked the morgue, but nobody with his description had been brought in over the last week." Rosengren took out copies of Westberg's photo and passed them around.

Turning to Rosengren, Ekman asked, "What was your impression when you both interviewed Lindfors?"

"She's hot," answered Rosengren with a grin, as some of the others smirked.

Ekman stared at him. "That's not quite what I had in mind."

"Only kidding, Chief. She seemed to be really broken up about his vanishing. It could have been an act, but if it was, it was a good one."

"I agree with Rosengren. She seemed very upset," put in Alenius. "But when I asked about any problems, she was quick to mention there were no financial ones, seeing how much money he and his family have."

"A not unusual response for an accountant," Ekman said.

"Yeah, perhaps. But Rosengren and I would like to look at Westberg's finances, and hers, just to see what the real situation is."

"Good idea, however, be careful to stay clear of anything about the father, Eugen Westberg. We're focusing only on his son, and Lindfors. See if you can find what you want about Rodger at his office. He probably drew up his own will. Let's get a copy of that. Also talk to the Tax Agency people about him, and her as well, and get the names of their banks. Then let's look at Westberg's bank statements from his office or apartment. We'll also want Lindfors's statements from her bank. If you need me to speak to the agency or the banks let me know."

"Do you think Westberg's been killed, Chief?" asked Rapp.

"Yes, it's begun to feel like that. We've eliminated the best reasons for a voluntary disappearance. If this were an abduction, we'd probably have had a demand from the kidnapper by now. What's left is homicide. How about the rest of you?"

"When we started on these missing-person cases I didn't know what to believe, but after this latest disappearance, I think we may be dealing with a serial killer," said Vinter.

"But we shouldn't jump to conclusions too fast," said Rapp. "Even if some or all the missing-person cases turn out to be murders, different killers may be involved. Look what's happened in the Thomas Quick affair. He confesses to being Sweden's only known serial killer, and then retracts. Now the evidence is being questioned."

"Alrik is right, Gerdi. To say it's a serial killer, even with Grendel in the background, is much too quick," Ekman said, with a straight face. Holm stifled a laugh.

"Nevertheless, Gerdi's point is important to keep in mind. We may be looking at four murders. Since Westberg's disappearance, this is no longer an investigation into a crackpot letter writer, whether or not he's involved.

"Enar, why don't you start us off with the map?"

Holm went over to the corkboard. Enlarged photos of the three previously missing men, plus Rodger Westberg, ran in a row across the top. Different colored push-pins had been used to mount each photo, with the same color pins showing the locations on the map where they'd gone missing.

"As you can see from the map, there doesn't seem to be any particular geographic pattern made by the disappearances," said Holm. "They're widely dispersed: one north of here; a second, northwest; the third, east; the fourth, here in the city. But all are within one hundred kilometers of Weltenborg. This suggests to me the city is where we're most likely to find the person, or persons, responsible if these are connected cases. If they're unconnected, however, there's no location more significant than any other."

"Does anyone disagree?" asked Ekman. No one spoke.

"All right. Then we're agreed. If these are linked cases, then we have a possible location for the person we're looking for. Thanks, Enar. Alrik, why don't you take us through the information on the whiteboard?"

Across the top were the names of the missing men: Alman Gustaffson, Bertil Henriksson, Rudy Bohren, and Rodger Westberg. The last had been added just before the meeting. Beneath were the dates they were reported missing, the weather on those days, their ages, occupations, schools attended, and names of family members, business associates, and friends.

"Sorry the information on Westberg isn't as complete as the others. We added him in at the last minute," said Rapp. "The differences in occupation are clear, ranging from the store manager, Bohren, to the lawyer, Westberg. They each went to different schools and have no family or friends in common that we could discover. Looking across the lists, there appear to be only two similarities: their age group, mid to late thirties; and the weather on the days they went missing . . . it was raining heavily."

"There's another thing they seem to have in common," interjected Ekman. "Even though their faces are quite different, three of them have brown hair and brown eyes. Bohren has blond hair and blue eyes."

"You're right, Chief. It's so obvious we missed it," said Bergfalk.

"It may not be significant," Ekman said, "but we should keep it in mind. Everyone did a good job getting these lists together so quickly. There's one category missing, however."

"What's that, Chief?" asked Bergfalk.

"Their interests outside of work. Did they have any hobbies in common?"

"Why would that be helpful?" inquired Vinter.

"They might belong to the same club, or business group, or might have met at the same favorite sporting event," replied Ekman. "These are possible connections worth looking into."

"I agree, Chief," said Rapp. "We'll try to fill in that gap, let's say by Tuesday's meeting?"

"Good. Something may surface. Now let's take another look at Stina Lindfors." Ekman told them about his meeting with Westberg's parents and their quite different opinions of Lindfors.

"Did Fru Westberg have any factual basis for her uncomfortable feeling?" asked Vinter.

"No, just a sense Lindfors was somehow phony. Herr Westberg thought his wife was being an overly possessive mother."

Ekman began distributing the blown-up ID photo of Lindfors. "For those who haven't seen her, this is Stina Lindfors. It occurred to me that it might be a good idea to have Lindberg look at this to see if she could be the woman who brought back my briefcase. While he couldn't say it wasn't her, he couldn't make a positive identification."

"It could be Lindfors," said Holm. Rapp and Bergfalk nodded their agreement.

"Yes, I also agree," said Vinter, "but while I can't say it's the same person, I can't say no either. Like Lindberg, I'm uncertain."

"We need to know more about her," Ekman said, turning to Holm and Vinter. "While Alenius and Rosengren are checking finances, I'd like you two to find out everything you can about Lindfors's background. Mats and Alrik will be pursing the common interests angle. Because many offices are closed today, all of you work with each other on whatever's available. And since we'll be taking a break tomorrow, and you'll be developing information on Monday, our next meeting will be Tuesday, unless something important comes up. There's one other thing."

They looked at him with questioning expressions.

"Someone has been leaking information. Alenius and Rosengren were aware of what the rest of us have been doing because it has gotten around the office. It won't take much more before the media is on our backs. That could slow our investigation and cause unnecessary public alarm." He looked at each of them. "Have I made myself clear?" Everyone was silent.

"Does anyone have anything to add? No? Then I'll see you on Tuesday. Have a good Sunday," Ekman concluded, getting up.

29

A Connection

Holm followed him into his office.

"Yes, Enar?"

"Chief, I didn't want to bring it up at the meeting, but I've finished running down the last names on that list from your past cases."

"Did anything stand out?"

"Not exactly. You wanted me to look at released guys who might have a grudge against you. But all those who got out in the past three to five years seem to have settled down to law-abiding lives elsewhere in the country, at least as far as we know. You didn't ask me to, but I went back over your major cases for twenty years, looking for a direct threat. There was just one where the defendant claimed he was railroaded by the police, and swore openly in court that he'd get revenge. He mentioned your name—you were in charge of the case."

"When was this?" asked Ekman, trying without success to remember the incident.

"It was seventeen years ago. The guy's name was Anderberg, Bo Anderberg, thirty-four years old. He was convicted of assault and armed robbery at a grocery store, and sentenced to four years. He never got out. Six months later, he was killed in a fight with another inmate."

"Well that eliminates Grendel being an enemy from my past. Thanks for the good work, Enar."

"Glad to do it," said Holm, and headed out the door.

That decided it for Ekman; Holm would definitely have to be promoted because he clearly deserved it. He always went the extra mile, even when not asked. But it couldn't be done until Ekman promoted Rapp. The two couldn't make chief inspector at the same time, so Holm would have to wait until next year. These bureaucratic personnel rules aggravated him, but they were the constraints he had to work with.

Returning to his memo, Ekman summarized today's meeting and their next steps. He ended by saying that he now believed Rodger Westberg, and the three other missing men, were dead. There was, however, no evidence confirming Westberg's death, so informing his family would be premature. He addressed the memo to Malmer and Edvardsson, with a copy to the commissioner, signed it, and printed off five copies.

Ekman got up, stretched, and walked to the window. The weather was still nasty, with rain coming down harder than ever. He hoped tomorrow would be better for their visit to Erick. The phone rang.

"I figured you'd be in today, Walther," said Malmquist. "Overdoing it, as usual."

"Well, so are you. How are you, Ludvig?"

"Tired of this rat race, frankly. I'm thinking seriously about retirement."

"For God's sake don't do that. Who'd I have to turn to for favors?"

"I'm sure you'd find some other sucker," replied Malmquist. "I just wanted to let you know the lens covers have only smudges on them. He must have worn gloves."

"Damn," said Ekman. "I thought they might give us something concrete to work with."

"So how are your investigations going, anyway?"

"Now we've got what feels like at least one, and possibly four, homicides. The new one's the politically sensitive missing-person case involving the lens covers. We've eliminated the good answers to the disappearance, and only the worst one is left. We don't know yet whether that maniac we discussed is implicated."

"Four possible murders? Jesus, that's bad. But something's bound to break soon."

"I just hope you're right. Thanks for the call, Ludvig."

Ekman was disappointed and frustrated. He'd harbored hope for a traceable fingerprint on the lens covers. It would have been just the sort of small, careless error that tripped up many criminals.

He reread his memo, wondering if he should say something about Malmquist's negative results. Since he'd already mentioned the lens covers to Malmer, he was going to have to revise it. He added the information and made new copies.

Ekman had the nagging feeling that something else had been overlooked. He got up and went back into the conference room. Scanning the whiteboard, he slowly reread the categories listed there. Then it suddenly came to him.

He looked to see if Holm was still at his desk, and found him at work on his computer.

"Enar, sorry to interrupt, but I'd like you to get hold of Alrik and Mats."

Holm looked up from his screen. "Yes, Chief?"

"I want them to find out if the missing men's homes, or their parents' places, were broken into like Westberg's before they disappeared, and if a family photo was taken."

"Sure, Chief. Is this important?"

"It may not be, but similar break-ins and thefts would be a hell of a coincidence. It would help confirm our suspicion that there's some kind of underlying link tying these cases together. If we persist, maybe we can find it."

Holm looked thoughtful. "You're right. That would confirm a link. We all missed it, except you, Chief."

The in-box seemed to have a life of its own, Ekman thought, contemplating the overflowing basket he had earlier reduced to a manageable pile. Maybe it will distract me from the case. He now believed the four missing men represented a single problem. The information he'd asked the team to gather would, he hoped, make that clearer.

When he next looked up from his desk, the clock was striking two, and he realized he was ravenous. He considered going across the square to the restaurant, but seeing the paperwork he still had to plow through, decided on the cafeteria. He thought of asking Holm to join him, but his cubicle was empty so Ekman would have to eat alone, as usual.

Hours later, looking with satisfaction at the empty in-box, the full out-basket, and the heap of discarded junk mail in the trash, he decided he'd done enough for a Saturday and, grabbing his coat and hat, headed for the door. Rain was still a steady downpour on the drive home and traffic was light.

Ingbritt and he had a quiet dinner of meatballs, beets, and boiled potatoes. She'd been curious about what had happened since Westberg's disappearance.

"I think he's dead," Ekman told her. "I've no idea how I'm going to break that news to his parents." This was always the worst thing about his job. He dreaded having to do it, although over the years it had become a too-frequent duty.

"Walther, you don't know for certain. Don't worry about it. You need a day off and tomorrow's supposed to be sunny. Think about seeing Erick and the children."

"You're right. There's no sense in being morbid. There'll be time enough for that, I'm afraid."

In his study, Ekman tried to divert his thoughts by immersing himself in the eighteenth-century history he'd been reading. It didn't work.

30

~~~~~~~~~~~~

Two Positions

Sunday, October 16. It was eight A.M. Sunlight crept through the blinds, waking Gerdi Vinter. She rolled on her side, threw off part of her covers and stretched. Leaning over, she nudged the shoulder of the man lying next to her.

With a grunt, Enar Holm opened his eyes. Thank God for Sunday, was his first thought, and then, thank God for Gerdi. He turned toward her and pulled their covers all the way off. Although her face was plain, Gerdi Vinter had a gorgeous body and flawless, silken skin.

"Are you ready?" he asked with a smile.

"What did you have in mind, sir?" she replied, laughing.

"Whatever you like. But I was thinking about breakfast. I'm starving."

"That's understandable, after all your exertion last night."

"That wasn't exertion, that was pleasure. If I could just get some coffee and pancakes, I'll show you real exertion."

"Promises, promises. I guess you expect me to make those pancakes?"

"Not at all. They're my specialty," he said, getting up and heading to the bathroom. "I'll be right out, and then you can shower while I put on an apron."

"And that's all you'll be wearing?"

"Underpants and an apron. There's no point in getting dressed only to get undressed," he said, grinning at her.

Over breakfast they planned their day. They'd made a resolution yesterday not to talk about work for at least this one day, and just devote the time to themselves.

It was warmer, and bright after yesterday's gloom. They wanted to get out and enjoy the good weather before it got colder. Biking through the large city park, around the fifteen-square-kilometer lake at its center, and a nice lunch somewhere would be perfect, then back to Holm's apartment to fix dinner.

Gerdi and Enar had been lovers for three months. At first, she'd been flattered that this handsome man was attracted to her. As they got to know each other better at work, over several dinners, and then in bed, she discovered that he seemed to care for her. Cautiously at first, and then with her whole heart, Gerdi fell for him. She'd been hurt two years before and dumped hard, leaving her resolved to just have casual affairs. But this was different. She trusted him.

For his part, Enar had had the many relationships available to a man who is not only handsome, but charming and intelligent. Gerdi moved him as no one else had for a long time. Beneath her quiet, controlled exterior, she was passionate and smart, with a sassy sense of humor that delighted him. We're a match, he thought; I'm falling in love with her.

Before they went out, Gerdi pulled off his apron, and with no persuasion at all, dragged him back to bed. After an intense half hour, they showered again, this time together, and then headed down to the basement to get their bikes.

∞ ∞ ∞

At eight that morning, Ekman and Ingbritt were enjoying a late breakfast. They weren't leaving to see Erick and the grandchildren for another hour, so they lingered, looking through the Sunday papers. It was a pleasant, unhurried morning, without the pressure of his having to get to the office.

Rising and checking his watch, Ekman said, "I guess we'd better be going." He was anxious to see Erick, even more than the grandchildren. Although he loved both his children, Erick was his favorite, just as Carla was Ingbritt's. He knew that taking pride in having a son to carry on the family name was old-fashioned, but it meant a lot to him.

Ekman was dressed in his casual clothes: a soft, light gray shirt, with a dark red tie; dark gray tailored trousers; polished, tasseled black loafers; and a black double-breasted blazer with gleaming brass buttons and a bright red pocket silk. Tucking his large gold watch into a pocket sewn into his trouser top, he thought with satisfaction that he looked quite relaxed.

They took the E4 southwest, and then followed Route 25 to Halmstad, the beach town where Erick lived. Turning south on the E6/20, they took the off-ramp to Ginstieden, and then made their way to Erick's home on Vibrytargatan. It had taken a little over an hour.

Erick had a large, 420-square-meter, two-story stone house on a rise overlooking the harbor, the result of his successful practice with two other orthopedic surgeons. The sun gleamed on the waves below as they pulled up. The front door was flung open, and Erick's girls—Ina, five, and Maj, seven—came running down the steps.

"Grandma, Grandma," they yelled, rushing up to Ingbritt who tried to gather both of them in her arms at once. After they'd kissed and hugged their grandmother, it was Ekman's turn to hold them. Maj looked up at him and said, "Grandpa, how big you've gotten," in the inno-cent way children have of telling an uncomfortable truth.

Erick, tall and with a long face like his father's, and his wife, Disa, a heavy-set redhead with an easy laugh, stood smiling in the doorway watching the scene. As Ekman and Ingbritt came up the steps holding the chil-dren's hands, Erick and Disa came out to meet them. After exchanging hugs, they led the way into the house.

"It's so good to see you," said Erick. "It must be almost two months since we've been able to get together."

"Far too long. But it's wonderful to be with you, the children, and Disa," she said, turning to her daughter-in-law, whose smile filled her round face.

"Come into the living room," said Erick. "And let me get you something to drink. Would you like coffee, or something a little bubblier?" he asked with a grin.

"Now bubbly sounds good," said Ekman. "With per-haps some orange juice added, since it's still morning."

"You've got it. The same for you?" he asked his mother.

"That will be wonderful. Why shouldn't we give our-selves a treat? This is such a marvelous Sunday," Ingbritt said with a delighted smile.

As always, Disa made them feel very welcome. After a long, heavy lunch, Ekman and Erick decided to walk it off on the beach. Ingbritt and Disa spent most of that time talking about the girls, who were engrossed with the folk-costumed dolls Ingbritt had brought for them.

"So how is your practice going, any interesting cases?" asked Ekman, as they strolled down the sand, glittering in the sunlight.

"It's doing very well, Pappa, but quite routine, although I did have a tricky compound femur fracture last week. But how about you? I'm sure your cases are much more interesting than mine," Erick said with a smile.

"Well, there's a possible homicide. Perhaps even as many as four. They may be connected to bizarre threats from someone a colleague of yours has told me should be referred to as 'a seriously disturbed person,' but I prefer to call him 'the maniac,'" Ekman deadpanned.

"I'd say that's a whole lot more than just 'interesting.'"

"It's challenging. But let's talk about something more pleasant," said Ekman, smiling and changing the subject to the wonderful weather, as they headed back toward the house. He put his arm around Erick's shoulders, and his son looked at him with a warm smile. Although Ekman didn't often use the word, he loved Erick very much. He believed Erick knew that, and returned the love and respect he felt.

The day had proven wonderful for everyone. It was just after sunset when Ekman and Ingbritt got home from Halmstad.

31

A Gift To Remember

*M*onday, October 17. At breakfast Ingbritt was still talking about how much she'd enjoyed yesterday's visit. Ekman nodded and grunted agreement as he finished his toast and jam. Draining a last cup of coffee, he got his coat and hat from the hall closet, and kissing her goodbye, went into the garage.

It was seven A.M. as Ekman began backing his Volvo down the drive, when he noticed sunlight glinting off something on the front stoop. He braked, put the car in park, and got out to see what it was. Wrapped in a transparent plastic bag was a small white box.

Looking through the plastic, he saw that it was addressed: *"To Walther Ekman,"* in the, by now familiar, black marker printing. He froze, and then backed away looking over every centimeter of the stoop, the walkway, and the ground all around. There was nothing. He reached into his overcoat pocket and took out his driving gloves. Pulling them on, he went back to the box and lifted it, peering at the stoop underneath. Again, he saw nothing.

*P*arked down the street, Grendel watched with delight as Ekman cautiously dealt with the surprise he'd been left.

Just wait until he opens it, Grendel thought; it will drive Ekman and the rest of them up the wall. That was one reason he'd prepared the 'gift'; the other was to send a message of how dangerous it was to challenge him. Grendel wanted Ekman sweating and squirming before the final curtain came down on the drama he'd scripted.

Carrying the box to his car as though it might contain an explosive . . . although he thought that extremely unlikely . . . he opened the front passenger door and placed it with great care on the seat. Getting back in, he pulled out of the drive, and headed well below the speed limit to headquarters. Taking out his mobile, he called the front desk.

"This is Ekman. I need two crime scene technicians and a photographer with lights and video equipment to meet me at my office in one hour. I don't care if they're probably not up yet. Get them up, and moving. Now," he said, and shut the phone off. Right away, he regretted being so abrupt with the hapless desk sergeant.

Ekman's face was red and his lips compressed in a grim line. He was furious that this creep had had the gall to violate his home, his family's sanctuary. In all his years on the force, nothing close to this had ever happened. Jarl is right, he thought, somehow this is very personal.

Carrying the box in both hands, he said "God morgen," to Holm, who looked up surprised at what he was carrying.

"Come in, Enar," Ekman said, going to his conference room door.

"Open it for me, please."

Holm followed him in as Ekman placed the box, still in its clear plastic bag, on the table.

"This was on my front stoop this morning," he said, answering Holm's unspoken question.

Holm peered at the address on the lid. "It's Grendel, isn't it?"

"Yes, I think so. Crime scene techs and a photographer should be here soon," Ekman replied, taking off his gloves, and putting them in his overcoat.

"Let's sit down," he said, heading back into his office, and hanging up his coat and hat.

"You must have been shocked, Chief, finding that on your doorstep," Holm said in a quiet voice.

"That's putting it mildly. I'm still having a hard time believing he had the nerve to do it."

"It feels like a message," said Holm.

"A really personal one. He's upping the ante again. We'll see how much."

It was no use wondering what this new package meant; they'd find out soon enough. Patience Ekman, he thought, patience. He wants to get you angry and flustered. Don't play his game.

"Did you have a good Sunday, Enar?" Ekman asked with a smile.

For a moment, Holm thought Ekman knew about Gerdi and him, but dismissed it. It was just a routine question but Holm hesitated before replying.

"Yes, it was fine. How about you?"

"We visited my son and his family in Halmstad. It was a pleasant day. A much needed break. Neither of us may get another one very soon, Enar."

A knock on the door announced the crime scene techs and photographer.

"Why don't you set up in here," said Ekman, leading the way into the conference room.

Turning to the senior tech, a short, forty-year-old woman he had worked with before named Asa Taube, he explained how he'd found the box on his doorstep and had examined the surrounding area.

"There was nothing there, so it seemed best to bring it in," he concluded. Ekman hadn't wanted a crime scene van in his drive and technicians with lights on his door-step panicking Ingbritt and alarming the neighbors.

He thought he knew enough about crime scenes to have done okay.

Taube didn't say anything, just nodded, but she looked skeptical. The photographer positioned his screens to reflect the field lights he'd set up on tripods around the table. He turned on the lights and camera, and began recording.

Taube, wearing white, crime scene overalls and gloves, picked up the package, and her assistant, a young man dressed the same, spread a white plastic sheet on the table, where she replaced the box.

Taking surgical scissors from her kit, Taube cut away the plastic bag from the box and then the twine, taking care to avoid the knot in front. She lifted the cover, putting it beside the box. Seeing a note on top, she used a pair of tongs to remove it and placed it on the white sheet.

Ekman bent over, and read:

To Walther Ekman
With the Compliments of Grendel,
His Fervent Admirer.
Please Permit Me to Introduce
The Distinguished
Advokat Rodger Westberg.

"Let's take a look," Ekman said to Taube. He was now very afraid of what they'd find.

Reaching into the box, Taube pulled back the tissue, revealing a bubble-wrapped object, which she removed from the box. Taking up the scissors again, she cut the wrapping away so they could see what lay beneath.

"Jesus Christ," exclaimed the photographer, as every-one stared, horrified at the shriveled male genitals.

Recovering from the shock, Ekman said to Taube, "Thank you for your help. Please prepare everything for the forensics lab, including a copy of the video. I'll let Malmquist know it's on the way."

Asa Taube had thought she was immune to brutal crimes, but she found herself immobilized, staring fixedly at what she'd uncovered. She pulled herself together enough to say, "Yes, Chief. You'll want a courier I suppose?"

Ekman nodded, as he and Holm went back to his office, while the crime team finished up.

"What do you think, Enar?"

"We don't know if it's Westberg. Grendel could be lying."

"You're right. But the only way to find out will be to get a DNA sample from his parents. That should be done today, although it'll be some time before we can be certain. They'll want to know why we need it, and I dread telling them."

"If it turns out to be Westberg, we still can't say if he's alive or dead."

"I don't think we should hold out any hope to them. My strong feeling is he's dead. And I want to believe pathology will tell us the mutilation was done after death."

"What I don't understand, Chief, is why Grendel's done this at all."

"He wants to increase the pressure. By giving us the first real evidence he's committed a crime tying him to one of the missing, he's pushing for public disclosure. He wants the publicity, and I'm afraid we're going to have to provide it."

"We should have more information at tomorrow morning's meeting on the other missing men."

"Good. I'll talk with Malmer and Edvardsson today about whether they want to hold a press conference. I'm going to recommend we have one tomorrow afternoon because I think Grendel's next step will be to go to the media. We need to preempt him."

Holm left as Ekman picked up the phone to call Malmquist.

"Ludvig, I'm sorry to tell you I'm sending a horrific package," Ekman said, explaining what had happened.

"My God, you really are dealing with a maniac."

"I'll also be sending along later today a DNA sample from the parents, so you can see if there's a match."

"I'll look for it. We'll rush it as much as we can."

"Thanks, Ludvig. This is going public tomorrow, so be ready for media inquiries."

"Something to look forward to," Malmquist said with his usual dry humor. "My only consolation is I know it'll be worse at your end. Good luck, Walther."

Ekman looked over the memo he'd drafted Saturday. It was already outdated. Sighing, he started to revise it yet again. When he'd finished, he reread it, made new copies, and called Malmer's office.

"Is he in Annika? Yes, I need to see him right away. Okay, I'll be up in fifteen minutes."

"What is it now, Walther?" said Malmer, without bothering to greet him.

Ekman handed him the memo and sat down.

Five minutes later, Malmer looked up, his face drained of color. "What on earth are you going to tell Westberg?"

"The truth. We need a DNA sample from him in case we have his son's body part."

"There's no way around that?"

"Westberg is an intelligent man. It would be pointless to try to deceive him, especially in view of the press conference I recommend. We'll be very general and not go into details, except to say that a crime has been committed involving Rodger Westberg. I'm going to speak to the father at his office so he can break the news to his wife."

"You think we should hold a press conference?"

"It's become unavoidable. I believe Grendel will go public. He wants the publicity. We need to do it first."

"I'll have to speak with the commissioner. If he agrees, we'll both be there, but you'll do most of the talking, of course."

"Understood," said Ekman, getting up. If things went wrong, Malmer and the commissioner wanted to be in the background, not out front fielding pointed questions.

"I'll let you know whether the commissioner wants to go ahead. And Walther, for God's sake, be gentle with Westberg." He paused. "I don't know how you tell a man his son is dead and mutilated. I wouldn't know where to begin."

"Neither do I," replied Ekman.

32

Visits

Looking up her number, Ekman called Taube. "Has the package gone? Good. Could you please get me a DNA swab kit? Thanks."

He next called Westberg's office. "It's Walther Ekman. Is Herr Westberg in? He's not free right now? I'd like to meet with him today. Yes, I understand he has a busy schedule. Yes, it's important. All right, I'll be there at two."

Westberg's secretary was accustomed to running interference. If she'd known why he needed to see Westberg, he'd have gotten in right away. Ekman didn't mind the delay. He would have postponed the meeting forever, if he could have.

It was time to see Edvardsson. He called on her direct line and got her in.

"Malin, it's Walther Ekman. I'd say 'god morgen,' back, only I'd be lying in my teeth. Yes, I'll be there in fifteen minutes."

As he was getting his hat and coat, Taube knocked and came in with the DNA kit. "Thanks," he said.

"You're going to get a sample from his relatives for a match?"

"Yes."

She looked at him. "Would you like me to help with the DNA swab?" she asked in a quiet voice.

"Thank you, Fru Taube, but this is something I have to do myself."

"I understand," she said, closing the door softly behind her.

This time, Ekman was in luck and found a parking space around the corner from the courthouse. He didn't want to deal with the officious parking police again.

Coming into Edvardsson's office, he saw the receptionist had gone out, and knocked on the inner door.

"Come in," Edvardsson said, getting up from her desk and coming to meet him.

"Walther, you look very tired. Are you all right?"

"I didn't know it showed already. I was fine at breakfast," he replied with a wry smile.

Sitting beside her on the couch, he handed her his memo. After reading it, she looked up at him.

"That poor man," she said, shaking her head.

"The son or the father?"

"Both. It's all too horrible. And how dreadful for you, Walther. First, the discovery at your home, and now, having to tell his father," she said, touching his shoulder.

"I'm seeing Westberg this afternoon to get some DNA. Until there's a match, we can't say for certain it's Rodger Westberg. I've recommended we go public with an announcement about his abduction and possible death. I won't disclose the original letter from Grendel, or other details, especially the mutilation, unless we have to. Does that sound about right, Malin?"

She was thoughtful for a moment. "Yes, it does. We didn't have real proof of a murder before, just suspicions. Now there's clear evidence a terrible crime has actually been committed. If this . . . creature . . . were to go to the media first, it would look like we've been concealing a crime the public has a right to know about. We need to speak to people before then. I'll be there, of course, to help you answer questions."

"Thanks, Malin. I'm waiting to hear if the commissioner agrees with us. I believe he will."

"But Walther, what about the other missing men? Could Grendel be involved with those disappearances too? If he is, do you think there could be other . . . packages?" Edvardsson shivered as though she'd felt something cold against her spine.

"We're working on whether the cases could be connected. It's a possibility that might produce new leads. If this maniac's involved in those disappearances, who knows what he'll do next. In any case, I'm not going to say anything about the other men at the conference." He got up. "I'll let you know when it will be."

Edvardsson walked with him to the door and, looking up at him, took his hand. "You have to do one of the hardest things imaginable, Walther. But I wouldn't want anyone else to bring such awful news; you're a kind man."

Ekman just nodded and walked out of her office. He was steeling himself for the Westberg interview that afternoon.

He called Jarl Karlsson from the car. "Jarl, it's Walther. I need your advice again. Are you free for lunch? At your place? I was going to buy, but if you're pressed for time I can be there in half an hour. See you then."

Ekman pulled up in front of Karlsson's door thirty minutes later. Jarl answered the doorbell.

"I'd have liked to take you up on your lunch offer," he said, as they walked toward the kitchen, "but I've got a full schedule of patients today." He looked at his plain, steel watch. "We've got a little over an hour. I've set out some herring and gravlax, and a couple of bottles of Dugges. I hope that will be all right."

"That sounds fine. Thanks for going to the trouble," Ekman replied, as they sat down at the large white kitchen table set for two.

"Please help yourself," Karlsson said, gesturing at the plates of assorted smoked fish, brown bread, fresh dill, mustard, cheeses, and beer. They made sandwiches for themselves and between bites, Ekman brought Karlsson up to date.

"It's become much worse than I would have guessed," Karlsson said.

"Does that mean you didn't take the cannibalism threat as real?" asked Ekman, surprised.

"Although I believed it was quite real when we spoke, the more I've thought about it, the more the letter began to sound too theatrical. It seemed like a ploy to get your attention, as well as an expression of his own inner needs. But now that he's engaged in mutilation, and flaunts it, I'm not so sure my second thoughts were right after all. Maybe if he wasn't a cannibal when he wrote the letter, he's become fascinated by it, and has moved in that direction."

"So what do I tell Westberg? That's the main thing I need your help with Jarl. Too many times in thirty years I've had to tell people their family member was dead, but never under such bizarre circumstances."

"The most intractable problem is that you have no body for his parents to grieve over. There would be some consolation and perhaps closure, if they could just see their son's body. And to make matters worse, you want to take a DNA sample. Westberg will ask what it will be matched against. I think here you must be careful. To tell him the truth would be cruel. I suggest you say you've exhausted the possibilities of finding their son alive, must assume he's dead, and need the DNA for reference when his body is recovered. He'll perhaps say that then he'll continue to hope his son is alive. So I'd be very clear that there's no hope."

"I agree with everything you've said, but there are two problems. First, the body part." Ekman couldn't bring himself to say genitals. "It may not be Westberg's, in which case, he could be living. And second, even if it is his, until we hear from forensics, it could have been taken when he was alive. So again, he might not be dead." Ekman didn't want to imagine what condition Rodger Westberg would be in if this second scenario were true.

"Yes, you're right," Karlsson replied, his words drawn out. "But since you can't spell all this out for the parents, you should just state his death as fact. I think, like you, that Rodger Westberg is dead. If one of your other possibilities turns out to be correct, you'll have to apologize and say you were too hasty. It's better now to be discreet and kind, and risk their anger later, if you're wrong."

"I knew speaking with you would help me get my thinking straight. Thanks for your advice, and the good lunch," Ekman said, getting up. "I won't take any more of your time."

"You're not taking up my time. I needed the company. Walther, by sending these genitals, and not an ear or finger, he's making this the most personal threat possible. He wants to emasculate you."

Ekman was very still for a moment. "I thought about that too. I guess I'll just have to wear Kevlar underpants from now on." His laugh came out as a bark.

Karlsson walked him to the door. "By bringing himself to your doorstep with that special gift, you realize Grendel's coming much nearer?" he said, concern for his friend written on his face.

"Yes, I've thought about that Jarl. I just don't know what to do about it, except to catch the bastard before he gets even closer," said Ekman, his jaw tight.

Parking on the steep hill near Westberg's office on Yakullsgatan, he angled a front tire against the curb and put on the parking brake. The building entrance was only a few doors away. He took the elevator to the top floor. It was almost two o'clock.

The receptionist recognized him. "You remember where his office is?"

"Yes, thanks," said Ekman, heading down the hall.

He knocked and entered the huge office with its spectacular city view, as Westberg came forward to meet him.

"Herr Ekman," he said, shaking his hand. "I hope you've good news for me." He led Ekman to the sitting area they'd used before.

"Councillor Westberg, I wish with all my heart I had such news. But after exhausting every avenue that could lead to finding your son, I must tell you that we're forced to conclude he's no longer alive."

Westberg sat very still for a long moment. "But if you haven't found his body, how can you be sure?"

"You're right. Without a body there can't be absolute certainty. But you should know our professional judgment is that there's no realistic likelihood of his being found alive."

"How am I, how is my wife, going to be able to accept this?" His face had become pale.

"It will be very difficult. But it would be better than clinging to a false hope."

Westberg had lost his usual composure. He ran his hands through his hair and turned away from Ekman. After a few minutes he turned around, his face wet with tears that he slowly wiped away with a handkerchief.

"Excuse me," he said getting up, "I need to be alone."

"There's one very helpful thing you can do right now. When we recover his body, we may need DNA identification," Ekman said, standing and taking the kit from his pocket.

"Would you please give us a DNA sample by rubbing the inside of your mouth with this swab," he said, extending the plastic bag to Westberg.

"My God, won't I be able to identify him?"

"It may be some time before we discover his body," Ekman replied in a quiet voice.

Westberg took the bag and, opening it with shaking hands, used the swab. Replacing it in the bag, he gave it back.

"Thank you, Herr Westberg. Believe me, you and your wife have my sincere condolences. There will probably be a media conference tomorrow about your son's case, since we're treating it as a homicide."

"I know you can't keep this a private matter now. But on top of our loss, you're telling me we'll have to deal with the media?"

As he was about to leave, Westberg added, "I believe you, Herr Ekman, but I don't know if my wife will be able to accept this as final."

"I understand," said Ekman, as he walked out.

33

Norlander

When Ekman got back to his office, he found a message that the commissioner wanted to see him. He was somewhat surprised. The commissioner usually dealt with him through Malmer. He called the office to say he'd be there in a few minutes, and then phoned Fru Taube.

She came up immediately, and he handed her the DNA kit. "Please send this by courier to Malmquist. He's expecting it."

She looked at him with a question in her eyes. "Yes, it was as bad as we thought it might be. Westberg is distraught," he said. Taube just nodded and left.

Knocking, Ekman entered the spacious corner office on the top floor. Unlike ordinary police offices, Norlander had decorated it at his own cost with expensive antiques and Persian rugs. Ekman found the commissioner talking with Malmer. They broke off as he entered.

"Walther, it's good to see you," the commissioner said, rising and coming toward him with hand extended.

Elias Norlander was forty-eight, slender, of medium height, with light brown hair slicked straight back over his handsome head. He was always dressed in dark, custom-made Savile Row suits, set off by bright Hermès ties on cuff-linked shirts.

Where Malmer was needlessly abrasive, he was smoothly polite, but like his childhood friend, he had an ear sensitively tuned to the political winds. Having been county police commissioner for just the past year, he depended on Ekman's experience. Ekman, for his part, treated him with wary respect, as though he were a dangerous animal that could turn on him at any moment.

Shaking Ekman's hand, he led him to an armchair facing his and Malmer's.

"I've been reading your latest memorandum with great interest," he said. "I know this morning's events must have been much more shocking for you than they have been for Olov and me. How are you feeling?"

"Rather worn, Commissioner, I must confess."

"That's understandable," said Norlander in a sympathetic voice. "I understand that you've just come back from speaking with Westberg. How do you think that went?"

"About as well as could be expected under these horrendous circumstances. I told him we would now be treating his son's disappearance as a homicide, but, of course, didn't mention today's package."

"Good. That's information we need to keep very much to ourselves." He looked at Ekman. "Now that we know this 'Grendel' has committed a crime, do you have enough investigators?"

"Yes, I think so. There're seven, including myself. We're pursuing every lead. I should have some more information for both of you after tomorrow morning's team meeting. If other people are needed as we go forward, I'll let you know."

"I see," said Norlander. "Westberg called me after you spoke with him. He was beside himself with grief. He wants to be able to assure himself and his wife . . . he hasn't spoken with her yet, I think he's afraid to . . . that everything possible is being done. He's still hoping his son may be alive, although I agree with you he's no doubt dead. But still, we need to take Westberg's concerns seriously, especially in view of the media conference you recommended. Again, I agree that with such a high profile disappearance and likely homicide, we need to inform the public."

"I met with Edvardsson after I spoke with you," Ekman said, turning to Malmer. "She also thinks that Westberg's son is dead and that we need a press conference. She's willing to be there tomorrow."

"That will be very helpful," said Norlander. Malmer, however, didn't look so pleased.

"In view of all this," he went on, "I've been giving serious thought to our overall approach. You should know that Westberg has very influential connections in Stockholm," he said in a confidential tone. "He wants heaven and earth moved to either find his son or confirm his death. If we don't ask for assistance from the National Criminal Investigation Division, he will. You have friends there I'm sure. Am I right?"

"Yes, but their help isn't needed now," protested Ekman.

"I understand that. And believe me, I have every confidence in you and your team. The actual need for outside help isn't the issue, however. We have to prove to Westberg that we're pulling out all the stops in this investigation. Rather than have Stockholm send in someone you don't know, it would be better if we called on one of your friends. Wouldn't you agree?"

Ekman was silent. This unexpected development surprised him and filled him with resentment. He'd been a respected criminal investigator for decades and this came as an undeserved slap in the face. Norlander, however, had a point. If Westberg was that connected, it would be better to preempt him and get someone from Stockholm he could work with. His mind raced through names until it stopped at Garth Rystrom, a superintendent at CID, and an old friend.

"I think I know just the man, Commissioner. Let me give him a call, and if he's available perhaps you could make a formal request for him," Ekman said in a neutral voice that concealed his feelings.

"An excellent idea," said Norlander with enthusiasm, as though Ekman had proposed calling the CID himself.

"I'll have our communications officer let the media know we're holding a conference about an important new case, tomorrow afternoon, say at three. Will that work for you?" asked Norlander.

"That will be fine, Commissioner," said Ekman, as Norlander stood.

Ekman called Edvardsson to let her know the conference would be at three in the large auditorium at headquarters.

"How did your meeting with Westberg go, Walther?" she asked.

"Badly. I tried to tell him we've explored all the good alternatives, and the only conclusion left is that his son is dead, but he's not persuaded. He's hoping against hope that somehow he'll be found alive."

"It's impossible news for anyone to deal with. Maybe, in time, he'll come to accept it."

"Maybe, but not right now. I'm going to have to call in National CID to satisfy him."

"You've done such excellent work, Walther. Please don't feel slighted."

"I'm trying not to, but it still bothers me, Malin."

"That's only natural. I think you'll solve this case, and I know you don't need any help from Stockholm to do it."

"Thanks for those kind words. I'll try to deserve them. See you tomorrow."

He next phoned Rystrom. They were not only personal friends, but had worked together on several cases over the last twenty years.

"Garth, it's Walther Ekman. How are you? And the family? Good. Yes, we're all well, thank you. I'm calling because I could use your help on a difficult case." Ekman sketched out what had happened since last Tuesday.

"Do you think this would be of interest to you? Great. And do you think you could come down here as early as tomorrow? We're holding a press conference, and it would be helpful if you could be there. Our commissioner will be making a formal request for your services later today. I'll see you tomorrow then. And Garth, thanks very much. It's really appreciated."

Then he called Norlander. "Commissioner, I've just spoken with Garth Rystrom, a superintendent at CID I've worked with before, a very good man. He's available and is planning to attend the conference. Yes, that's right, 'Rystrom.' I think you'll find he's the right person to assist us."

Ekman sat back in his chair and, taking out his needlepoint, thought about what he'd say at the conference. He had to satisfy the media without going into sensitive information. Putting the stitching to one side, and taking a sheet of paper, he jotted down the key points he'd make, and answers to probable questions.

34

Castling Queenside

When he came in, Ekman's drawn face made it obvious something was very wrong.

"What is it, Walther? What's happened?" Ingbritt asked.

Ekman hung his coat and hat in the hall closet, and turning, gave her a kiss.

"Let me get us a drink and then we'll talk. What would you like? Some wine? I'm having vodka."

"Vodka will be fine."

They went into the kitchen and Ekman poured stiff drinks for them. He'd decided to tell her everything about the day's events, starting with his discovery of the box.

"It's been a strange day, Ingbritt," he began. As he told her all that'd happened since that morning, he saw shock, horror, and compassion flit across her face like successive shadows.

"You knew something awful was going to happen, didn't you, Walther? And it would be directed at you. That's why you started to carry a gun."

"No, I didn't know, only guessed from the letters and talks with Jarl. Now there's proof a dangerous lunatic has probably killed someone. I didn't tell you before because I wasn't certain and didn't want you to worry. There'll be a press conference tomorrow in which some of this will come out, but not all the details I've told you. We needed to talk before that happened. And, there's another reason as well."

"What?" she asked.

"I want you to stay with one of the children until we catch him. It's become too dangerous for you to be here. He's come too close."

Ekman had considered asking her to stay at a hotel. She would be safest in some anonymous place out of town, but he knew she'd never agree to that. Staying with one of the children would make the separation more bearable for her, and make her more willing to accept it.

"Walther, I won't leave you to face this alone. We've shared everything, and we'll share this too." Her expression was adamant.

"No, Ingbritt, you have to leave. For a while, until he's found. I can't function, I can't do my job properly, if I'm worrying all the time about whether he might decide to harm you in order to get at me. Please do this for me."

She was silent for several minutes. "You're right. You have to be able to concentrate on finding this monster. I'll do it, because someone else may die unless he's caught quickly. But you have to promise me you'll call every evening without fail. As it is, I'll be a wreck worrying about you."

Ekman went to her and they hugged for a long moment. "Thank you," he said. "Now I'll be able to really focus on finding him. Who will you call, Erick or Carla?"

"I haven't seen Carla in weeks and weeks. I'll tell her I'd like to stay and have a good long visit with her. I've been wanting to see Johan, too."

"I'm sure she'll be delighted, and so will Johan. I'm sorry I can't go with you. Why don't you call her now and tell her you'll be there tomorrow?"

Her face was stricken. "So soon, Walther? Can't we wait a few days?"

"I'm afraid not." He kissed her. "I'll miss you like crazy, but I'll be very relieved you're safe."

Hesitating for another moment, Ingbritt picked up the phone and called Carla.

"Yes, I'm planning on staying for a while. I'm not quite sure how long, perhaps a few weeks. Is that all right? I don't want to interfere with your work. No, your father won't be coming with me. He's very wrapped up in a new case and won't be home much, I expect. I should be with you before lunch. I'm looking forward to seeing you, Johan, and Gunnar." She hung up the phone and turned to Ekman.

"There. It's done. Now, let's have dinner and put all this aside. I think I'll have to reheat the chicken," she said, going to the kitchen.

After dinner, they made love, and then lay holding each other for a long time until sleep overtook them.

35

Black Widow

Tuesday, October 18. Watching Ingbritt as she started to pack after breakfast, Ekman felt much relieved. He wanted to stay until she'd left, but needed to get to the office early. It was going to be a hectic day.

"You'll remember to call me when you get there?" he asked.

"Of course," she replied. "And you'll call me this evening, remember?"

"I won't forget," he said, kissing her, and giving her a long hug. "Drive safely," was his parting admonition, as he went out to his car.

The sun had been up for almost half an hour, but heavy cloud cover dimmed the light. It promised to be another dark, rainy day. He was happy Ingbritt would be safe; however, he was bitter and angry that he'd been forced to send her away. It made him more determined than ever to find Grendel.

Ekman arrived at his office by seven, ahead of Holm. He was reviewing his notes for that afternoon's conference when Holm knocked and entered.

"God morgen, Chief," he said in a cheerful voice. Ekman returned the greeting in a preoccupied manner.

"I'm not disturbing you, am I?" Holm asked.

"No, not at all Enar," said Ekman, looking up. "Please sit down. I was just going over what I'll say. The commissioner has agreed we need a press conference. It's been scheduled for three, and you'll want to be there." He hadn't had a chance before to tell him about his meeting with the commissioner.

"Also, you should know that because of pressure from Westberg, Norlander has insisted on bringing in CID. I've invited Superintendent Garth Rystrom to come down for the conference. I don't think you've met him before. He's an old friend of mine and a first-rate investigator."

"He's not going to take over the case is he?" asked Holm with a troubled expression.

"No way. As I said, CID will be here to satisfy Westberg that we're doing all we can to find his son alive, or confirm his death. Rystrom's going to 'assist' us. We can always use another person's perspective, and he's quite sharp. I think you'll like him."

"That's a relief. For a moment I thought the case was going to be handed over to Stockholm."

"Not if I can help it," said Ekman with a grim smile. Another thing he liked about Holm, besides his sense of humor, was his loyalty.

Ekman and Holm moved to the conference room, and when the food arrived, poured themselves coffee, as Ekman took a sweet roll.

"Not hungry?" he asked Holm, who had skipped the pastries.

"I had a big breakfast," he replied. Ekman knew he'd probably had only a slice of dry toast, and didn't want to embarrass Ekman.

Just before eight, the other team members began to drift into the room, helping themselves to coffee and pastries. Ekman waited until they were all seated before speaking.

"God morgen, everyone. Before we begin reviewing assignments, I need to tell you what happened yesterday." He described the discovery of the second package and its contents. They were all astonished.

"On your doorstep?" asked Vinter in a voice that showed her shock.

"Unfortunately," said Ekman, in a flat tone.

"Then it's a homicide for sure, Chief," said Rapp.

"Probably," said Ekman. "Although we won't know until we hear from forensics. He could conceivably still be alive." Rapp's face paled. He hadn't thought of that.

"We also don't know if it's Westberg, do we?" asked Bergfalk.

"That's right," Ekman said. "We won't know until there's a DNA match with the sample I got from Westberg's father."

"So, at this point, all we really know is we have a body part from someone who may be dead or alive," put in Rapp.

"Then this may not be a homicide. It could be only a maiming," said Rosengren.

"'Only' may not be quite the right word," said Bergfalk.

"Although you're all quite correct that we don't know for certain, I propose we proceed as though this is a homicide and the victim is Rodger Westberg," Ekman said. "Until we find out otherwise."

Then he told them about the press conference. "Everyone who wants to can be there, but you're not to tell anyone you're on the investigating team. If one of the media people asks you a question, just refer them to me." He looked around the table. "There are to be no leaks now, or in the future. Is that understood?" They all nodded agreement.

"I should also mention there'll be a new person joining the team later today: Superintendent Garth Rystrom from National CID. But this is still our case and

I'll continue to head the investigation. Rystrom is a top-flight detective, and I think you'll like him. He's also an old friend of mine."

Ekman didn't want to go into the politics behind bringing in CID, and just left it at that.

"Now, let's get started. Alenius and Rosengren, what have you discovered?"

Rosengren answered, "Chief, we went back to Westberg's office and found his will, his grandfather's trust agreement, bank and brokerage statements, and tax returns. He was really loaded."

Ekman looked at him with raised eyebrows.

"According to the latest statements, his combined accounts total almost fifty million kronor. On top of that his trust is worth another twenty million. See what I mean about loaded," said Rosengren.

"What about the terms of his will?" asked Ekman.

"Now, here's the really interesting part," said Rosengren, almost smacking his lips. "Everything had been left to his parents if they survived him, otherwise, to a charitable foundation for poor university students. That includes the trust money, because he had the power to dispose of it in his will after he was thirty-five. But three months ago, he drew up a new will. Guess who's the sole beneficiary? Yes, the beautiful Froken Lindfors. How do you like that?"

"It's a hell of a motive," put in Bergfalk, unnecessarily stating the obvious.

"And what about Lindfors's finances?" asked Ekman.

"She's got a good salary as an accountant, and considerable savings, about 800,000 kronor. She rents a one-bedroom apartment and drives a new Volvo. No debt to speak of, but also no other assets that we could find," Alenius answered.

Ekman was quiet for a moment, digesting this information.

"Gerdi and Enar, you were looking into her background. What did you find?"

"She's not who she seems, Chief," said Holm.

"For starters," Vinter continued, "her name is Lindfors all right, but she was born Stina Ernstsson in Lund, thirty-four years ago. She looks a lot younger than she is. Her parents died within the last six years. She was married at nineteen to a Carl Stillen, who was two years older."

She handed around a license photo of Stillen. He looked back at the camera without expression. His brown hair was cropped short, his brown eyes deep set.

"That marriage lasted six years and ended in divorce. There were no children. One year after that, she married again, in Malmö, this time to Eberhardt Lindfors, forty-nine, almost twice her age, who owned a successful women's apparel business."

She passed out a photo of Eberhardt Lindfors. He had loose jowls, gray hair, and light blue eyes.

"Three years later, he died. He was a heavy drinker with heart problems and, apparently by mistake, took an overdose of barbiturates he used to help him sleep. He left her about a million kronor. His widow now began to call herself 'Froken' Lindfors. This is the Stina Lindfors we know." Gerdi looked around the table. The others were quiet, digesting this information.

"So, as you pointed out, Mats, there's ample financial motive, and now we have an interesting background that raises additional questions," Ekman said.

"However, because she's had a husband and a fiancé both die on her, it may simply mean she's been unfortunate. Yet, it's troubling that in each instance, she's come away wealthier. This last time, very wealthy, indeed. But it's not a crime to inherit large amounts of money, so I don't want us to make any assumptions about her. She may be quite innocent."

"Can we tie her to Grendel?" asked Rapp. "We've got evidence he's the one who's killed Westberg. Perhaps she's the accomplice who delivered the briefcase."

"Maybe we're looking at this case upside down, Chief," said Holm. "Suppose Lindfors is the one really in charge. Let's say she's a 'black widow,' who murders her men . . . she has a clear motive . . . and this man 'Grendel' is simply her accomplice, who does the killing. All the cannibalism talk, and the mutilation, could just be camouflage to persuade us we're dealing with a maniac. It's intended to distract us from what's really going on: a garden-variety murder for money."

"Enar, you could be right," said Ekman. "But we just don't have enough information yet to reach that conclusion. Still, what you've suggested fits together. You've come up with a strong theory of the case that clears away the confusion.

"We need to find out more about Lindfors. Gerdi and Enar you've made a very good start. She doesn't know you, so for the next few days, I'd like you to follow her, starting right after the press conference. We need to know everything she does from the time she leaves for work until she goes to sleep at night. You can spell each other. Take a camera with a long lens. And make sure she doesn't see you.

"Now let's turn to the other missing men. Alrik and Mats, what can you tell us?"

"As you asked, Chief, we tried to find some interests that would link the four missing men. We talked to family members, people in their offices, and any friends we could identify. All of them liked to travel, mostly to southern Europe. Just like the rest of us, when we can afford it," Rapp said with a smile.

"Except for Bohren, who preferred television, Henriksson and Gustaffson liked going to the movies and played at their local chess clubs. We couldn't find out if they knew each other, however. There were no other common social or charity organizations. And that's about it. I'm sorry it doesn't help much."

"Then, apart from travel, two of them shared an interest in movies and chess?" Ekman asked.

"Yes," said Bergfalk. "By itself, it's not a lot to go on. But we also looked into that question you had, Chief, about break-ins at their homes, or their parents' places, and here we found something. That was a sharp question, Chief. How on earth did you guess?"

"Dumb luck," Ekman said with a shrug.

"Gustaffson and Henriksson had their apartments broken into a couple of weeks before they went missing. We talked to their relatives, who remembered that among the missing items, each had a family photo taken, just like Westberg's parents."

"So far then, we have a number of common elements that join three of the missing men, Gustaffson, Henriksson, and Westberg," Ekman summarized. "Age group, hair and eye color, the weather when they went missing, and now, the break-ins and missing photos. Although two shared an interest in movies and chess, we don't yet know if Westberg did.

"Some of these factors, if not every one of them, may be significant. At least they begin to provide a pattern of sorts. From what you've told us, I think we should conclude Bohren is an outlier for now, and focus on the three remaining men.

"We need to know more about this chess connection particularly. How often did they play? Were they good at it? Did they play together? Who were their opponents? Were there any arguments at their chess clubs? Who was involved? And so on. Alrik and Mats, take another crack at it, and see if you can get answers to those questions.

"I'll speak with Westberg's father about his son's interests." Ekman was not looking forward to the conversation with the bereaved father, but it had to be done to see if Rodger fit the pattern they'd uncovered.

"At the conference, we'll be handing out Westberg's picture and asking anyone who saw him last Tuesday or Wednesday to call us. Alenius and Rosengren, I'd like you to field those calls." They looked at each other with dismay.

"Yes, I know it's a difficult assignment, but I have confidence you two can ask the right questions to sort out the crank callers we're bound to get. Maybe someone will have seen something helpful."

"Chief, it looks like we've got two tracks going here," Rapp said. "One involves Lindfors, and the other, Gustaffson, Henriksson, and Westberg. I think Enar's onto something. This is really all about money. Should we keep on with this second track when the first looks so good right now? There doesn't seem to be any connection between Lindfors and the two other missing guys, so maybe it would be better to drop the second approach."

As Ekman looked around the table, the others nodded their agreement.

"You may be right, Alrik. Enar's theory could explain a lot of what's been happening. And the connections we've found among the missing men are sketchy right now. But there still seem to me too many coincidences to just ignore. So let's keep on with both tracks for a while.

"Are there any other comments or questions? No? We're making real progress, thanks to the good work all of you have done. We'll meet again tomorrow," Ekman said, getting to his feet.

As the others trickled out, Enar followed Ekman into his office. "Do you think my idea is dead wrong, Chief?" Holm asked.

"No, Enar, not at all. It clarifies a great deal, just not everything. What we need to keep looking for is a way of explaining every element of what I think is a single case. Perhaps Lindfors will provide the answers we need. You and Gerdi keep a close eye on her. Let's find out where she goes, what she does, who she sees. Then we may get a better understanding of what's going on."

"We'll be watching her every move, Chief," said Holm, leaving.

36

The Adulterer

As Ekman reached for the phone to call Westberg, it rang. It was Ingbritt.

"Walther, I'm calling from Carla's. The trip here was uneventful. How are you doing?"

"Missing you, already."

"You're a terrible liar, Walther Ekman," she said with a laugh. "You're wrapped up in that case of yours and haven't thought about me at all."

"That's just not true. I've thought about you at least twice since kissing you good-bye."

"Well, that's better than not at all. I guess I'll have to settle for that. All right, I'll let you get back to what you were doing. Remember, call me tonight when you get home. It doesn't matter if it's late."

"I won't forget. Have a good time. I wish I were there," Ekman said, and meant it.

They hung up and he called Westberg.

"Herr Westberg, it's Walther Ekman. I know this is a difficult time for you, but you can help with our investigation. Yes, it won't take long, I have just a few questions. No, I think it would be better if I speak with you in person rather than over the phone. At your home, in an hour? I'll be there."

Ekman was just about to leave when the phone rang again.

"Walther, it's Ludvig. I have some answers for you on that gruesome package you sent. There are no finger-prints, and the knot again is a bowline. We're still work-ing on the DNA and I should have something for you soon. Whoever the genitals are from, it was done post mortem. And it wasn't done with surgical precision. I'd say he used a large scissors of some kind. Perhaps, garden or kitchen shears."

"I don't know whether I'm relieved or not. Now we're definitely dealing with a homicide, rather than a maim-ing. At least we don't have to worry about what kind of condition the victim is in."

"I know what you mean. How is the case going?"

"We may have a potential suspect, and there are a lot of disjointed leads. But it's progressing. I feel better about it than when we last spoke."

"That sounds encouraging. The sooner you catch this madman, we'll all breathe easier. Good hunting."

When Ekman pulled up in front of Westberg's house, the door opened and Westberg came out to meet him.

"God morgen, Herr Ekman," he said, shaking hands. "I didn't want you to ring the doorbell, my wife is rest-ing. The doctor had to give her a sedative." His face was drawn and red-eyed. He looked like he hadn't slept either, Ekman thought, and could use a sedative himself.

"We can talk in my study," Westberg said, leading the way down the wide hallway to a large, book-lined room in the rear of the house.

When they were seated in chairs facing each other, Ekman said, "Again, Herr Westberg, I apologize for dis-turbing you, but you may have information that can help with our investigation."

"I don't know what that could be, but of course, I want to do anything I can to help."

"I have just a few questions. They may seem unconnected to your son's disappearance, but you can be sure any information you provide will assist us."

"Yes, go on," said Westberg, shifting in his chair.

"Did your son like to go to the movies?"

"Why on earth can that matter?" Westberg replied, exasperated. Ekman realized that this irritability was not really directed at him. It was just a way of releasing pent-up anger over his lost son.

"Please answer the question," said Ekman in a mild voice.

"As a matter of fact he dislikes films. He prefers the theater. He thinks most movies today are garbage. I agree with him." Ekman noted that Westberg was still using the present tense. He hadn't accepted that Rodger was dead.

"Thank you, that's useful to know. And does your son like chess?" asked Ekman, using the present tense on purpose.

"He's a chess enthusiast. I taught him to play when he was seven. He's been an active player ever since. He's quite good too," Westberg said with pride.

"Is he a member of a local chess club?"

"Why, yes, he is. They meet every third week."

"If you have the name and address of the club, and a phone contact, that would be helpful."

"I'll get that for you," Westberg said, going to his desk and rummaging in a drawer for his address book. He took out a piece of paper and jotted down the information.

"Is that all you wanted?" asked Westberg, handing him the paper.

"There's just one other thing," said Ekman in an offhand manner. "Do you know how Rodger met Stina Lindfors?"

"Stina? Why do you need to know that?"

"In a homicide investigation, anything may be important."

Westberg was silent for a moment. "Is she a suspect?"

"At this stage, Herr Westberg, I wouldn't say that. We're simply gathering information of all kinds, as you can tell from the questions I've asked."

"I introduced them."

"How did you first meet Froken Lindfors?"

"Her company did some accounting work for my firm. She was one of the junior accountants assigned to the job."

"When was this?"

"I first met her about two years ago."

"What was your impression of her then?"

"She's intelligent, quite charming, and of course, very good looking, as I mentioned when you were here the other day. She was also good at her job."

"Did you meet with her often?"

"A few times, as the accounting work required. Is this much detail really needed?" He paused, frowning. "What are you really asking?" He got up, and going to the door, closed it.

"I'm sorry to pry into personal matters, Herr Westberg, but I'm sure you can understand this is a necessary part of my job. Your answers will be kept confidential." Ekman knew he wouldn't be able to keep this promise, but he needed Westberg's cooperation.

"You want to know about our relationship, Stina and me?" Westberg responded in a low voice. His usually aggressive manner with Ekman had vanished.

"Yes, please," said Ekman.

"I'll tell you right out then. We were lovers. I'm not proud of it. It started one evening when we were working late."

"How long did this relationship continue?"

"About four months. Then I broke it off. Nothing could come of it. It couldn't go on any longer without arousing my wife's suspicion. And I could never leave her, we've been together too long. She doesn't know anything about it." Ekman wondered if his wife's unreasonable aversion to Lindfors wasn't instinctive dislike of a rival.

"Did Froken Lindfors suggest you should leave your wife for her?"

"No, never. It was my idea. I thought about it briefly and decided I couldn't do it." Maybe he was deceiving himself, thought Ekman. The idea may have been so subtly planted he thought it was his.

"After the affair ended you introduced Stina Lindfors to your son?"

"Yes. Rodger needs to settle down, to marry. She's perfect for him." You should know, after you gave the car a test drive, Ekman couldn't help thinking.

"Did you know that three months ago your son altered his will?"

"No," said Westberg, his face showing his surprise. "How did he change it?"

"Rodger left everything to Froken Lindfors," Ekman replied, watching Westberg's face, which betrayed astonishment and then dismay that changed rapidly to anger.

"That scheming bitch. I've been an imbecile, an absolute imbecile," Westberg said, turning his anger on himself as he got up and paced about the room. It's suppressed guilt, as much as anything else, Ekman thought.

"Everything, even the trust fund?"

"Yes," said Ekman, standing and facing him.

"That's family money and meant to stay in the family. I won't accept this. Rodger will have to change his will again. Most of what he has is money I settled on him when he turned thirty." His expression was pained.

"I certainly understand your feelings."

Westberg pulled himself together, trying to restore his frayed dignity and sense of self-importance. "Have I now told you all you wanted to know, Herr Ekman?"

"You've been very helpful, Herr Westberg. Thank you for speaking so frankly. I won't trouble you further."

Westberg walked him to the front door.

"This was a private conversation, Herr Ekman. I was open with you only because my son is in danger. You will remember that, won't you?"

"Of course, Herr Westberg," said Ekman as he left.

At the bottom of the front steps, he turned and saw Westberg looking after him with narrowed eyes and tightly compressed lips. I've made an enemy, Ekman thought. He's told me too much.

37

<hr />

Rystrom

On the way back to headquarters, Ekman called Rapp.

"I have some information for you and Mats," he said, reading from the paper with the chess club details Westberg had given him. "Find out all you can about Rodger Westberg's involvement with this club. Also, we can forget about the missing men's interest in movies being a common link. Westberg wasn't a fan."

Garth Rystrom was waiting for him in his office. At fifty-three, he looked more like forty. Six feet tall and very fair, with thick blond hair that hadn't begun to gray, he had light blue eyes and pale skin. A snub nose on an unlined face, and an energetic manner, added to the youthful impression.

"Walther," he said smiling, as he got up and came toward Ekman with hand extended, "it's good to see you."

"Thanks for coming down, Garth," replied Ekman, shaking his hand.

Once they were seated, Rystrom said, "It sounds like you have an intriguing case on your hands."

"Perhaps too intriguing. We can really use your help."

Ekman began to describe, in more detail than he had in their phone conversation, what had happened since last Tuesday when the first letter arrived.

"I'd like to take a look at the letters you've received."

"I thought you'd like to see everything, so I've a complete file for you, including a psychological profile of Grendel, photos, and my memoranda, right here," he said, taking out of a drawer the three-ring binder he'd had Holm prepare, and handing it to him.

"I'll need to study this. Why don't you go ahead and fill me in?"

As Ekman spoke, Rystrom leaned forward in his chair.

"Fascinating," he said. "Unlike anything I've heard of."

"You and me both," said Ekman, as he told Rystrom of the personal turn the case had taken since it began.

"But there seems to be no reason for this apparent fixation?"

"None we've been able to discover, and we've even looked at twenty years of cases for an old enemy," replied Ekman.

"You've taken precautions, I assume?" Rystrom asked, concerned for his friend.

"Yes. Believe it or not, I'm going around armed, and after this last package was delivered to my front door, I even sent Ingbritt out of town," Ekman said, shaking his head in disgust.

"Well, you've done all you can to deal with that. What about this potential suspect you've found?"

"She's only a possibility at this point," said Ekman, telling him what they'd discovered about Lindfors's marital history. "One theory we've come up with is that she, and a male accomplice, who's using the name Grendel, have created this fictitious maniac. They're using him as a ruse to distract us from the money motive that would otherwise have become obvious. What I found out this morning strengthens that theory," Ekman said, telling Rystrom about Eugen Westberg's affair with Lindfors.

"What this may mean," he said, "is that she made a calculated decision to become involved with the elder

Westberg, but when he wouldn't leave his wife for her, shifted her attention to his unmarried son. After over a year together, Rodger is intent on marrying her, changes his will leaving her everything, and she finds this out. Three months later, he vanishes. When his body surfaces, which will probably be not too long from now, she inherits. On its face, it would look suspicious to us, so she needs a distraction: enter Grendel.

"Knowing what we do now, it makes even more sense to concentrate on Lindfors. The problem with this theory is that there are two other missing men with similar circumstances that seem to link them to Rodger Westberg's disappearance," Ekman said, explaining these in more detail.

"I agree with you. Those are tenuous connections, but there seem to be too many to be just coincidences. They need to be explained." Rystrom paused, looking thoughtful. "Could these other killings be additional tricks designed to confuse us?"

"You mean perhaps Lindfors and Grendel also murdered these two other men? And Westberg is supposed to look like the most recent victim in a maniac's killing spree?" asked Ekman.

"I admit it sounds extraordinarily cold-blooded, but it would make sense if Lindfors is ruthless, intent on misleading us, and planned everything some time ago. She could have selected Eugen Westberg as her next lover years before, and schemed to marry and then kill him. If that didn't work out, she could have already had his bachelor son in mind as backup.

"The other killings and seeming coincidences, like the stolen family photos, are just part of a carefully thought-out scheme to throw a possible future police investigation off track. With tens of millions at stake, she might be willing to go to vicious extremes in advance, trusting her seductiveness to succeed with one man or the other.

It also might explain Grendel's apparent personal interest in you from the beginning. It could be a clever part of their plan, intended to distract the person who would head any investigation."

Ekman was silent for several moments, as he considered this from every angle. "It could work. You may have hit on a way to tie everything together. I'm impressed, my friend."

With a laugh, Rystrom waved off the compliment. "They're just a series of wild-ass guesses, Walther."

"But very shrewd guesses. If you're right, we're dealing with a pair of exceptionally dangerous psychopaths. Now we need to gather hard evidence to confirm your theory. I've already assigned a team to watch Lindfors starting later today, and we'll keep her under close surveillance. If they come up with anything, I'll ask the prosecutor for a warrant to wiretap. In the meantime, let's pursue the ties among the three men. If Lindfors and Grendel killed all of them, they may have slipped up on something that could point to them."

"It sounds like a plan. What can I do to help?"

"You've already made a major contribution by coming up with how the puzzle pieces might fit."

Although he was willing to go along with Rystrom's theory for now, Ekman had strong reservations. While it covered all the known facts, the theory depended on Lindfors and her accomplice, Grendel, executing an elaborate long-range, murderous deception to throw off a future investigation. In all his years as a police officer, Ekman had never heard of, let alone encountered, such farsighted, bloody-minded criminals. He knew he might have met them now and Rystrom could be right, but he was skeptical.

"What we need to do before the press conference is introduce you to Commissioner Norlander, and Olov Malmer, the DC," Ekman said, reaching for the phone.

"But let's keep your theory to ourselves for now, Garth. Otherwise, Norlander and Malmer will jump the gun and think the case is already solved, when we've just begun to figure it out." Rystrom nodded his agreement.

An hour later, they entered Norlander's office. Malmer was already there.

"Superintendent Rystrom, it's a pleasure to meet you," said Norlander, shaking his hand. "You come very highly recommended by an unimpeachable source." He smiled at Ekman as he said this.

"I'm glad to be of any help I can, Commissioner," replied Rystrom, turning to shake hands with Malmer.

Norlander led them to a seating area. "As you know, there'll be a press conference this afternoon, Superintendent, where you'll be introduced. Were you planning to say anything?"

"No, I hadn't intended to do anything except be there."

"After I make a few brief remarks then, I'll turn the conference over to Walther. What are the main points you're going to cover?" he asked, turning to Ekman.

"I'll focus on Rodger Westberg's disappearance last Tuesday afternoon or Wednesday morning, and say we need the public's assistance in locating him. We'll distribute a photo and ask the media to print it and show it on TV with a phone number. I've already assigned two inspectors to answer the calls. Then I'll field questions, but don't intend to be very responsive. That's about it. I don't think it should run more than half an hour."

"They won't be satisfied with that," said Malmer, critical as usual.

"You're right. Of course, they'll push for more information. All I'll say is that the investigation is ongoing."

"At this stage you really can't say anything else," put in Norlander. "But perhaps you can promise them some more details at a later time."

"I'll do that, Commissioner."

Norlander got up. "Thanks again for coming down, Herr Rystrom. I'm sure that with CID involved our investigation will have added credibility. And your presence will also help satisfy Rodger Westberg's parents that we're doing everything that can be done," he added.

Seated in the restaurant across the square from headquarters, Ekman and Rystrom watched pedestrians hurrying to avoid the increasing rain, unsuccessfully trying to shield themselves with umbrellas that the wind, whipping around them, threatened to turn inside out. They'd both ordered the luncheon special: pea soup, Swedish sausage and brown beans, with ale.

Over their food, Ekman asked, "Where were you planning to stay, Garth?"

"I've already checked into the Thon on Strandgatan."

"With Ingbritt away, I'm rattling around in the house. We've got a couple of guest rooms and I'd welcome the company."

"Thanks for the offer. Maybe I'll take you up on it after I've had a chance to explore the town a little, okay?"

"Sure," said Ekman, somewhat hurt that Rystrom hadn't jumped at the chance to spend more time with him. Perhaps it was best. After the long days to come working the case, they'd probably each need some time alone.

"This is good," said Rystrom, holding up a forkful of sausage. "Thanks for suggesting this place, and for the lunch. It's not only convenient, but the food's great."

"My pleasure," said Ekman, digging in himself, and taking a sip of ale.

"So, tell me," asked Rystrom, "what do you *really* think about my theory?"

Ekman was startled, and then smiled. His friend was very acute at assessing people's moods.

"Okay, you've got me," Ekman replied. "It just seems a little far-fetched that Lindfors and her accomplice could be that astute. Setting up two killings, and those other coincidences, to cover the Westberg murder, and making up this Grendel character as the murderer, pushes the limits of my credulity. It's too neat, and gives them too much credit for creativity. In my experience, criminals aren't that smart."

"Walther, it's only a preliminary theory," said Rystrom. "I'm not sold on it, but I'm willing to consider it a working hypothesis until we come up with something better. That's all."

"Good," said Ekman, much relieved. He wanted both of them to be on the same page, and was glad Rystrom wasn't committed to his theory.

"I hope we'll know more soon," he said. "Keeping our judgment suspended until we have better information seems essential to me."

"I agree," said Rystrom.

38

Press Conference

Thirty media people, including several photographers and two television camera crews, were already milling about the front of the auditorium when the police communications officer, Lena Sahlin, a tall, red-haired woman of forty, led Norlander, Malmer, Rystrom, Ekman, and Edvardsson onto the small stage. While the others sat down in a row at a table behind her, Sahlin went to the podium microphone.

"Ladies and gentlemen, please take your seats so we can get started," she said. It was five minutes past three.

After some shuffling about as the camera people positioned themselves, she went on, "Thank you all for coming. To begin, I'd like to introduce Commissioner Elias Norlander." She stepped away from the microphone and went to one side of the stage, as Norlander came forward.

"Let me add my thanks to Fru Sahlin's for your coming here on short notice. The police need your assistance, and the public's, in a new case, which you will soon hear more about. Joining me today are my colleagues whom I would like to introduce to you. Seated behind me, to my right, is our Deputy Commissioner Olov Malmer." He, and the others, stood and then sat as they were introduced. "Next to him is Superintendent Garth Nystrom, of the National

Criminal Investigation Division, who has kindly agreed to assist us with our inquiries. Beside him is Prosecutor Malin Edvardsson, and next to her, heading our investigation, is Chief Superintendent Walther Ekman. All of us will be glad to try and answer any questions you may have. Now I'd like to turn the conference over to Herr Ekman."

As Ekman stepped to the microphone, he looked around the room, and saw his own team standing around the back.

"Good afternoon. As Commissioner Norlander has said, we need your assistance, and through you, the public's, to try and locate a missing person, Advokat Rodger Westberg. He vanished Tuesday afternoon or early Wednesday, last week. Our investigation has revealed no reason for his disappearance and we've become increasingly concerned that a criminal act may have occurred. Fru Sahlin will be distributing a photo of Herr Westberg with a police phone number to call if anyone has information about his disappearance." He held up an oversized copy of the photo with a large red phone number across the bottom. Cameras flashed.

"We would appreciate your publicizing this as widely as possible, and hope it will lead to finding Herr Westberg. I, and my colleagues, will try to answer any questions you may have."

A hand shot up from a short, bald man in the front row. "How come all this brass," he asked in an aggressive bass voice, pointing to the stage, "is involved in a routine missing-person case? Is it because Westberg is the son of Councillor Westberg?"

"Not at all," replied Ekman, his voice neutral. "We treat every case with the utmost seriousness and my colleagues decided to make this clear to the public by coming here today."

He had a point, thought Ekman. This did look like overkill. It would have been better if I held the conference myself, but Norlander wanted to make sure Westberg's father knew we were pulling out the stops.

Hands were going up around the room. He gestured to a woman two rows back.

"Has Herr Westberg been kidnapped?" she asked.

"We don't think so at this juncture because no demands have been made during the past week. Of course, this could change," he replied.

"Has he been killed?" someone yelled out.

"We don't know that, but unfortunately, it's a possibility we must consider."

"I've a question for Superintendent Rystrom," said a well-dressed man in his forties. Rystrom got up and joined Ekman at the microphone.

"Why has CID been called in at this early stage? Does Stockholm think the case is that important, and if so, do you believe it's being mishandled?"

"I'm here only because I was asked by my good friend, Chief Superintendent Ekman, and your commissioner, Herr Norlander, to be of whatever assistance I can to the investigation. Every case is important, and far from being mishandled, in my professional opinion this investigation is being brilliantly directed by Herr Ekman. I hope that answers your questions," said Nystrom, and sat down again.

Ekman indicated a woman in the first row. "Does Prosecutor Edvardsson agree that a crime has been committed?" she asked. Edvardsson came forward.

"Yes, I share Herr Ekman's belief that, at this point, the most likely explanation for Advokat Westberg's inexplicable disappearance is that he has been the victim of a crime," Edvardsson responded, and without saying more, returned to her seat.

"Herr Ekman, you're not telling us anything about the actual investigation," a man called out, as he stood. Tall, unshaven, with sunken cheeks, Bruno Haeggman, at thirty-five, was the chief investigative reporter for *Sydsvenska Nyheter*, one of the largest newspapers in southern Sweden. Ekman had dealt with him before. They hadn't been pleasant experiences.

"At this stage, our investigation must remain confidential. When it's possible to release details, I can assure you, we will," Ekman replied in a flat voice.

"I guess we'll just have to discover what's really going on for ourselves," Haeggman said loudly, his voice abrasive, and stalked out of the room.

There were still a few hands in the air trying to get his attention, but Ekman ignored them. There was nothing more he could say.

"Ladies and gentlemen, again, thank you for coming," Ekman said, ending the conference. "Please make sure to get a copy of the photo from Fru Sahlin as you go out."

As he left the stage, Norlander turned to Ekman. "That went about as well as could be expected, although I don't think we've made any new friends in the media," he said. Malmer trailed after him without saying anything.

Edvardsson was talking quietly with Rystrom as Ekman joined them. "I arrived late and haven't had a chance to speak with you before," she said to Rystrom.

"It's a pleasure to meet you, Fru Edvardsson, I've heard so much about you. All of it extremely complimentary, of course." Rystrom grinned.

"It's kind of you to say so, even though some people in Stockholm might strongly disagree," she replied, as a sly smile brightened her small, wrinkled face.

"You received my latest memo?" Ekman asked her.

"Yes, and read it with great interest. Things are moving rapidly."

"Not fast enough for me. I'm hoping that between the two of us," he said, turning to Rystrom, "we'll be able to get you enough evidence to convict whoever's behind what's been happening."

"I know you will, Walther. It was good meeting you, Herr Rystrom," she said as she left.

Sitting in the office Rystrom had been assigned, two doors down from his own, Ekman was discussing the next steps in the investigation.

"Lindfors will be watched, beginning this afternoon. We may learn more at tomorrow's meeting. We've been holding them at eight in the morning, in my conference room."

Rystrom nodded. Joining an investigating team after it had been working together would be awkward. It would require an adjustment by everyone to an outsider from Stockholm who outranked them.

"Walther, I don't want to be just window dressing to satisfy Norlander and Westberg," he said.

"Believe me, you won't be. You've already hit on a theory that ties everything together, and I want you to feel free to bring it up. At these meetings, everything is open for discussion. We need everyone's views."

"That's good. It's the approach I like to use, too."

"Well, then," said Ekman, getting up, "I'll see you in the morning, Garth."

Rystrom opened his desk drawer, took out the "murder book," and resumed reading where he'd left off.

39

~

Johan

At home that evening, Ekman finished the pad Thai he'd picked up for dinner, and phoned Ingbritt.

"You see, I didn't forget to call. How did your day go?"

"Carla and I took Johan to the park. We had a wonderful time with him, but I'm frankly exhausted. Trying to keep up with a six-year-old boy has become difficult for his aging grandmother."

"Nonsense. You haven't aged a day since I first met you."

"You lie like a well-trained husband should, Walther Ekman. But I'm still flattered you find me attractive."

"And miss you more than ever," he said, meaning it.

"And how did your day go?" she asked.

Ekman described his meeting with Westberg.

"That must have been very difficult for you."

"Yes, but necessary, and now we have even more evidence that Stina Lindfors may not be what she first seemed."

"Do you really suspect she could be that scheming?"

"Don't all women have a graduate degree in that?" he asked with a laugh.

"You're a hopeless misogynist," she replied in a stern voice to his teasing.

Ekman told her about Garth Rystrom's arrival and the press conference.

"It sounds like you handled that well, and Garth will be good company for you. Why don't you ask him to stay with you while I'm away?"

"I did, but for now, he prefers a hotel. Otherwise, it might be too much togetherness."

"I hate to think of you being all alone, Walther."

"I'm managing so far."

"Well, don't get to enjoy it too much."

"That'll never happen. I'll talk with you again tomorrow night. Sleep well."

Ekman went to his study and once again tried to immerse himself in eighteenth-century history. In some ways, it seemed a more civilized time than today, he thought, but knew he was deluding himself. The world was brutal then and hadn't changed.

40

Watching

Wednesday, October 19. Enar Holm was dead tired. It was seven thirty A.M. and he hadn't slept more than five hours the night before. He and Gerdi Vinter had sat in his car watching Stina Lindfors's office building starting at four thirty the previous afternoon. When Lindfors finally appeared at six, they'd split up. The rain had stopped and Gerdi followed her on foot, staying a discreet distance behind, while he followed in the car.

Six blocks later, Lindfors entered a grocery and came out with a large shopping bag. The store was two streets away from her apartment building at 78 Homsgatan. After Lindfors went in, Gerdi checked the names on the building directory outside, and found that she had an apartment on the third floor. There was no way to tell if it faced the street.

Back in the car, diagonally across from the building entrance, she said to Holm, "I guess we'll just have to wait and see if Lindfors goes out. This is the first time I've done surveillance since the academy, what about you?"

"It's the second time, so I'm no expert at this. Do you have the camera?"

Gerdi reached into the backseat for the camera bag, and took out a high-speed digital Nikon D800E with a long 200-m.m. lens.

Holm said, "Let's photograph everyone who goes in or out. We can't know if they're connected to Lindfors, but they could be."

"Okay, for now," she said. "But I've a better idea. Why don't I take a photo of the directory? Then we can get driver's license pictures of the residents and only photograph visitors."

"Great idea. Go ahead," said Enar, watching her cross the street and use her mobile to take a picture of the directory.

When Gerdi came back, she called headquarters and transmitted the directory photo, asking for license pictures of the residents at 78 Homsgatan. While they waited for them, Enar snapped pictures of several people entering and leaving the building. Two hours later, they had twelve license photos and started comparing them with the ones Holm had taken. All the people he'd photographed lived in the building.

It was a long and boring day.

At eight P.M., Holm said, "Why don't you grab something to eat? I'm not that hungry."

They'd stocked up on bottles of water and snacks before they started watching Lindfors. "I do need to use the bathroom again. Can I bring you anything from the restaurant?"

"Only your sweet self," said Enar, with a grin. Gerdi kissed him on the cheek and stepped out of the car.

She'd been gone a few minutes when a man approached the doorway to Lindfors's building. It was dark now, but there was a street lamp nearby, and the building entrance was well lit. Holm took several quick frames as the man went in. Looking at them afterward, most were shadowy, but there was one clear head profile.

When Gerdi came back from a small restaurant down the street, she brought sandwiches and hot coffee for both of them.

"Thank you, my guardian angel," said Enar. "I was starving."

"I thought so, you liar. You're always hungry, even though you hide it."

"While you were gone, I took some pictures of a guy going in. Let's compare them with the residents' photos."

It soon became clear that the man was the first stranger they'd found so far. But he wasn't the last. Two other men who went in and a woman who came out didn't live there either. Enar took photos of all of them.

By ten, two of the three male visitors had come and gone. The lit apartment windows went out one after the other.

An hour later, when the building was totally dark, Enar asked, "How long do you want to keep watching for that third guy?"

"I'm ready to call it a night," Gerdi replied. "Nothing seems to be happening. How about you?"

"Okay, let's go to my place, and be back here by six."

"It's a good thing I've a change of clothes at your apartment, or people might begin to talk," she said with a mischievous grin.

"Let them," he said, kissing her hard on the mouth.

After a quick breakfast of coffee and pastries, Enar and Gerdi drove back to Lindfors's building and parked in a slightly different place, with a good view of the entrance. It was six thirty. The sun would be up in an hour. The weather report had promised a dry, cloudy day.

By seven, people were leaving for work. At seven thirty, Enar said, "Why don't you go to the meeting? I'll stay here and watch for Lindfors."

"Afterward, I'll find you near her office, and you can take a break," she replied.

They kissed, and he watched her head down the street toward a taxi rank on the corner.

At seven forty-five, Lindfors came out and started walking in the direction of her office building. Enar followed her in the car keeping a half block back. Near her office, she stopped at a coffee shop and came out a few minutes later with a small bag. She entered her office building at eight ten. Holm was in luck. There was a parking space a short distance across the street from the entrance. He settled down to wait.

41

Case Theories

The evening paper and last night's television newscasts had carried stories about the press conference. Westberg's photo, the police request for information, and the number to call had been prominently displayed. Ekman had glanced through the morning papers to make sure they carried the same information. This should keep Alenius and Rosengren busy sorting out the crank calls, he thought. There was a chance somebody who had seen something useful would phone. He hoped they could tell the difference.

Ekman half expected Holm to be at his desk, but remembered that he and Gerdi would be watching Lindfors. He wondered how that had gone. One of them would probably be at the meeting.

He had just hung up his hat and coat, when Rystrom poked his head in.

"God morgen, Walther. I assume you saw the TV and papers?"

"God morgen, Garth. Yes, they gave it the coverage we wanted. We'll see if it bears some fruit. Alenius or Rosengren should be filling us in at this morning's meeting."

"I'm looking forward to meeting your crew," Rystrom said, sitting down.

"I think you'll find they're a good team. Don't be disturbed if some of them seem a little distant at first. They'll soon adjust to your joining us. I don't expect everyone to be there. A few have ongoing assignments that will keep them away, but you'll meet most of them."

"I'm sure they'll get used to me soon enough. I've been thinking about that theory I came up with."

"Yes?"

"Maybe it's too soon to mention it at the meeting. There's not enough evidence yet to make it credible."

"No, Garth, don't hesitate to bring it up. Whether it's right or not, it will get everyone thinking along different lines. We need to stimulate them to come up with ideas about what's behind all that's happened. Your theory will help do that."

"I just don't want everyone seizing on it prematurely and running off in the wrong direction."

"Don't be afraid of that. Between us, we'll keep things on the right track," Ekman said with a smile. "We should be getting more solid information about connections among the missing men."

They sat in the conference room chatting about mutual acquaintances until a little before eight, when Bergfalk and Rapp came in, followed by Vinter and Alenius.

Ekman and Rystrom got up, as Ekman said, "Please shake hands with Superintendent Garth Rystrom of CID, who's joining us, as I mentioned before. You heard him speak at yesterday's conference."

Once everyone was seated, Ekman turned to Rystrom. "Gerdi and Enar Holm have been watching Lindfors since yesterday. What can you tell us, Gerdi?"

"We trailed her from her office to her apartment building," she said, describing the photos they'd taken and how they'd figured out a way to sort visitors from residents.

Ekman was impressed. "That was very clever, Gerdi. When Enar comes in, we'll have to check those photos."

"There's no need, Chief. I asked him to hook up the camera to his mobile and send the photos to me. They're being run against our facial recognition database right now."

Rystrom's raised eyebrows showed he was impressed.

"Thank you, Gerdi. You're moving things along quickly, as usual," Ekman said, pleased. Technology did have its uses, he thought.

"Alrik and Mats, what have you found?" he asked, trying not to stare at Mats's shimmering, florescent blue shirt.

"We went back, Chief, to Gustaffson's, Henriksson's, and Westberg's chess clubs," said Alrik. "They were all good amateur players, but not grand masters, or anything like that. They were well liked at their clubs and didn't have problems with anyone. None of the three clubs played matches against the others. And we ran the names of the opponents each man had at his club over the last three years, and none matched at the other clubs. So we think the missing men and the people they played with were strangers to each other, outside of each man's club. There don't seem to be any connections. Mats and I think it's a dead end."

"That's too bad," said Ekman, stroking his chin. "I'd hoped we'd find a real link."

"Have you checked if they played on the Internet?" asked Rystrom.

"No," replied Bergfalk. "We didn't think about that."

"Is there a lot of chess playing on the Net?" asked Rapp.

"A huge amount," responded Rystrom. "I've played chess that way, myself."

"How would we find out what they did on the Net?" asked Rapp belligerently.

"There's only one way," said Ekman. "We have to get the men's computers from their former homes and offices. I'll talk to Edvardsson today about warrants to bring them in so our IT expert can check them out. If they played on the Net, it should still be on their hard drives." He was showing off a little that he wasn't completely technologically illiterate.

"If it would help speed things up," added Rystrom, "I can bring in some of our tech people at CID."

"A great idea," said Ekman with real enthusiasm; but he also thought that too much CID involvement in his case might become a problem for him at some point.

Ekman asked Alenius, "Any luck so far with the calls?"

"A lot of people think they've seen Westberg, not only in Weltenborg, but in Stockholm, Lund, Malmö, you name it. But after Rosengren or I questioned them, they turned out to be either mistaken or cranks. Rosengren is still taking calls. Maybe something will turn up." He shrugged.

A mobile phone rang; it was Vinter's. "Yes. Please repeat that," she said, scribbling notes on a pad. "Okay, got it. Thanks for being so quick. I appreciate it."

Everyone looked at her.

"We got a hit," she said, grinning. "Do you remember when we spoke about Stina Lindfors's background that she had an early marriage? The name of her first husband is Carl Stillen. I've just been told he has a criminal record: assault with grievous bodily harm. He served four years. The conviction probably led to their divorce. He was one of three male visitors we photographed going into Lindfors's building last night. When I double-check the photos, I think we'll find he's the one who didn't leave. My guess is he spent the night with her."

Alenius looked surprised. "When we interviewed her, I thought she was genuinely upset about Westberg. She sure fooled me."

"Because she may be seeing her first husband," said Vinter, "doesn't necessarily mean she's not upset about Westberg."

"Yeah," put in Bergfalk, "she's grieving all the way to the bank."

"But does she know Westberg changed his will in her favor?" asked Rystrom. "If she does, her involvement with Stillen gives added support to a theory I've come up with," he said, explaining how the entire case, including Grendel and all the missing men, could fit together.

Everyone, except Ekman, was stunned. It was an improvement on Enar's approach.

"Garth's theory of the entire case could work," said Ekman. "But before we jump too far ahead, let's consider alternatives. What Gerdi has just found out can lead in a couple of different directions. For example, Stillen may have been Lindfors's lover since he came out of prison. She may be involved with him, but it may not be as her accomplice in the complex, multiple murder scheme Garth has outlined. She could have truly loved Westberg, and may just be unfaithful.

"A second theory is that Stillen became intensely jealous of her relationship with Westberg, and without her knowledge, killed him. So her grief may be quite genuine, even if she knew about the changed will, and it's not certain she did.

"As a third theory, she could have loved only Westberg's money. If she didn't know he'd already changed his will, then it would explain her being upset, seeing the money slipping away with his disappearance.

"Now we need to gather evidence to tell us which of these theories is true." He looked around the table. There was silence for a few moments while they digested this.

"But Chief, how do Grendel and the other missing men fit in?" asked Alenius. "In Rystrom's theory, Stillen is Grendel. Stillen has a history of serious assault; maybe now he's become a killer. It all works, with money the prime motive, and getting rid of a rival for Lindfors a possible secondary motive."

"We don't know how Grendel and the other men fit in yet," replied Ekman. "Grendel may be a real person acting for reasons we don't understand, or simply a useful fiction created by Lindfors and Stillen to cover up their real motives. Garth's theory has very helpful explanatory power," he said, looking at Rystrom. "All I'm saying is that we have to reduce any theory to hard facts. Otherwise we won't have a case that will stand up in court."

"I agree," said Rystrom.

"What should we do next, Chief?" Rapp asked.

"We need to keep watching Lindfors and find out where Stillen goes when he's not with her. If he's simply killed Westberg out of jealousy, he could lead us to Westberg's body. And if he's indeed Grendel, perhaps the bodies of all three men. Gerdi, I want you and Enar to keep watching Lindfors until Stillen appears again, then follow him. Let's discover where he goes, what he does, who he meets.

"I'm going to ask Edvardsson for warrants for the missing men's computers so we can search for a possible link. Alrik and Mats, I want you to confiscate those computers. There could be six or more. Most have probably been moved. You'll have to find out where they are and who has them. We'll need that information for the warrants.

"Alenius, you and Rosengren keep on with the phone calls. We may turn up something that will help us, if we just persist." Alenius nodded, but everyone could see he was unhappy.

"Is there anything else?" Ekman asked. When no one responded, he got to his feet. "We're making exceptionally good progress. See you tomorrow."

42

Edvardsson Intervenes

Ekman was back in his office on the phone with Edvardsson as Rystrom sat across the desk.

"Malin, Garth Rystrom and I need to see you. I want to bring you up to date, and speak to you about some warrants. We'll be there in fifteen minutes. Thanks."

In his car on the way over, Ekman said to Rystrom, "Malin may want to take over the investigation herself, but I don't think so. We've always worked well together, and she usually just gives us general guidance. But now that we've reached the warrant stage, she may want to be more actively involved."

"You know, she has a reputation in Stockholm for being abrasive and difficult to work with," said Rystrom.

"I'm really surprised to hear that. I've always found her to be a good colleague, ready to listen, not just give orders. She's also a decent person."

"Now I'm the one who's surprised," said Rystrom. "But I'm glad to hear it. Sometimes things get distorted at a distance. Perhaps some people in the Prosecutor General's Office have decided she's not deferential enough."

"That's probably it," said Ekman, as they pulled into a reserved police parking space at the courthouse. He pulled down his visor with the police ID, as they got out.

Ekman had decided he wasn't going to take the time to hunt for a space, parking police be damned.

The same officer was on duty in front, and saluted Ekman as they went in. Doesn't he ever get time off? thought Ekman. As they came in to Edvardsson's outer office, the receptionist got up.

"Please don't trouble yourself, Froken Sundquist, we're expected. This is Superintendent Rystrom from the National CID," Ekman said, introducing them.

"A pleasure to meet you, Superintendent," she said smiling, and then went back to her desk.

Ekman knocked on the inner office door, and they entered. Edvardsson came forward to meet them holding her hand out to Rystrom.

"It's good to see you again, Garth," she said, and then turned to Ekman. "It sounds like things are progressing, Walther," she added, as she led them to a seating area. They took the couch and she sat in an armchair facing them.

"Yes, Malin, we've had some new developments," he said, briefly sketching out for her the results of that morning's meeting, and the important discovery of Carl Stillen.

"So you now have two potential suspects to follow. You also want warrants for several computers, but you don't know how many?"

"There are probably at least four, and could be six, if we count the three men's office computers, as well as those they used at home. Westberg's will be easy to get hold of, but because the other men have been missing for some time, the computers will probably have been moved. I'll get you the names of current owners and addresses."

"I'll need affidavits supporting the warrants as soon as you have that information. Now, tell me more about your case against the two people you'll be following."

"Garth has come up with a comprehensive theory that has become stronger after discovering Stillen's possible involvement. Why don't you describe it, Garth?" he asked, turning toward him.

Rystrom laid out his idea as Edvardsson listened with an intent expression.

"What will it take to prove your theory?" she asked.

"Apart from getting outright confessions, which seems unlikely, it won't be easy," Rystrom responded. "We both hope following them, particularly Stillen, will lead us to hard evidence," he said, looking at Ekman.

"That seems to me, too, all you can do at this point." Glancing from Rystrom to Ekman, she added, "You realize, of course, that you have no evidence whatsoever against either of these people? Legally, they must be considered innocent until something actually implicates them. You're proceeding simply on the basis of a theory that, while it's comprehensive and exceptionally clever," she smiled at Rystrom, "frankly, seems to stretch plausibility. Your suspects have to be not only extraordinary planners, but brutal killers, as well."

"Garth and I agree it may be overreaching," Ekman said. "But his theory does answer all the key questions we have, and therefore has to be pursued. What we're trying to do by examining the missing men's computers is determine if there's something linking all of them that can lead us to the killer who calls himself Grendel. This may help us develop an alternative explanation for what Garth and I believe are three murders, or possibly five, if we include the guys on the scooter."

"It makes sense to pursue both approaches. At this juncture, I have no suggestions. I believe you're doing all that can be done. Walther, please keep me informed of your progress in writing, on a daily basis," Edvardsson said, getting up.

Turning to Rystrom, she said, "I'm glad you're helping. You have a creative mind, Garth. It's definitely needed in this strange case," she added with a faint smile.

43

~~~~~~~~~~

Haeggman

Ekman was at his desk when the phone rang.

"Herr Ekman, it's Bruno Haeggman of the *Sydsvenska Nyheter*. Do you have a few minutes for a telephone interview? I'd like to get your comments on a story we'll be running tomorrow."

Ekman was immediately on his guard. Haeggman had made clear his antagonistic attitude at the press conference.

"I don't do telephone interviews, Herr Haeggman, but can you tell me what the story's about?"

"Does the name 'Grendel' ring a bell?"

Shit, thought Ekman. Here it comes. I've been expecting this since it began, but now that it's here, I still don't know how to handle it.

"Herr Haeggman, I'm not certain what you mean. However, if we could meet, perhaps you could give me a better sense of what your story is about."

"It will need to be soon. I can meet you in half an hour at Volkmann's. It's a German restaurant at 620 Ullevigatan."

"I've never been there, but I can find it. I'll see you then."

Ekman called Norlander's office.

"I need to speak with him and Malmer immediately," he said to Annika. "Yes, it's extremely urgent."

Norlander and Malmer were waiting when he came in.

Without even shaking hands, Ekman said right away, "I just got a call from Haeggman at the *Sydsvenska Nyheter*. They're going to run a story tomorrow naming Grendel. I'm meeting him in less than thirty minutes."

Norlander took the news in his usual calm manner, but Malmer's face tightened.

"Can you get him not to print it?" Malmer asked, totally disregarding Swedish dedication to freedom of the press.

"I doubt it. I wanted you both to know that Grendel's involvement is going to come out now, as I was afraid it would when we first discussed this case."

"Do you think they'll take a balanced tone?" asked Norlander, pacing slowly about.

"I don't know. I'll have to see what Haeggman says."

"Caution him against the danger of going off half-cocked. He has a reputation for digging up government scandals, but there's none here. We're not covering up anything. An intensive investigation into the Westberg case is going on. I think that's the line to take with him, Walther."

"That's what I'll say then. If he agrees to keep a lid on the Grendel angle, can I promise him an exclusive when we find out more?"

"No, I don't think so. There's always the possibility that if Grendel is communicating directly with Haeggman, and if a story doesn't appear, he'll go elsewhere. Then Haeggman won't get his exclusive. He's well aware of that possibility, so he's likely to turn down any offer. Maybe some variation on it would work, however," Norlander said, always the media expert. "Perhaps if he strikes a neutral tone in the story, we can suggest he'll have an inside track later."

"I'll try that," said Ekman, impressed with Norlander's insight.

"I hardly need to tell you to be careful how you word things. He'll be recording everything you say, even if he shuts off a visible recorder. Thanks for the heads-up, Walther," he said, shaking his hand.

"Don't screw it up," added Malmer, his face anxious at the nightmare of bad publicity.

Norlander turned with a surprised look at Malmer.

"I'll try not to," responded Ekman, with just a hint of sarcasm.

Haeggman was waiting for him at a back table of Volk-mann's. He had a stein of dark beer and a small tape recorder in front of him. It wasn't busy in midafternoon. There were a few couples scattered about the restaurant and a single woman, sitting with her back to them several tables away, who had turned to watch him. Ekman wondered if she might be a photographer. He wouldn't put it past Haeggman.

Unshaven as usual, he got up as Ekman came over. "Herr Ekman," he said, offering his hand. Ekman shook it and sat down.

"Can I get you a beer?"

"No, thanks." That would be all he needed: a damaging story, illustrated by a fat, beer-swilling cop.

"Do you mind?" asked Haeggman, pointing to the recorder.

"Not at all." Although he very much did mind. But he remembered what Norlander had said, and assumed another recorder was already running in Haeggman's shirt pocket.

"What can you tell me about Grendel?"

"Can I ask how you came across that name?"

"You can ask," he smiled ironically.

"But you won't say."

"Actually, I don't mind telling you. It will be in the story anyway. I received a short note from Grendel this morning. He enclosed a copy of a letter he said he sent you last week about his . . . what shall we say . . . unusual tastes. This is one very weird character. He also enclosed notes he'd sent you about a stolen briefcase, and Rodger Westberg. I don't suppose you care to tell me what that was about? It has a bad sound. Did he enclose something gruesome, an ear, or finger? My guess is he did, which might make this a murder case."

Ekman's face was immobile, giving nothing away, even though he was surprised Haeggman had leaped so quickly to the correct conclusion. "Herr Haeggman, as you know from the press conference we held yesterday, we're conducting an intensive investigation into Westberg's disappearance. A story that sensationalizes the internal workings of our investigation won't assist us in locating Westberg. I know the Westberg family, as well as the police, would appreciate it if your story didn't speculate about fanciful grim details, and struck a more balanced tone."

"Are you questioning the public's right to know?"

"No, far from it. That's why we held the conference to ask for media and public assistance to find Westberg."

"Look, let's stop dueling over this. We're going to publish a story about Grendel's involvement. You can't stop us."

"You have every right to print whatever you want. All I ask is that you also state that there's a major investigation going on, involving not only local police, but National CID, and it's still in the early stages."

Haeggman paused, then shrugged his thin shoulders. "I intended to do that anyway. But you refuse to say anything about this Grendel?"

"It's always been police policy not to comment on the details of an ongoing investigation. You know that Herr Haeggman."

"Okay," he said, getting to his feet. "You can't say I didn't give you a chance to tell your side of the story."

Ekman rose, and as he did, the woman a couple of tables away also got up, and rapidly aiming a camera, took several photos of him. It was exactly as he'd guessed. He grimaced in disgust, and strode quickly out to his car.

44

Listening

When Haeggman's article came out, Ekman knew there would be even more intense attention focused on the Westberg case. He couldn't let the investigation hinge on just following Lindfors and Stillen, hoping something linking all the disappearances would turn up on the missing men's computers. A more aggressive approach was called for now.

He phoned Edvardsson. "Sorry to do this twice in one day, Malin, but I need to see you again. No, it can't wait. I'll be there in twenty minutes."

"You sounded quite urgent, Walther," Edvardsson said, as she led him to a seat on the couch.

Ekman told her about Haeggman's call and his meeting with him.

"It's what we've been afraid of, Malin. The whole Grendel angle is going to become public."

"What do you propose we do about it?"

"We have to move the investigation along a lot faster, now that Grendel's going to get the attention he wants. We have to resolve Lindfors's and Stillen's possible involvement as fast as possible. Following them and hoping for a solid lead isn't enough. If they're as clever as we suspect, a phone tap won't do it either. They'd never speak about their plans over the phone; everyone knows they're vulnerable to hacking. I think we need to hear what they're talking about in Lindfors's apartment."

"You want a warrant to put listening devices in her flat?" Malin asked, surprised. In past cases, Ekman had never proposed anything this extreme with so little to go on.

"Yes. I can understand your reluctance because there's no evidence yet that either of them had anything to do with Westberg's disappearance, let alone the other men's. But there doesn't seem any other way to find out what we need to know right away."

Edvardsson was silent for several minutes. "Walther, I don't have to tell you that this would be an extraordinary invasion of privacy of someone who may be innocent of any crime. And any evidence uncovered won't be admissible in court."

"I know, and I wouldn't ask, except that with all the publicity the case will get now, you, Norlander, and I will be pushed very hard to show immediate results. Look at it this way: If we don't learn anything that connects Lindfors and Stillen to the case, we can clear them of involvement and look elsewhere."

"I'll try and persuade myself to see it that way, and hope that my friend the district judge will go along with me." She paused for a long moment.

"All right, Walther. I'll need your affidavit supporting the warrant. Be careful not to be too creative."

"You'll have it today," Ekman said. "I'll ask Rystrom to bring in some of his technical people to plant the microphones tomorrow while Lindfors is at work."

Edvardsson got up. "I hope we're doing the right thing, Walther," she said, with a troubled frown.

"We'll soon find out, Malin. Believe me, I share your misgivings, but I don't think we have much choice."

Her small, lined face looked up at him. "There's always a choice, Walther. Let's hope we've made the correct one."

When Ekman walked into Rystrom's office, he was on the phone. Covering the mouthpiece, he said, "I'll be with you in a minute, Walther."

Ekman sat down and when Rystrom hung up, said, "Garth, I need your help," explaining what had happened in the last few hours.

"This case is already hot, and going to get much hotter, starting tomorrow," Rystrom said, shaking his head in surprise at the rapid developments. "So you want a couple of my 'black bag' techs to bug Lindfors's apartment?"

"Is that going to be a problem?"

"No. I'll have them here first thing tomorrow morning."

"Thanks, Garth. I knew bringing you in would be a great help. It's appreciated," he said, standing up.

But Ekman wasn't happy about it. It was Rystrom who'd come up with a broad theory of the case that explained almost everything, and his people would be all over the place—deciphering information on the missing men's computers and now, planting listening devices. Rystrom's assistance would move things forward much more rapidly. For Ekman, bringing a killer to justice as fast as possible was by far the overriding consideration, and justified cutting legal corners. Protecting his own control of the case had to be a distant second.

45

~~~~~~~~

The Story

Bruno Haeggman was standing in the second floor, glass-fronted office of his paper's editor at 875 Ullevigatan, a nondescript building two blocks from Volkmann's restaurant.

Haeggman had outrage written all over his tight-lipped face. When he'd handed in his story about Grendel's involvement in the Westberg disappearance, he knew it was a huge scoop and would be major news all over Sweden. Now he was being told to do a drastic rewrite.

"Bruno, it can still be a front-page story, but any connection to Westberg has to be dropped," said his boss, Arne Trest, a big, bluff man of sixty with a ruddy complexion and watery blue eyes.

"Tell me again exactly why," said Haeggman, daring him to repeat it.

"You know why. It would traumatize the Westbergs. You're suggesting in your story that this cannibal, Grendel, has sent part of their missing son to the police, and the cops won't discuss it. You write as though it's some kind of cover-up, but they're acting the way you'd expect police to act in any investigation. And they're incidentally doing the decent thing. So should we."

"Your deep concern for the tender feelings of the Westbergs does you credit, although it wouldn't have anything to do with the fact that he owns 20 percent of the paper, and is a friend of the publisher, right?" asked Haeggman.

"Sure it does. Don't bullshit me. You know better than pretend to be shocked; it's the real world. And how do you even know these letters are related to the case? Ekman didn't say they were, did he?"

"No, but when I mentioned the name, he sure offered to meet very fast."

"So what? It's still pure speculation based on this character who's calling himself Grendel."

"Look, it's not speculation. I told Ekman that Grendel sent me those letters, but it was someone else, someone on his investigating team. And the last note Ekman got from Grendel did enclose a piece of Westberg: not an ear, his genitals."

"My God, that's gruesome . . . Who's your source?"

"I can't tell you, but he's gold. I promised I wouldn't say, and I don't want to compromise getting more info."

"I can't accept that. We're on the same team and you work for me. Who is it?"

Haeggman was reluctant to give up the name, but if the story was going to be printed, he had to. "It's a police inspector named Rapp."

"You talked to him?"

"He called me and said I'd be receiving some information from inside the investigation."

"Did he say why he was doing this?"

"I asked. He said he had personal reasons."

"So you checked him out?"

"Of course. He's a senior inspector named Alrik Rapp. He's pissed about something, and this is his way of getting back at his boss, Ekman."

"How does he know that what Grendel sent is from Westberg?"

"They're doing DNA testing and should find out soon."

"So, for now, it's just a guess?"

"Yes," Haeggman acknowledged, biting his lip, "but probably an accurate one."

"That's not the kind of reporting we do here. Even with inside information, that's not good enough, and you damn well know it. We need at least two reliable sources before we can print anything, and there's nothing at this point that involves Westberg at all. We're not some scandal sheet, for God's sake," said Trest.

"Look, I'll accept Rapp as a source, and that Ekman's eagerness to meet with you when you mentioned Grendel's name confirms there's a dangerous nut out there calling himself that. But you cut the story way back to eliminate any reference to the note about Westberg, or speculation about how Grendel is connected, or I'll do it myself, and drop your byline."

It was the ultimate threat for someone like Haeggman who lived for headlines over his name.

"Okay, okay. But without referring to Westberg, it's lost its punch," said Haeggman, with a downturned mouth.

"What are you talking about? Just say we've received the Grendel material from 'a reliable police source,' that the threat of cannibalism makes us concerned for the public's safety, especially since a senior police officer has been the victim of a theft connected to this maniac.

"Follow up with some quotes from the letter and briefcase note. You can ask what the police are doing about it. Period. No reference to Westberg. It's still going to shake things up and grab headlines everywhere. Hell, TV news will want to interview you. If they do, by the way, you, of course, will say, 'No comment, my article said it all.'"

"All right, you win. I'll give you the rewrite in half an hour," he said, and walked stiffly out of the office, slamming the door behind him.

46

Home

It was after eight when Ekman got home. He'd gotten the information from Rapp and Bergfalk for the computer warrants. Then he'd spent hours writing out affidavits for them and the listening devices. He'd sent them over to Edvardsson before the end of the day. Usually he'd have Holm prepare drafts for his review, but now he had to do it all himself. He missed having him around, not only for his assistance, but because he enjoyed their kicking ideas back and forth.

Ekman knew that if the surveillance of Lindfors and Stillen was going to continue much longer, Holm and Vinter would have to be relieved before they became exhausted. He was going to have to get more people involved, and because his best people were stretched thin, would have to ask Rystrom for help . . . again, much as he didn't want to.

When he pulled into his drive, the contrast between this dark, empty house, and the warmly lit, welcoming one when Ingbritt was there, made him feel her absence all the more. After a quick meal of warmed-over sausages and beans, Ekman sipped an ale at the kitchen table, trying to relax. Looking at the clock, he saw it was past nine, and picking up the phone, called Ingbritt.

"I was wondering when you'd call," she said.

"Sorry, it's been another busy day. I just got in a little while ago. I really miss you."

"I miss you too, Walther, even though I've been busy too."

"What've you been doing?"

"Running around this morning at a playground, trying to keep up with a very active little boy. It's fun, but exhausting. This evening Carla got a babysitter, and she and Gunnar took me out to a really nice French restaurant."

"It sounds great. Again, I wish I were with you."

"How is your case going?"

In a few words, Ekman told her what had happened.

"Do you feel you're getting closer?" she asked.

"Yes and no," he replied. "Yes, we're developing information, but no, nothing that brings Grendel into sight yet. Maybe tomorrow we'll have something that will give us greater confidence. But you'll be hearing more about this case." And then told her about Haeggman.

"So this will be in the paper?"

"After the morning, I expect in a lot of papers and on TV."

"That will make things harder for you, won't it," she said, concerned.

"Yes, but we'll get through it. Maybe the publicity will turn up new leads. That's the bright side I'm trying to keep in mind."

"I love you, Walther Ekman."

"I know. I love you too. Say hello to everyone for me. I'll talk to you tomorrow. Good night, Ingbritt."

After they'd hung up, Ekman thought about reading for a while, but was too tired. His mind kept churning through the day's events. He tossed about fitfully before finally falling asleep.

47

Midgame

*T**hursday, October 20. Grendel was both elated and disappointed. The bold headline plastered across the front page of the Sydsvenska Nyheter, "Cannibal Stalks City," delighted him. The story named him, quoted his first letter to Ekman, and the briefcase note, and speculated about what the police, and in particular, Ekman, the victim of the theft, were doing about it. Centered in the middle of the page was a photo of a glowering Chief Superintendent Ekman, whom the story cast as his nemesis. This was as he'd planned. But he was frustrated there'd been no mention of the third letter making the connection to Westberg's disappearance.*

Later that day, tomorrow, and for many days, Grendel's fame would light up the media sky in other papers and on TV. He'd long hoped for this. But even more publicity would come. He could see the entire plan in his mind's eye. Soon it would be reality and the focus of the world's attention.

That fool Haeggman, so greedy for a big story, for his small taste of fame, was ready to be deceived with little effort. Grendel had initially called and said he was Inspector Alrik Rapp and wanted to give Haeggman an exclusive, with written material, from inside the investigation. And Haeggman hadn't inquired too closely, blinded by ambition for a blockbuster scoop.

When he spoke with him again after sending copies of the letter and notes, Haeggman had eagerly fastened on the link between the cannibal, Grendel, and Westberg's disappearance, followed by the arrival of a body part, presumably Westberg's. The story had all the lurid qualities that would make it an absolute media sensation. Yet someone at the paper had squelched it. Grendel was surprised. He shrugged off his annoyance and disappointment; the problem would be fixed later.

For the next scene in the drama he'd constructed, Grendel needed to do one more thing. He picked up the same untraceable temporary mobile he had used to phone Haeggman, and made another call.

The two newspapers Ekman picked up from his front stoop on a cold, gray morning were wet from the blustery downpour despite their plastic wrappings. The heavy rain promised to continue for the rest of a dismal fall day.

Haeggman's story was on his paper's front page, where Ekman was afraid it would be. But as he read it over toast and coffee, he was surprised to see that while he was named in the briefcase theft, there was nothing about the Westberg case. How did we dodge that bullet, he wondered?

He knew other media would be calling about the story looking for more details, and Ekman considered holding another press conference, but decided against it. He was afraid someone besides Haeggman would put two and two together and ask point-blank if Grendel was connected to Westberg's disappearance. The communications officer would have to field inquiries, acknowledge there was an ongoing investigation of the Grendel matter, and say that, therefore, the police had no comment at this time.

At seven thirty that morning, Garth Rystrom was briefing the two technicians and two detectives from CID who would be putting devices in Lindfors's apartment and listening.

"You're authorized to enter the building and Stina Lindfors's apartment, using 'whatever technical means are necessary,'" Rystrom said, reading from the warrant.

"That won't be a problem, Super," replied the senior tech, a short, bald man in his fifties, with thick-lensed glasses.

"Where will you put the mics?"

"We'll use three: one in the living room, one in the kitchen/dining area, and one in the bedroom. If there are two bedrooms, one in each. These mics will be invisible the way we'll plant them, and they're state of the art, sensitive enough to pick up anything in a room, even a whisper. We'll be in and out in ten minutes."

"And where will you be listening?" Rystrom asked the detectives.

"We've brought a van with recording equipment that'll be parked on a side street two blocks from the apartment," responded Hans Bergner, the lead detective, small, thin, with wispy brown hair, looking a decade older than his thirty-four years.

"You'll need to coordinate with the team watching Lindfors and a guy named Carl Stillen, who's been visiting her, to make sure they're both out of the apartment. I'll give you the team's mobiles," he said; consulting a list and writing down Vinter's and Holm's numbers, Rystrom handed the paper to Bergner. "They'll be in touch with you."

"Sounds like we're good to go," said Bergner, standing up.

After they'd left, Rystrom phoned Gerdi Vinter, telling her she and Holm would need to contact Bergner and giving her his number.

"Enar is taking the meeting this morning, so I'll call Bergner when they've both gone," she said.

48

The Leak

Rystrom was reviewing the Lindfors and Stillen bios that had been e-mailed to him from CID headquarters that morning when the phone rang.

"Rapp is the leak," said the man's voice on the phone, and repeated it again before Rystrom could interrupt.

"Who is this?" demanded Rystrom, but he was talking into a dial tone. The man had hung up.

Rystrom got out the newspaper with Haeggman's story under the screaming headline. Looking through it, he found the reference he remembered to 'a reliable police source.' Could it be Rapp? If it was, then who called? Certainly not Rapp or Haeggman.

Perhaps there was someone on the investigating team who knew, or suspected, that Rapp was the leak, and wanted to alert them. But why didn't he call Ekman? The caller might think he'd be reluctant to act, because he'd worked with Rapp for many years, and so instead, called Rystrom, the outsider. Possibly, the man didn't identify himself to avoid becoming involved in an investigation and the focus of the intense police dislike for internal whistle-blowers.

∾ ∾ ∾

Ekman looked up as Rystrom knocked and entered. Rystrom told him about setting up the listening surveillance, and then, the phone call.

"There have been some leaks from someone inside the investigation, but they've been circulating only in the department," said Ekman. "I never would have guessed that it was Rapp, and that he'd go outside to the media. And especially not to Haeggman; he doesn't like him any more than I do. But let's get him in now and ask him point-blank." He picked up the phone.

When Rapp came in he saw Rystrom and Ekman regarding him with tight faces. Ekman didn't ask him to sit down.

"Alrik, we've been told you're the source for this morning's headline," Ekman said in a harsh tone, holding the front page of the paper up to Rapp.

Rapp was speechless, and then his face reddened. He said in a rush, "How could you think I'd do something like that, Chief? After all the years we've worked together? Who told you I had?"

Ekman looked at him for a long moment. "Sit down, Alrik. Let's go over this carefully," he said in a quiet voice. Rapp sank into a chair, and Rystrom told him about the call.

"Maybe it's somebody in the department who has it in for me. But I can't think of anyone who'd do something this low."

"Neither can I," said Ekman. "When I met with Haeggman yesterday, he said Grendel had sent him the letters. But think about it. If that were so, the paper wouldn't have printed the story; there would be no way to confirm the letters weren't from a crank. However, if a police inspector provided the information that would be very different. Haeggman was trying to mislead us to protect what he still thinks is a solid, inside informant. He couldn't get the paper to print the story without it containing a reference to a 'reliable police source' to give it credibility."

"So it really was Grendel?" asked Rapp.

"It has to be. And he's the one who called me," said Rystrom.

"Now the question is why did he do it? Not the act of sending the letters to Haeggman; I've thought all along he'd eventually go public. He wanted the attention and we didn't make his involvement known, so he went to the paper. But why did he phone Garth?" Ekman asked, puzzled.

"He's just stirring the pot, that's what he's doing," said Rapp, his face getting even redder. "And he's made me the fall guy. That bastard."

"Yes, you're exactly right, Alrik," said Ekman. "He wants us to suspect one another and have confrontations like this. He enjoys the idea of us squabbling among ourselves. It weakens us, and strengthens him. He likes to see himself as the ultimate trickster and in control of the situation, and us. Karlsson warned he would do something like this, and be very good at it.

"But now we know something we didn't. Haeggman thinks he's been getting information from inside the investigation. We may be able to use this at some time to tilt the playing field in our favor by feeding him false information, using your name, Alrik," Ekman said with a smile. But then he became serious.

"I owe you an apology for even considering you could be the leak. I know you better than that, my friend."

"That apology goes for me too," said Rystrom.

"I understand. You didn't really have a choice. You had to ask me."

Ekman stood up. "Now that's settled; I think we're keeping the others waiting."

49

Stillen

Bergfalk, Holm, and Rosengren were discussing the lurid newspaper story when the other three entered.

"So now Grendel is public knowledge," Ekman said. "No matter what today's story said, it didn't originate from a police informant. It's a plant by Grendel himself."

"Other papers and TV will pick up the story and speculation will be running wild. I expect everyone here could get a direct inquiry as the media tries to find the 'police source.' The uniform answer will be to tell them to talk to Lena Sahlin, the communications officer. I hope that's clearly understood." Everyone nodded agreement.

"Enar, what's happening with the surveillance?" Ekman asked.

"I checked with Gerdi just before the meeting and Lindfors has left for work, but Stillen, who came back last night, hadn't come out yet. When he does, Gerdi will follow him."

"You and Gerdi have done good work identifying Stillen, but you look worn out, and I'm sure Gerdi is too. We're getting you some backup." Turning to Rystrom, he asked, "Your people should be here later this morning?"

"Yes, four of them should be getting in shortly. I'll brief them and get them into position so Enar and Gerdi can take a break."

Rystrom told them about the other crew waiting to plant the listening devices in Lindfors's apartment as soon as Gerdi gave them the all clear.

"We may know, perhaps as early as tomorrow," he said, "what Lindfors's and Stillen's relationship is, and whether they're involved in the Westberg murder, or the others. Here's Stillen's bio, with some additional info on Lindfors." He handed copies around.

Ekman was surprised. Again he felt he was losing control to Rystrom, but reproached himself immediately. Garth was accustomed to leading investigations and taking initiatives. He was simply doing what Ekman had asked him to do: helping move the case forward.

Carl Stillen's profile was headed by the most recent front and side police identification photos taken when he was twenty-four. He was a very good looking, muscular man with brown hair and eyes, of medium height and weight, born in Lund thirty-six years ago to parents who were divorced when he was six. His father had abandoned his wife and son, and after the divorce, his mother put Carl up for adoption. He was a difficult child, given to uncontrollable temper tantrums, was never adopted, and was raised by a succession of foster parents. He'd left school, and his last set of foster parents, at sixteen, and taken a series of odd jobs as a carpenter's helper, roofer, and later, as a delivery van driver.

At twenty-one, he'd met and married Stina Ernstsson. During their marriage, she'd worked as a waitress. Over the next five years, Stillen had several misdemeanor arrests for drunk and disorderly, for which he received warnings. One night in a bar brawl, he rammed a broken beer bottle into a man's face, taking out an eye. This led to the felony conviction Vinter had reported. Stina was working in that same bar the night of the fight, and witnesses said the victim had made a rough pass at her that precipitated Stillen's assault.

After he'd served a year of a four-year sentence, Stina had divorced him. She was twenty-five when she moved to Malmö where she continued working as a waitress, this time in an upscale restaurant. It may have been at the restaurant that she met the well-to-do Eberhardt Lindfors. They'd married a year later, and three years after that Lindfors was dead. The death had been ruled accidental.

When he got out of prison, Stillen had also moved to Malmö. He'd gotten a job as a clerk in a naval supplies store. Whether he'd been in touch with Lindfors was unknown but likely in view of his moving to wherever Stina was, and their current contact. After Stina's husband died, she'd moved back to Lund to enroll in the accounting program at Lund University. Shortly afterward, Stillen had quit his job and also moved there becoming assistant manager of a hardware store.

Three years later, Lindfors graduated with a bachelor's degree in accounting. She next moved to Weltenborg and had worked for the last two years at an accounting firm, where she needed another three years before she could become an authorized accountant. Stillen had followed her again, as they'd already learned from surveillance.

"It looks like Lindfors and Stillen have never really broken up, even after their divorce," Holm said.

"And except for his prison time, they may always have been together as lovers, even when she was married to Lindfors and engaged to Westberg," interjected Rosengren with a knowing smirk.

"So what we're looking at now is an unusual couple," said Rystrom, summarizing. "One is an ex-con with a history of extreme violence—the other, a smart woman who has used her looks and brains to get a rich husband. He soon conveniently died, leaving her a small fortune. A few years later, she became engaged to an even wealthier man, who inexplicably vanishes and is probably dead, leaving her with a much larger fortune."

"It's certainly suggestive," said an expressionless Ekman. Holm looked at him with a half-concealed grin.

"Where are you with those computers?" Ekman asked Rapp and Bergfalk.

"We should have them all by the end of the day, Chief," said Rapp.

"Yeah, two of the owners we've visited so far kicked up a real fuss, even though we promised we wouldn't harm their files and they'd get them back in a few days. I think they may have some stuff on their systems they'd rather not have us looking at," added Bergfalk.

"My computer techs will be down here this afternoon and start right in on them," said Rystrom.

"Good," Ekman said. "Then we should find out if the chess connection among the missing men leads anywhere or is another dead end."

"How are those phone calls going?" he asked Rosengren.

"Alenius and I are working through them, Chief," replied Rosengren. "It's amazing how many nuts are out there. The Westberg calls had been tapering off, but with all this Grendel publicity this morning following right behind the Westberg story, people are connecting the two. Some are panicking."

"Do any calls look promising?"

"Two of them may give us something. Alenius spoke to an old woman who lives up the street from that hill overlooking the Westberg place. She didn't know if it had anything to do with Rodger Westberg's disappearance a few days later, but decided to call anyway. She'd read about the Westberg break-in, and said that day she saw a silver car she believes was a Volvo, parked near the bottom for hours. She didn't think much about it, until we asked the public for information about Westberg.

"A guy had gotten out, gone up the hill, and didn't come down for a long time. She couldn't see him clearly, but said he was slender and thinks he was young. But she's almost ninety, so everyone looks young to her. She saw you too, Chief. She said a big man in black, driving a black Volvo did the same thing a few days later. That's why we think she's believable."

"And the other call?"

"It may back up her story. Early Wednesday morning, a man who may have been Westberg was seen walking toward downtown where Westberg's office is located. He would have taken that route from his apartment. The guy who called said a car stopped, the man leaned over to talk to the driver, and then got in. The caller was almost a block behind the car so he couldn't see the man's face or the driver. But from the body build he described, it could have been Westberg. And get this . . . the car was a newer model silver Volvo."

"This could be the lead we've been looking for," Ekman said, his voice steady, not betraying the excitement he felt. "You and Alenius have done good work. I'd like you to run all the cars currently, or previously, owned by Lindfors, Stillen, Westberg's parents, and the people who work in Rodger Westberg's office. Let's see if we get a hit."

"Right away, Chief," said Rosengren.

∞ ∞ ∞

Gerdi Vinter was fighting off her urge to fall asleep, when she saw Carl Stillen leave Lindfors's apartment building at eight forty-five A.M., turn right and head down Homsgatan. She started the car and slowly drifted after him. Two corners down, he turned right again on Eklangsgatan and kept going for six blocks before heading into a Clas Ohlson store. Vinter drove past, looking for a parking space, and found one halfway down the street.

Taking out her mobile, she called Hans Bergner. "Stillen's out, and I'll let you know if it looks like he's coming back."

"Thanks, Gerdi. We're going in now. We should be done in fifteen minutes max."

She walked back to Ohlson's and entering, looked around to see if she could spot Stillen. It was a big store and crowded even early in the morning. Not seeing him in front, she walked toward the rear. There he is, she thought, behind the hardware counter. He works here. He'll probably be here for hours, and I'm starving. I'll wander around the store, keeping an eye on him for half an hour to make sure Bergner and the techs have time to finish, and then I'll get something to eat before coming back.

50

A Deception

After two rings Ekman picked up his phone.

"Walther, it's Ludvig. I've got the DNA on that 'item' you sent. We broke every speed limit on this. Our lab worked literally day and night to finish the analysis in record time."

"Ludvig, you've got my sincere thanks, and I'm ready to pin a medal on you, but what are the results?"

"It's not Westberg."

Ekman was surprised. He could have sworn it would be. "I hesitate to even ask, but are you absolutely certain?"

"Nothing is 100 percent, but this is as close to it as anyone is likely to get. Based on the cheek swab from his father, I'm ready to testify under oath that the genitals are excluded from being Rodger Westberg's. Is that good enough for you?" Malmquist asked, sounding annoyed his work was even questioned.

"More than good enough, Ludvig. Sorry I asked, but I felt certain it was Westberg. Now, the question becomes, who is it?"

"Well, get me something else for comparison, and I'll try to give you a more satisfactory answer," he said, still annoyed.

"Okay, it's back to the drawing board for us. And Ludvig, thanks again for the quick results."

"Even if they're not what you wanted to hear?"

"Even so," said Ekman, hanging up.

That damn Grendel, he thought. Tricked us again, sending his 'gift' with that note telling us it was Westberg. He loves to get us running around on wild goose chases. This was a lesson I won't forget, he promised himself.

Now who do the genitals belong to? If he's right about the connection among the missing men, it should be Gustaffson or Henriksson. We'll have to get DNA samples from their relatives. I'll ask Enar to do it, if he feels up to it, now that we'll have a larger surveillance team watching Lindfors and Stillen.

Before he could call Holm, the phone rang again. Norlander wanted to see him.

The commissioner was pacing back and forth in his office. He was no longer his usual smooth, unruffled self. Ekman observed that, interestingly, Malmer was nowhere to be seen.

"Walther, come in. Please sit down. That story has caused even more of a furor than we expected. I've been on the phone since it came out. I've had to assure the National Police Commisssioner that we're on top of it. Thankfully, I could tell him CID is already involved. It was a good idea to bring in Rystrom. Bring me up to date on what's happening."

Ekman told him about the listening device techs, surveillance team, and computer specialists Rystrom had brought in to help them. Norlander seemed somewhat relieved.

"So, we're doing everything we can."

"Yes, I believe we are," he said, describing what they now knew about Stillen and Lindfors, and their possible motives.

"That all sounds very positive, Walther. Good work. Now I'm going to have to call Westberg back. He's going ballistic. He said when his wife saw the story, she immediately thought their son was a victim of this crazy cannibal, Grendel. He's afraid she may be right."

"It's possible, but there's one new piece of information that could be reassuring. I just got off the phone with Malmquist at the forensics lab: the genitals are not Westberg's, despite what it said in Grendel's note. He was trying to mislead us."

"That's helpful for us to know, but I don't think I'm going to mention that to ease Westberg's mind," Norlander said with a wry grin.

Ekman hadn't told Norlander about Grendel's call to Rystrom accusing Rapp of being the source of the newspaper story. He didn't want any hint of suspicion, however mistaken, falling on Rapp; Ekman was convinced he was innocent.

"I think all you can really tell Westberg is that we, and CID, have large teams working on every possible lead," he said.

"You're right, but it won't satisfy him."

Ekman shrugged. He was less concerned about Westberg's feelings now that he knew about his affair with Lindfors. Apart from Rystrom, he'd kept that information to himself so far. But it was bound to come out sooner or later, he thought, if the case against Lindfors became stronger.

"Walther, please keep me informed directly about your progress. Also, I've asked Olov to take on some more administrative responsibilities, so you needn't keep him involved," Norlander added in a casual manner.

Ekman nodded, and shook hands with Norlander. Well, well, he thought, Norlander's finally woken up to the fact that Malmer is more of a hindrance to his career than a help.

51

~~~

Volvos

Ekman was working on a report for Norlander and Edvardsson when there was a knock and an excited Rosengren came in.

"We found two silver Volvos in that group of people you wanted me to check on, Chief. One belongs to a paralegal in Westberg's office. I remember questioning her. She's sixty-three and uses a cane. I called her to ask whether she might have forgotten she picked up Westberg that morning, and she swears she didn't. I believe her." He paused.

"And the second car?" asked Ekman.

"This is the really interesting one. It belongs to Lindfors. But that's not all. It was signed over to her five months ago, and you'll never guess by who."

"It's 'whom,'" Ekman replied. "And the car belonged to Eugen Westberg."

Rosengren was crestfallen. "How did you guess, Chief?"

"The stars told me," said a straight-faced Ekman. He now believed Westberg had lied to him about the affair with Lindfors being over a long time ago. His admission had come too quickly, Ekman thought. I'm going to have another chat with Councillor Westberg.

"That was quick work, Rosengren. Thanks."

"Do you think Lindfors picked him up? It would fit," said Rosengren. It would tie up the case neatly. "She kills Westberg, or her boyfriend, Stillen, does the dirty work, and they walk away with millions."

"Yes, it works. But let's find out what surveillance and the mics give us before we bring her and Stillen in for questioning. It may give us more leverage. Then we'll take a look at that car."

"We're getting real close, Chief," said a pleased Rosengren.

"Perhaps," said Ekman. "We'll see."

52

Overheard

Rystrom had been receiving reports from his surveillance teams whenever Stillen or Lindfors were on the move. When either of them headed back to her apartment, the listening van would be in place. It was twelve thirty. Stillen had gone to get lunch at a small takeaway around the corner from his store. Meanwhile, Lindfors was having lunch with two women from her office at a Thai restaurant down the block from her building.

At six Lindfors left work. The surveillance team tracked her walking directly to her apartment. The listening crew in the van was ready and poised. The mics had been checked out immediately after they'd been planted. The recording equipment was now up and running.

Both Lindfors's and Stillen's surveillance teams had been given pictures of the apartment buildings' residents, and told to photograph only strangers. At seven, an unknown man was snapped going into the building. Right after this, the van picked up a knock on Lindfors's door.

Two hours later, Rystrom and Ekman were sitting in Rystrom's office listening to the conversation.

"Who is it?"

"It's Eugen."

Sound of the front door opening. Footsteps. The door closed.

"What do you want?"

"We need to talk."

"We were talked out four months ago. There's nothing more to say."

"It's not about us. It's about Rodger's money."

"What about it?"

"Don't tell me you didn't know he left everything to you?"

"He told me he was going to, but I didn't know he'd actually done it."

"Well, he did. If he's alive, I'll get him to change his will. But with this news story about a maniac on the loose, so soon after he disappeared, I'm beginning to think he may not be."

"I read it. It's awful. You don't really believe he's been kidnapped by some crazy cannibal?"

"The longer he's not found, it's becoming a real possibility. The police told me they thought he was dead. They're probably right."

Sound of Lindfors crying.

"This isn't the time to talk about money. It's wrong."

"It's exactly the time. Before his body's found and the will takes effect. That money is Westberg family money, not yours."

"Rodger wanted me to have it."

"Yes, as a marriage present, for your future security. But that won't happen now. I want you to agree not to take the money."

"Why on earth should I?"

"You've got no right to any of it. Look, because Rodger wanted you to have something, I'll let you have 5 percent, not including the trust fund. All the rest stays in our family. In return, I'll agree not to tie up everything in a lawsuit. Otherwise it would be years before you'd see a krona."

Long pause.

"This isn't the time to even bring this up, Eugen. But if you insist, I'll tell you what I'll do. I'm willing to let you have all the trust fund because that money has always been in your family. Five percent of the remaining money is ridiculous. I won't be victimized by you. However, I don't want to go to court, even though I think I'd win. So, I'll agree to take 75 percent."

"That's really my money you're talking about. I gave Rodger most of it. I won't give you 75 percent. For nothing. That's absurd."

"It's not for nothing, Eugen. A scandal about your years-long affair with your son's fiancée wouldn't do your marriage, your business, your political career, or your precious reputation any good, would it? But I'm a fair-minded person. Let's agree that I'll keep two-thirds of Rodger's money."

"You're blackmailing me?"

"Not at all. You know I'm legally entitled to 100 percent of everything, including the trust fund. You're getting a terrific deal. You haven't got a legal leg to stand on. Let's say I'm willing to do this in memory of our time together, and what Rodger might have wanted."

Long pause.

"All right. I'll have the papers drawn up. With a confidentiality clause. You drive a hard bargain."

Pause.

"I loved you very much."

"Not enough to leave your wife. Not enough to stop me from becoming your son's lover. Those were your mistakes. It's only right you should pay a penalty."

Sound of the front door opening and slamming shut.

Rystrom looked over at Ekman. "What do you think?"

"I'm not sure yet. Let's hear the other recording after Stillen came back to the apartment."

Rystrom turned the machine back on.

Sound of the front door opening and closing.

"Hi. It's me."

"Carl. I'm so glad you're back."

"Me too."

Sound of kissing.

"Eugen left a little while ago."

"What the hell did he want?"

"Money, believe it or not."

"What? The money Rodger left you in his will?"

"Yes. All of it. Then he offered me 5 percent, but nothing from the trust fund. We finally agreed I'd get two-thirds, except for the trust—and no lawsuit."

"You let him off easy. He's got balls, I'll give him that. He's also one cold son of a bitch."

"I'm becoming more convinced of that every time I talk to him. I don't know what I ever saw in him."

"Sure you do, baby. The same thing he came here for: money."

"That's not fair, Carl. I really fell for him."

"The money just made the old guy look younger, right? Just like Lindfors."

She laughed.

"Anyway, everything is working out as planned. Actually, it's a good thing you've already got a deal with Westberg. Now we don't have to worry about him trying to stop us from getting the money. It'll be ours, and no argument, as soon as Rodger's body is found."

"And when will that be?"

"Soon enough. (Pause.) Bodies have a way of turning up."

"Your plan's working out honey."

"Hasn't it always?"

"So far." Pause. "Why don't we see what you can plan for me?"

Footsteps. The bedroom mic picked up the sounds of their lovemaking.

Rystrom shut off the machine. Ekman was quiet for several moments.

"She lied to Westberg," said Rystrom. "She told him she wasn't sure Rodger had changed his will. But she seemed certain of it talking with Stillen."

"Yes, that's the key," Ekman said. "If they murdered Westberg, they'd have to be very sure they could get the money, otherwise there'd be no point in risking it."

"She's extremely calculating about using her sex appeal to have simultaneous affairs with Stillen and both Westbergs. Just as she apparently had with Stillen when she was married to Lindfors."

"She's not the world's most moral woman. But that's not a crime," Ekman said.

"She and Stillen did have a plan, however, to get their hands on the Westberg money. Stillen as much as admitted it. He also seemed to hint about an earlier scheme to get Lindfors's money."

"You're right, Garth. They schemed; however, it's still not clear they murdered anyone."

"How about Stillen's response to her question about Rodger's body? He seemed pretty sure it would be found."

"I thought her question about that was interesting. From her tone, it was a real question, not a rhetorical one. If Stillen is the killer, she may not know it."

"She's been with this man her entire adult life, except when he was in prison for almost killing that guy. She's not stupid. Lindfors has got to know whether he's a killer, even if she won't admit it to herself."

"Knowing someone else is capable of murder, and being an accomplice to an actual murder, are very different things."

"You're right, Walther. But remember that although Eberhardt Lindfors's death was ruled accidental, it may not have been. If it was murder, she's more likely to have done it than Stillen because she had easy access, and he didn't."

"So what we may have here are two murderers who don't openly acknowledge each other's crimes?"

"It's possible."

"Let's agree that it is. And let's say your general theory of the crime is close, but a little off. Suppose Stillen is Grendel. But even if Lindfors killed her second husband for his money, she doesn't know how insane Stillen is. There's no carefully thought-out, ruthless, long-term plan by both of them to get their hands on the Westberg money—and distract our investigation with extraneous killings and threats against me.

"Stillen is crazy, did those other killings on his own for whatever mad reason, just as he tried to get my attention with the Grendel character he later invented to focus our investigation elsewhere. When Lindfors met Eugen Westberg, events just gradually led to a plan by Stillen and Lindfors to somehow get hold of the Westberg money.

"Lindfors may not know that for Stillen, the plan always involved killing either the father or the son, depending on who would leave money to Lindfors. That actually makes more sense to me. What do you think?" He thought this approach fit in better with life's coincidences and general messiness.

"It sounds right to me too, Walther. What's our next move?"

"You haven't met him yet, Garth, but tomorrow I think we should talk to Jarl Karlsson, our profiler, and run all this by him. I want to get his take on Stillen and Lindfors."

"Sure, I'd like to meet him," Rystrom said as he looked at his watch. It was just past nine P.M. "Why don't we call it a day?"

"You're right, I hadn't realized how late it was getting. After we talk with Karlsson, we'll decide when to bring in Lindfors and Stillen for questioning."

Before leaving, Ekman phoned Karlsson.

"Jarl, I hope I'm not calling too late. I need to see you tomorrow, in the morning, if at all possible. Yes, eleven is fine. I'm bringing someone with me: Garth Rystrom from National CID. He's working the case with me. See you then."

Then he remembered to call Ingbritt.

"I'm just leaving the office and wanted to get you before it was too late. Yes, I'm fine. How is everyone? Good. Several new developments today and things are looking clearer. No, not yet. Yes, I hope we'll resolve this one soon and you can come home. I miss you, too. Good night, dear."

Ekman had only grabbed a sandwich from the cafeteria for lunch. That was eight hours ago and he was starving. He looked up the number of the pizza place near his home and ordered a large with everything on it, to go, before heading out the door.

53

~~~~~

Chess

Friday, October 21. It was a clear, increasingly cold fall day under a bright, Prussian-blue sky. At seven fifteen, Ekman was sitting by himself, one of the few people in the police cafeteria, eating a second breakfast of waffles and sausage. The toast and coffee he'd had at home had barely lasted the drive in and he'd felt the urgent need for a hot meal.

Looking up from his plate, he saw Holm and Vinter standing uncertainly just outside the doorway. They finally made their way to the counter to place their orders. After getting their food, they glanced around the room and spotted Ekman sitting in the back at a corner table.

"Can we join you?" asked Holm.

"Please do," he said, smiling up at him and Gerdi. Who do they think they're kidding, he wondered? He'd known they were a couple ever since they'd first started going together.

"That looks good," said Gerdi, glancing at Ekman's rapidly shrinking stack of waffles. Her own tray held just orange juice, coffee, and toast.

"It's too good. I don't usually do this," he said with a guilty look at his plate. "Ingbritt is out of town and I'm not much of a cook.

"Have you both rested up?" he asked, and then realized this could be taken as innuendo.

"From the surveillance," he added, making matters worse.

Holm started to laugh. "We know what you mean, Chief." He looked over at Gerdi. "I guess there's no use trying to hide anything from you," he said to his boss.

Ekman looked from one to the other. "Actually, I've known for quite a while. And you needn't worry, you have my paternal blessing. Also, I know how to keep a secret," he said with a straight face.

They both grinned back at him. The air had cleared and they relaxed.

Ekman turned to Holm and asked, "Did you get the DNA swabs?"

"I got one early yesterday from Gustaffson's father in Växjö. It didn't take any persuasion. He's anxious to do anything he can to help solve his son's disappearance. I drove it over myself to Malmquist to compare it with the 'sample' Grendel sent."

"Have you been able to get hold of Henriksson's parents?"

"I haven't been able to locate his father yet. His parents divorced years ago, but his mother lives up in Norrköping and is expecting me today. It's a bit of a drive. I thought I'd go up right after the meeting."

"Good," Ekman said, and looked at Gerdi. "Why don't you go along with Enar? It will make the trip less boring," he added with a smile. "Don't worry about the surveillance. We've got Rystrom's people covering that."

Looking at each other, they couldn't help smiling. Ekman was being kind.

"Thanks, Chief," they both said.

At the morning meeting, the others were transfixed as Rystrom played yesterday's conversations in Lindfors's apartment. There was dead silence for a moment after he turned off the machine.

Rosengren couldn't help commenting, "I knew it, when I first saw her. She's hot."

"You can say that again," said Bergfalk. "Screwing three guys at the same time."

Ekman glared at them. "Let's keep this professional. We're investigating a series of murders. This is not the place for those kinds of comments. Keep them to yourselves."

Bergfalk and Rosengren looked down at the table without saying anything. Ekman sounded offended. He wasn't a prude, but demanded respect for the victims and the seriousness of the investigation.

Ekman laid out for them the current theory of the case he and Rystrom had agreed on. "This may change as we get new evidence, but so far, it seems to fit what we know."

Rapp said, "You may want to adjust that theory again, Chief. The computer techs have come up with something."

All eyes focused on him.

"We asked them to search the hard drives on the computers of the three missing men, looking for any-thing connected with online chess. There were six computers, but they worked fast and got hits on two of them. These were Gustaffson's and Henriksson's personal computers, rather than ones from their offices. They both played chess on the same site, a special one, with pass-word protected access, set up for higher-level players. You were right, Chief. This was the connection. And it gets better."

He paused for effect.

"Players posted some personal information, including photos of themselves. The two men played with several opponents, but only one was the same for both. It was Stina Lindfors. She'd posted a photo. They not only played chess with her; they sent her personal messages. They flirted by e-mail, and she flirted back. They both asked to meet her, and she said she'd call if she was interested. They gave her their mobile numbers. What do you think of that, Chief?"

Ekman was quiet, thinking over this unexpected information. The link among the other two missing men and Lindfors, and through her, Stillen, was now firmly established. And Lindfors had met Rodger Westberg, the third chess player, through his father, putting Lindfors at the center of all three disappearances.

"What this seems to indicate," he finally said, "is that Stillen may not have acted alone in killing the men as we thought. Lindfors may have not only known he's a killer, she may have been a willing partner. There have been a number of two-person teams of murderers in the past. It looks like we could be dealing with that here. And there's the motive in Westberg's case of money."

"I agree," said Rystrom. "But this is the first time we've had a serial killer duo in Sweden."

"What we need to do now," Ekman said, "is gather more evidence against them. First, we have to find the computer Lindfors used to play chess with the two victims. I'll ask Edvardsson for warrants for Lindfors's home and office computers, her car, and also her phones and Stillen's, in case they were used to contact the men. Now seems like the right time to bring in Lindfors and Stillen for questioning and see if either will crack. While we're doing that, Alrik and Mats will execute the warrants."

Turning to Rystrom, he said, "We'll need your techs to reconfirm the computer evidence tying her to the two men. Then they'll need to check all the calls to the two men's mobiles against Lindfors's and Stillen's phones."

"You're right. Those are the next steps," Rystrom said.

"Also, we need to maintain surveillance of Lindfors and Stillen, physically, and through the listening devices," Ekman said. Rystrom nodded agreement.

Alenius had been silent throughout the meeting. Ekman asked him if he had anything to add from taking calls from the public.

"Nothing new, Chief. I think it's tapped out. That's why I came to the meeting. I turned on the answering machine, just in case."

"Okay. I want you and Rosengren to join the surveillance team. That makes six, so there'll be enough people to share the watching without anyone becoming exhausted.

"Enar and Gerdi are heading to Norrköping today to get a DNA sample from Henriksson's mother. Is there anything else?" No one spoke.

"We're closing in. This is no time for us to let up. So plan on working through the weekend. On the bright side, everyone is still authorized overtime pay," Ekman said, getting to his feet.

Ekman phoned Edvardsson.

"Malin, it's Walther. Planting the listening devices paid off," he said, telling her the gist of what had been heard. "So, yes, she was well aware that Rodger had left his money to her. She and Stillen, her first husband, have apparently been planning to get their hands on the Westberg money, one way or another, all along.

"We can't be certain yet that Stillen is Grendel, but it looks more like it with every new piece of evidence. And computers from the two missing men prove Lindfors was connected to them, as well. What we need now are warrants for Lindfors's home and office computers, her car, and both her phone and Stillen's, to confirm the link. Yes, I'm sending over a transcript of the intercepts along with the warrant applications. You'll have them in the next hour."

54

Duo Killers

Ekman had just finished giving the papers for Edvardsson to a police courier, when Rystrom came in.

"When did you want to leave for that meeting with Karlsson?" Rystrom asked.

Looking at the clock, Ekman saw they'd just be able to get there on time.

In Karlsson's study, the three of them sipped coffee and sampled the cake his wife had prepared yesterday when she learned Ekman would be visiting. She and Karlsson had greeted them at the door, and then she'd left them alone.

Jarl said, "Our friend Grendel has become quite a sensation."

"Just as you and I thought he would, sooner or later," said Ekman, and he sketched out what they'd discovered since he last spoke with Karlsson.

"So you suspect Lindfors and Stillen may be serial killers working together?" Karlsson asked.

"It's becoming more likely."

Stillen could be a good candidate for Grendel, Karlsson suggested. With his poor childhood, all the foster homes, and his uncontrollable temper, it all fit.

Karlsson conjectured that Lindfors could have been a victim of sexual abuse, which could have led to her promiscuity. He ticked off the sudden death of her second husband, her link to the two other missing men, and her long relationship with Stillen, along with her plan to hang on to Westberg's money.

"Taken together," he said, "she could be participating in these murders."

"But there's nothing conclusive?" Rystrom asked.

"That's right. And I'm going out on a limb without further evidence. I don't think we should push these conjectures too far."

"Yet nothing we've told you would exclude her from being an active participant?" asked Ekman.

"Again, you're right. I'd say on balance, with what you know now, it's more likely than not."

"We know the motive for Westberg's murder, but what about the other two?" asked Rystrom.

"That's difficult to say, but something about these men led to their being killed."

"Should we warn all the chess clubs then?" Rystrom laughed.

"I don't think chess players are at risk," Karlsson replied with a slight smile. "The online chess club seems to have been just a convenient way to select victims and draw them in. There's got to be something else."

"The other links we have are similar age, appearance, and marital status," said Ekman. "Gustaffson and Henriksson were in their thirties, single, average height and weight, not bad looking, with brown hair and eyes."

"What about Rodger Westberg? Did he look like them?"

"Yes, he did."

"Then that's it," said Karlsson.

"But there are hundreds of thousands of men in Sweden who fit that description," objected Rystrom.

"The others were lucky. These men weren't," Karlsson replied in a somber voice.

"But why were men who fit this description selected in the first place?" Ekman asked.

"I think it has nothing to do with these men, of course. It's something from the past, probably something in Stillen's or Lindfors's backgrounds. Perhaps Stillen, Lindfors, or both of them, were abused as children by someone who looked similar, and all that pent-up rage and hatred has been transferred to these other men. The real motive for these two, apparently pointless, killings could be in their distorted minds," Karlsson said, looking at the ceiling and then back at his guests.

"Remember when we first talked about this, Walther, I said there would be a reason for Grendel's behavior. There would be a rationale behind the madness that would explain, and would, at least for him, justify his actions?"

"Yes, I haven't forgotten. So, simply stated, what we have here is a twisted, misplaced revenge motive, plus in Westberg's case, his money. Do you agree, Garth?"

"It's the only explanation that begins to make any sense of these killings."

"Nothing I've told you would exclude them from being duo serial killers?" Ekman asked.

"No, not at all. What you've told me is very sugges-tive of other serial duos—particularly, Lindfors's sexual relationship with Stillen and at least one of the victims, Westberg."

"Right now, we can connect her to the other missing men," said Rystrom.

"What about the focus on me personally that we spoke about, Jarl?" Ekman asked.

"It could be a way first of getting your attention, since Grendel needed that for his game, and then later, a means of distracting your investigation—a dueler's feints. And for some reason we don't yet understand, it could also be that Grendel has grouped you with the other victims. Although your coloring is the same, your size doesn't quite fit the victim profile we've developed," Karlsson said with a glint of amusement in his eyes.

"Well, I'll try and take some comfort from that," said Ekman, getting up.

"Thanks for your help, Jarl. As always, you've made things clearer."

In the car, Ekman said to Rystrom, "What do you think about Karlsson's analysis?"

"It seems on target to me. But it wasn't unequivocal. He painted a vivid picture of Stillen, but he wouldn't commit himself on Lindfors."

"He's cautious. That seems appropriate. After we question them, we should be able to be more definite."

"If they're the psychopaths we suspect, that may not be easy. They're very convincing."

"We'll soon find out. I doubt they'll be able to trick both of us," Ekman said with a wink.

55

Interrogation — Lindfors

Back at headquarters, the warrants had arrived. Ekman called in Rosengren and Alenius.

"First, bring in Stillen for questioning. Don't tell him why. When you have him, take his phone. After he's in an interview room, let him just sit there. Then pick up Lindfors at her office. Tell her we need her help with the Westberg case. She's not to use her phone. Take it from her and get her fingerprints and Stillen's from their phones. Put her in a different room. They mustn't know the other one is here. Okay?"

"Got it, Chief," said Rosengren. Alenius just nodded.

"Stillen was convicted of extreme violence. He could be armed. Have two surveillance team people with you, just to be safe. Lindfors shouldn't be a problem. And you can tell the others watching her they can take a break while she's here."

"Right," said Rosengren, pleased they were finally seeing some real action.

Stillen was working behind the counter at the rear of the hardware store with a wall of shelves behind him when the four detectives approached. Two faced him and the others stood at each end of the counter in case he should try to run.

"Carl Stillen?" asked Rosengren.

He showed no surprise, just looked at them without expression.

"Yes, what do you want?"

Rosengren flashed his identification. "Police. Please come with us to headquarters, Herr Stillen."

"What's this about?"

"You'll find out at headquarters. Just come with us quietly."

"I need to let my boss know I'm leaving."

"We'll inform him," said Rosengren, turning to one of the detectives at the end of the counter.

Stillen shrugged, and reached for his leather jacket, hanging on a hook behind him.

"Don't touch the jacket," barked Rosengren. One of the other officers went around the end of the counter, took the jacket and patted it down. He nodded to Rosengren.

"Please come out from behind the counter, Herr Stillen," said Rosengren.

When he did, Alenius patted him down for weapons and took his mobile phone. Then Rosengren handed him his jacket. Several customers had turned to watch.

"What are you doing with my phone?" protested Stillen.

"It will be returned to you later," said Rosengren, as they walked him to their car.

At headquarters, they put Stillen in an interview room. The bright fluorescent lighting emphasized its starkness. It was painted a dull green, the floor covered with white linoleum tiles. A wooden table and four plastic chairs were in the center of the room and a large two-way mirror occupied one wall. Wide-angle video cameras were high up in opposite corners so the room could be viewed from different directions. On the table was a plastic bottle of water.

Stillen looked around. He took out a pack of cigarettes and some matches, but didn't resist when Alenius took them away from him.

"I need a smoke," he objected.

"There's no smoking allowed in the building," replied Alenius.

Stillen paced around the room and then sat in one of the chairs.

"Well? What's going on?"

"You'll find out soon enough," said Rosengren, as he and Alenius left, locking the door behind them.

At Lindfors's office, they asked for her, and she came down the hall to meet them. She was dressed in a simple, close-fitting light gray business suit without a blouse, and a knee-length skirt that set off her figure. Her golden hair shimmered in the sunlight from the windows; she looked stunning.

"Is there some news about Rodger?" she asked.

"We need some further help with our investigation," replied Rosengren, eyeing her with obvious admiration. "We'd appreciate it if you could come to headquarters with us. Chief Superintendent Ekman would like to speak with you."

"Right now?"

"Yes, please. It's urgent," said Alenius.

"All right. I'll just get my coat," she said, and turned away.

She looked surprised when they walked with her back to her office, but didn't say anything.

In the car she took out her mobile to make a call, and Alenius, sitting beside her, reached over and took it from her. She looked shocked.

"What are you doing?" she asked, angry now.

"I'm sorry," Alenius said. "But until you speak with Herr Ekman, he's asked that you not talk with anyone. Your phone will be returned to you later, of course."

Lindfors sat stiffly silent, radiating outrage, on the ride to headquarters.

The interview room they brought her to was a twin of the one Stillen was in farther down the corridor.

"Please sit down, Froken Lindfors," said Alenius. "Herr Ekman will be with you shortly and explain everything."

"He'd better," said Lindfors, and clamped her lips tightly as she sat on one of the hard plastic chairs.

Alenius and Rosengren left her to stew, locking the door.

Ekman and Rystrom had been watching through the two-way mirror.

"She's even better looking than her photo would have led you to think," said Rystrom.

"Yes, she's quite a knock-out, very sexually seductive. It's easy to see why these men have been so taken with her."

"If she's a killer, she certainly fits the description of a *femme fatale*."

"You can be the good guy," Ekman said. "It fits you better. I'll be the heavy," he deadpanned.

Rystrom smiled, as they left the observation booth and walked around the corner to the door of the interview room. Ekman unlocked it and they went in, followed by a woman constable who'd been waiting by the door. She took one of the chairs and moved it to one side of the room. It clattered against the wall as she sat down.

"Good afternoon, Froken Lindfors, it's a pleasure to meet you," said Rystrom, extending his hand, which Lindfors shook without getting up. Her hand felt soft in his palm. "I'm Garth Rystrom, superintendent, National

CID, and this is Walther Ekman, chief superintendent in Weltenborg." Ekman just nodded, his face expressionless.

"I apologize for the urgent request and want to thank you for agreeing to this meeting. Can I get you some coffee?" Rystrom asked, as Ekman sat down across from Lindfors.

"No thanks," Lindfors replied. "I was told you had some questions, and that I could help with your search for Rodger. I certainly want to do whatever I can. But for some reason my phone was taken away. I want it back."

"Again, I apologize for the inconvenience," Rystrom said in a soothing voice. "It will be returned after our meeting. We just thought it important that anyone you might speak with not distort your memory of events related to Herr Westberg's disappearance."

"That's absurd."

"We wanted to be certain. Now I think we need to begin the interview," he said, turning to Ekman.

"This interview with Froken Stina Lindfors is being recorded," Ekman said in a loud voice. "It's two thirty P.M. on Friday, October 21st at county police headquarters in Weltenborg. I'm Chief Superintendent Walther Ekman and with me are Superintendent Garth Rystrom, CID, and Constable Greta Sorrensson."

"This sounds really formal. Am I under arrest? If I am, I want to know why, and I want an attorney," she said in a tight voice.

"You're certainly not under arrest, Froken Lindfors," a smiling Rystrom replied. "So there's no need for an attorney. We really do need your assistance with the investigation. You are willing to help us aren't you?"

"Of course. That's why I dropped everything I was doing to come here as soon as I was asked," she said, somewhat mollified. "I want to do everything possible to find Rodger."

"Good," said Rystrom. "Please don't be put off by the formal interview. This is a major criminal investigation and a record has to be kept of all we do. We'll be asking a wide range of questions, some of which may not seem relevant to you, but are needed to provide background for the investigation. In a case like this, everything must be examined. I hope you can appreciate that."

"Certainly. I'm anxious to cooperate in any way I can."

"Then let's begin at the beginning," said Ekman. "You use the name Stina Lindfors. Is that your birth name?"

"No. I was born Stina Ernstsson, in Lund."

"How did it change to Lindfors?"

"I was married to Eberhardt Lindfors. I kept his name after he died in an accident."

"What kind of accident?"

"He drank a good deal. By mistake one night he took an overdose of a sleeping medicine. He had a heart problem and it was too much for him," she said, looking down at her hands that were now knotted in her lap.

"And where is he buried?"

"Of what possible importance is that?" she asked, startled. "He wasn't buried. He was cremated. It was his wish."

"That's convenient."

"How can you say such a thing?" she said, her face showing her shock. "It's terribly unkind."

"Sometimes we need to be unkind. It depends."

"On what?" It was clear she resented his harsh manner.

"On whether someone is being entirely truthful with us."

"But I am."

"Was that your only marriage, Froken Lindfors?"

"No. I was married before when I was very young."

"But you didn't mention that."

"You didn't ask."

"Why didn't you take your first husband's name?"

"I didn't want to at the time. I changed my mind about doing it when I married Eberhardt."

"By the way, who was your first husband?" interjected Rystrom.

"His name is Carl Stillen."

"How long were you married?"

"Six years. Then I got a divorce."

"And why was that, Froken Lindfors?" Ekman asked.

She hesitated. "He could be violent at times, especially when he drank. Never with me though. I was working as a waitress in a bar, and a man pawed me. Carl was there and saw it. They got into a fight and the man was badly hurt. Carl was sent to prison for four years. I waited a year and then filed for divorce."

"So you were horrified by Carl's violent tendencies? You wanted nothing more to do with him?" asked Rystrom.

"Yes. I decided he wasn't likely to change. I wanted to make a fresh start."

"Let's move on to your first meeting with Eugen Westberg. When was that?" said Ekman.

"About two years ago. I was working on an accounting assignment at his office."

"And what was your relationship with Eugen Westberg?"

"We became friends."

"What kind of friends?"

"What do you mean? We were just friends."

"Really? Weren't you more than 'just friends'?"

She paused and considered the question carefully. Lindfors had been staring at her hands in her lap, now she raised her eyes to look directly at Ekman. "Yes. We became lovers. I knew it was wrong, but I was very taken with him. He's charming and good looking."

"Then you met his son, Rodger Westberg?"

"Yes."

"And he also was charming and good looking. And considerably younger."

"Yes. Rodger was a more youthful version of his father. I fell deeply in love with him."

"Deep enough to give up seeing the father?"

"Yes. Of course."

"You're lying and you know it."

"How can you say such a thing? After I met Rodger, I stopped seeing his father."

"Then if Eugen Westberg has admitted he continued being your lover until four months ago, you'd say he's lying? Before you answer, remember this is a formal interview that's being recorded."

There was a long pause before she answered. "I said I'd stopped seeing him because I was ashamed of what happened. Yes," she raised her head and looked Ekman in the eye, "I did go on seeing Eugen. It's our personal business. It has no bearing on Rodger's disappearance."

"That's for us to say. Did you know Rodger Westberg had changed his will in your favor?"

"No. I'm very surprised to hear that."

Ekman hunched forward in his chair. His voice was menacing as he glared at her.

"You're lying again, Froken Lindfors."

She was silent for a moment. Turning to Rystrom, she said, "I'm really feeling threatened by these questions."

"Please don't be alarmed, Froken Lindfors," Rystrom replied, and turning to Ekman, said, "Walther, there's no reason to be so offensive. You need to change your tone."

Ekman pretended to look chastened. "All right," he said to Lindfors, "I apologize if I sounded harsh. But you should reconsider your answer."

She looked down before lifting her head to reply. "I didn't want to say I knew he'd changed his will because I could see it might make me look like some kind of gold digger, and that's not true. I never asked Rodger for anything, ever. He told me he'd changed his will several months ago. I asked him not to cut off his family, but he insisted they didn't need the money. He wanted to make sure I was financially secure in case something happened to him."

"That was very thoughtful of him," said Rystrom. "He must have loved you a great deal."

"Thank you for being so understanding, Superintendent," she replied, looking at him with glistening eyes.

"Do you own a silver Volvo, Froken Lindfors?" asked Ekman.

"Yes, what about it?"

"How did you acquire this car?"

"It was a gift," she said. "From Eugen Westberg, if you must know."

"How kind of him, too," said Ekman, with undisguised sarcasm. "And where is this car now?"

"It's in a garage on Sundgatan."

"And the address is . . . ?"

"Why is that important? It's 2740 Sundgatan."

"Let's turn back to Carl Stillen. What is your current relationship with Stillen?"

"We've been friends since our marriage," she replied; her expression was sullen.

"Didn't you say earlier you didn't want anything to do with him because of his violent tendencies?"

"I meant at that time. He's changed."

"Since when?"

"Since he got out of prison. It made him realize that more violence would ruin his life."

"So now he's a perfect gentleman?"

"There's no need to run him down. He's become a better person."

"So much better that you could resume a romantic relationship with him at the same time you were involved with both Westbergs?" Ekman asked, his voice grating.

She was quiet for a moment. "You must think I'm an awful person," she said to Rystrom, her eyes welling with tears, ignoring Ekman.

"Not at all," Rystrom replied. "You've known Stillen since you were young. You were married to him. It's perfectly natural."

"And when did you and Stillen first begin your plan to get hold of the Westberg money?" Ekman asked.

"We never did. Never. How can you say such a thing?" she asked.

"That's the third lie you've told us, Froken Lindfors," Ekman replied. "Maybe you don't want Rodger Westberg to be found."

"Above all I want Rodger back safe and sound." She paused. "You can't prove Carl and I wanted his money," she said, with narrowed eyes.

"You may find out differently what we can prove, Froken Lindfors. Do you know someone called Grendel?" Ekman asked, changing the subject.

"What?" she said, seeming surprised by this sudden shift. "That cannibal in the papers? How could I know anything about him?"

"You could know a great deal, if you and Stillen had made him up."

"That's absolutely ridiculous." She turned to Rystrom, "Your colleague has gone off the deep end with his wild accusation. He hates me. Can't you see that?"

"Walther, please. Froken Lindfors is upset," Rystrom said in a sympathetic tone.

"She has every reason to be upset," Ekman responded. "No one likes to have their lies found out."

Turning to Lindfors, Ekman said, "Lying to the police in a murder investigation is a serious offense. I'm tired of listening to you." He got up. "I need a break." And left the room.

Outside, he found Rystrom's technician waiting for him with Lindfors's phone in his hand.

"Well, what did you get?" he asked.

"We copied all the phone numbers and text messages. It'll take a little time to compare them with the missing men's phone calls. We're working on Stillen's phone now. And we've taken fingerprints from both phones."

"Okay, good," Ekman said, pocketing Lindfors's phone, and heading down the hall to the men's room.

Rystrom had leaned across the table, speaking to Lindfors in a low, confidential tone.

"I apologize for Walther. He's a good police officer, but he can get carried away and go off on a tangent when he feels frustrated."

"He's an unfeeling person. After all I've been through. He doesn't understand people the way you obviously do, Superintendent," she said in a soft voice.

"Please call me Garth, and may I call you Stina?"

"Of course . . . Garth."

"Stina, we're trying to solve a difficult case. Much more complicated than you or the public know. So we need your help. Please forgive me if I have to ask very personal questions."

"Ask whatever you need to, Garth."

"How long have you been romantically involved with Stillen?"

She hesitated. "Please try to understand, Garth. He was my first lover. After he got out of prison, where he was because he defended me when I was his wife, I felt I owed him something. So we've become attached to one another. But this was different from what I felt for Eugen, and then Rodger. Carl and I have become more like brother and sister."

Ekman was watching and listening in the observation booth. She's smooth, he thought. That was an interesting brother and sister act she put on in her apartment. I'm not surprised she's trying to charm the pants off Garth.

"I understand completely," said Rystrom.

"I know he seems changed, less violent, but is there some slight possibility that Stillen may have a hidden tendency to violence?"

She considered the question. "It's always possible, I suppose, Garth, but I've never seen any sign of it since he got out of prison."

She's hedging, Ekman thought. The question about Grendel got her thinking.

"Since there is a possibility, however small, that Stillen could be hiding his violent nature from you, knowing how repulsed you are by it, do you think he might have had something to do with Rodger's disappearance? Totally without your knowledge, of course."

"I can't believe that. I know him better than that. He wouldn't do such a terrible thing."

"Think about it, Stina. He knew Rodger was leaving you his money, didn't he?"

"I suppose I may have mentioned it," she said.

"Well, knowing that, and perhaps being secretly jealous of your relationship with Rodger, he could have decided to remove him to have you to himself. I could understand that, Stina. You're an incredibly desirable woman," Rystrom said, smiling at her.

She shook her head.

"No, don't deny it, you're very lovely. What man wouldn't want you?"

"He's never been jealous," she protested.

"He was in a jealous rage when he almost killed that man years ago, wasn't he?"

"Yes . . . but he's changed."

"Can you be absolutely sure?"

She hesitated. "No, not absolutely."

She's decided Stillen's a liability and is getting ready to cut him loose, thought Ekman. Good work, Garth.

"Well, that's something to think about, Stina," Rystrom said, as Ekman came back into the room and stood over her.

"Is there anything else you want to tell us, Froken Lindfors?" Ekman asked.

"I've told you everything."

Ekman said, "This interview is over. Here's your phone."

"And here are warrants for the computers at your home and office, and your car. They're being executed just about now," he said, looking at the clock on the wall.

"How dare you? You've no right to enter my home and office and invade my privacy. Can't you stop him, Garth?" she pleaded.

"Stina, I'm truly sorry, but it's out of my hands. The prosecutor has authorized the warrants."

"The computers will be returned when we've finished examining them," said Ekman.

Lindfors was speechless, her face red with outrage.

She got up, and Rystrom said, "Constable Sorrensson will drive you back to your office, Stina. Thank you for your time and for being so frank. I know it was difficult for you." He shook her hand, holding it a few seconds longer than he had to. "It was a pleasure meeting you. I hope to see you again sometime."

"It was good meeting you too, Garth," she replied with a dazzling smile. Ignoring Ekman as though he weren't there, she walked out of the room. The constable followed her.

In the observation booth, looking through the mirror at Stillen restlessly pacing back and forth, Ekman grinned and said, "What a performance, Garth. The stage lost a great actor when you entered the academy."

Rystrom bowed; "You weren't bad yourself, Walther."

"However, the Oscar must go to your dear friend, 'Stina.' She's a piece of work."

"Yes, but an extremely beautiful piece of work. If I weren't a happily married man, and a totally dedicated officer, I'd be tempted to follow up."

"And she'd probably be delighted if you did exactly that. Seriously, what do you think? Are she and Stillen killers?"

"That's still not clear. When I suggested he might be, she was willing to consider it. That doesn't mean she hasn't been his partner all along. Maybe now she thinks she needs someone to take the fall, and he's it. But the other possibility, of course, is that what I was proposing to her is exactly what happened. Stillen killed Westberg out of jealousy, and the other men . . . whom she doesn't know about . . . because he's deranged. She may be innocent of everything, except promiscuity and greed. But these are only biblical, not secular, crimes."

"Wait a minute, Garth. What about her involvement with the two men on the chess site?"

"I thought about that, but all we have is her photo and some e-mails. What if it's actually Stillen, pretending to be Lindfors, and she knew nothing about it?"

Ekman considered this for a moment. "It's possible. You don't think she's worked her magic on you, do you? Maybe you're bewitched?"

Rystrom laughed. "I'm not as vulnerable as all that, but she does exert a powerful amount of charm."

"Now, however, I'm afraid you have a less charming task ahead . . . Stillen. This time I'll be my usual benign self," Ekman said, with what he believed was a beneficent smile.

56

Interrogation — Stillen

Stillen got up as they came in.

"It's about time. I've been waiting here for two hours," he said. "What do you want from me?"

"Shut up and sit down," said Rystrom, his voice harsh.

Stillen hesitated and then sat, glaring at them as they pulled out chairs across from him.

"This is a formal, recorded interview with Carl Stillen," Rystrom said for the cameras. "It's four thirty P.M., Friday, October 21st, at county police headquarters in Weltenborg. I'm Superintendent Garth Rystrom, CID. With me is Chief Superintendent Walther Ekman."

"This is a murder investigation, Stillen," Rystrom said. "So I advise you to cooperate. You're not under arrest. Yet."

"Arrest? For what? Who's been murdered?"

"Rodger Westberg, for one, and perhaps several others," replied Ekman. "If we get the answers we need, you'll be able to walk out of here, a free man. If not . . ."

"I've got nothing to do with Westberg's disappearance. As for others, I don't know what you're talking about."

"Let's focus on Westberg for now," said Rystrom. "What's your involvement with him?"

"I've never met him. All I know from the papers and TV is that he's missing. Period."

"Don't you dare lie to us," said Rystrom, slamming his fist on the table.

"I'm not lying."

"Carl," said Ekman in a confidential tone, "we know all about you and Stina Lindfors, Westberg's fiancée. There's no point in lying. It just makes you look bad."

Stillen bit his lower lip. "Okay, okay. You're right. I didn't want to drag her into this."

"She's already in it up to her neck. And so are you," Rystrom said.

"Now wait a minute. We didn't have anything to do with Westberg's disappearance."

"You didn't know he'd left your ex-wife and current girlfriend a fortune?"

Stillen paused before he answered. "We'd heard he'd changed his will. But it's not our fault if he vanished. We were as surprised as anybody, and that's the truth."

"So you say. Why should we believe you?" Rystrom asked.

"Because we'd be stupid to do something to him soon after he changed his will, right?"

"Criminals always do stupid things. That's why they're criminals."

"How did you feel about Stina taking up with West-berg's father, and then the son?" asked Ekman. "I can understand if you were jealous. It's only natural."

Stillen shrugged. "I wasn't jealous. Stina and I go back a long way. We kept in touch over the years. After we divorced, she led her own life and met other guys. I was okay with that."

"Don't give us that bullshit, Stillen. You almost killed a man and went to prison over Stina," Rystrom said.

"We were married then. The guy grabbed my wife right in front of me. What would you do?"

"Not what you did. You were always crazy jealous of the men she was with, so when you saw a chance for her to get a fortune, too, you had a double reason for killing Westberg."

"You've got it all wrong. Yes, Stina and I've been lovers for years, no matter who else she was seeing. We always come first with each other. I'm the important guy in her life; they never were. So I don't have any reason to be jealous. Sure, I was glad Rodger put her in his will, but when she married him, she'd get everything she wanted, and so would I. Stina and I would be together after she married. That was our plan. Not to kill him."

"Why did you create Grendel?" Rystrom asked.

"That cannibal guy? I don't know anything about him."

"Just like you didn't know anything about Westberg? Grendel is the fall guy you invented to take the blame for your murder."

"You're out of your mind," said Stillen, his face tensing as his hands gripped the edge of the table. His words fell over themselves. "You're trying to finger me so you can get credit for solving the Westberg thing. But I'm not going down for it. No way. No way."

"You're a psychopathic killer, Stillen, and we know it. You can't lie your way out of this one," said Rystrom, standing up and going to the door. "I can't stand to be in the same room with you."

There was silence after Rystrom left. Ekman looked at Stillen with concern written on his face.

"Carl, Rystrom thinks you're guilty, but I believe he's mistaken. If you're honest with me, maybe I can help change his mind."

"What do you want to know?"

"Do you know how to tie a bowline knot?"

"Sure, I worked in a naval supply store. I know all the knots. What's that got to do with anything?" He looked puzzled.

"Do you play chess, Carl?" Stillen was startled.

"Yes, I learned in prison. Why? What's this about?"

"Tell me, does Stina play?"

"Sure. We've played sometimes."

"Is she good at it?"

"She beats me every time. Why do you want to know?"

"It's just something I was curious about. Let's drop it."

Stillen had a puzzled expression.

"Did Stina kill Eberhardt Lindfors?" Ekman asked all of a sudden.

"What are you talking about, that was an accident."

"That's what she may have told you. But can you be sure?"

"She'd never do something like that."

"I think you may not really know Stina, even after all these years." Ekman leaned over the table toward him.

"She was just here, Carl. We interviewed her, and when we asked whether you could have killed Westberg, she thought it was possible. She'd like to pin the killing on you, but you know what I think? Maybe she did it. After all, she's the one who'll benefit directly. And if you went down for the murder, she wouldn't have to share with you, would she?"

"You're lying."

"No, I'm not, and I have a recorded interview to prove it. I wouldn't trust her, Carl. She's getting ready to dump you now that there's the pressure of a murder investigation."

Stillen was silent and didn't move. He's considering it, thought Ekman.

Rystrom came back into the room.

"Here's your phone, Stillen. This interview is over. But we'll see you again. Soon. Now get out of here."

A constable standing outside the door led him out of the building.

"That was very neatly done, Walther. You got him thinking about Stina's loyalty. Maybe we'll learn something when they're arguing tonight over who said what here."

"If we can get them to really distrust each other, they'll probably tell us a lot more."

"We'll hope so. Your questions about chess and the knot were interesting. What do you think of his reaction?"

"He put on a good show of being bewildered. But Stillen could be a clever actor; psychopaths are."

"If he's Grendel, he's got to be really on guard now. He knows we've found the link to the other killings."

"Yes, I was hoping those questions might make him nervous. Nervous people, even psychopaths, are more likely to make mistakes."

"Do you still think we may be dealing with a serial killer duo? He could have lied and said he and Stina didn't know anything about chess."

"Yes, but he might be trying a double bluff—making us believe that Grendel wouldn't admit he and his accomplice know the game. Therefore, he couldn't be Grendel. It would be clever."

"He didn't seem that smart to me. Just an average jerk. If either of them planned the killings and created Grendel, my money's on Lindfors."

"You may be right, Garth. Her computers and their phones should tell us whether we're getting close."

57

~~~~~

Running

Ekman was writing summaries of the interviews for Norlander and Edvardsson when the phone rang. It was Malmquist.

"Walther, you're in luck. We worked through the night on your latest DNA swab. Gustaffson is a 99 percent match to that grisly sample you sent."

"Ludvig, what can I say. We're in your debt."

"If you really want to pay that debt, just don't send us any more emergency work, okay?"

"I'll do what I can to avoid it. And Ludvig, thanks, sincerely."

"You're welcome. God knows you're getting enough publicity on this. How soon before we see an 'Ekman Solves Another One' headline?"

"Perhaps we'll have results fairly soon. But I hope without that headline."

Ekman phoned Holm. "Where are you?"

"We've gotten the sample from Henriksson's mother and we're about to head over to Linköping."

"Hold off on that. Malmquist just called. They got a match to Gustaffson."

"That's great. I mean for us, of course."

"I know what you mean. It confirms the murder we expected. Make sure you preserve the sample you just got. We may have to match it later."

"We're heading back now. Is there anything we need to do this evening, Chief?"

"No. I think that's all we can do today. I'll see you both at tomorrow's meeting."

Ekman went back to finishing his report. By the time he was done it was eight P.M. The case seemed to be on track. Lindfors and Stillen had been interviewed with mixed success. Neither he nor Rystrom had actually expected them to break down and confess. If they were psychopaths, they were unlikely to. Of course, that was the problem. The murderer of Gustaffson and, he felt sure, of Henriksson, had to be a psychopath. There was no other explanation for the killings.

Westberg was another matter. There were obvious motives: money and jealousy. And there was the connection of all three men to Lindfors. Based on what they now knew, there seemed to him several possibilities: Lindfors or Stillen had killed the men without the other knowing; the two had worked as a team; or Grendel was simply a ploy used by one of them, or both, to distract and confuse the intense investigation that would inevitably follow Westberg's disappearance. But if none of these proved correct, they were back to square one. They would then have to develop new leads. He had no idea how they would do this.

The most likely explanation, Ekman thought, was that Lindfors and Stillen worked together. Lindfors would be the sexual magnet for the men. She'd admitted as much when confronted with her involvement with both Westbergs and Stillen. It also seemed to him that the double motive they'd suggested for Stillen was at work, probably with Lindfors's knowledge. As for the other killings, they simply demonstrated the psychopathy of the two.

His muscles were aching from fatigue and his stomach had begun to growl. Perhaps I'll go to the restaurant across the square, before heading home, he thought. He didn't feel like trying to pull together a dinner at the house, or even getting carry-out. Eating at home by himself was just too lonely.

In the restaurant with a glass of ale and a plate of roast pork loin, potatoes, and cabbage in front of him, he felt somewhat restored. He called Ingbritt and was surprised how moved he was just to hear her voice.

"Is everyone fine? Good. Yes, I'm okay. Working hard, trying to finish up this case. No, not yet. It may be another week. I miss you too. Very much. I'll be glad when this is over so we can be together. No, I'm not being unreasonably cautious. There have been at least three murders. I just wouldn't feel comfortable with you here until this is wrapped up. I love you too. Good night, Ingbritt."

On the drive home Ekman wondered if she wasn't right. After all Stillen and Lindfors were under close surveillance. Maybe if things moved along well, he should reconsider. He would decide in a few days. What he knew now was that her absence left a deep void in his existence.

Ekman had been in bed reading Braudel's history of Philip II's era until he gradually dozed off. He was startled awake by the phone. The bright green numbers on the bedside alarm clock told him it was eleven twenty P.M. He groped for the bed lamp's switch, blinked in the light, and picked up the phone.

"Chief, it's Rosengren. I'm sorry to disturb you, but I thought you'd like to know right away."

"Yes, go on." Ekman had a sense of foreboding. Was it another murder?

"Stillen's gone. The surveillance team lost him an hour ago. He went into a bar and never came out. When they sent a guy to check a half hour later, he wasn't there. The place had a back entrance. He's skipped."

Their interrogation had probably frightened him more than they'd realized, Ekman thought.

"Put out an all-points alert, using the best picture of him we have from the interview recording. Describe him as 'a person of interest, wanted for questioning.' He should be treated as dangerous and possibly armed. And keep a close watch on Lindfors and her apartment. She may decide to run too, or Stillen may turn up there."

"Got it, Chief," said Rosengren, and hung up.

It was one A.M. before Ekman managed to get back to a restless sleep.

58

<del>~~~~~</del>

Pursuit

Saturday, October 22. When Ekman walked into the conference room at eight that morning, everyone was standing around talking about Stillen's flight. He sat down and the others gradually quieted and took their seats.

Turning to Rystrom, he said, "Any sighting of Stillen?"

"Not yet."

"Has he contacted Lindfors?"

"No, although she's been trying to reach him. He's not answering his phone."

"We may have to involve the media, but I'm very reluctant. If we do, some of them are likely to jump to the conclusion that he's Grendel. They'll say we had him in custody and released the cannibal on the public. It could be a PR disaster."

"Don't you believe he's Grendel, Chief?" Holm asked.

"I'm not certain yet. What do you think, Garth?"

Rystrom looked around the table. "After yesterday's interrogation, I don't know. He didn't impress me as being smart enough to be Grendel. Although he could have been purposely playing dumb."

"For now, we'll keep the hunt for Stillen out of the media," said Ekman. "We'll maintain the surveillance on

Lindfors. Stillen will probably try to contact her soon, if only because he'll be running out of money and has nowhere else to turn."

"There's important new information about Lindfors," said Rystrom. "The techs have gone over her computers and phones. They can't find anything related to the chess club. There's nothing to tie her to the missing men."

Ekman looked around the table at the others. The room had become still after Rystrom spoke.

"Are you certain your people are right?" Ekman asked.

"Yes. They were very thorough. Unfortunately, there's no doubt. There's nothing incriminating and nothing has been deleted."

"And yet, we know the missing men were in computer contact with her." Ekman rubbed his chin, gazing at the ceiling. "How do we account for that?"

"There could be another computer we haven't found, Chief," said Vinter. All eyes turned toward her. "Maybe she has a storage locker."

"You're right, Gerdi. We need to find out if she has a locker, perhaps in the attic or basement of her apartment building. The warrant we have is broad enough to cover it. Alenius and Rosengren, talk to the building manager. If she has a locker and you find another computer, get it to the techs right away. Have forensics check it, and everything in the locker, for fingerprints."

"We'll get on it right after the meeting, Chief," said the usually silent Alenius, pleased they'd gotten this assignment.

"Until we can make the computer connection between Lindfors and the other missing men we can't move against her. As for Stillen, we need to get our hands on him and sweat him some more. His taking off makes me think that whether or not he's Grendel, he's done something criminal he's afraid we'll soon discover," Ekman said.

"I think you're right, Chief," said Rapp. "He has to know that running away makes him look bad. And we didn't really have anything on him. So why do it?"

"Alrik, you and Mats pay a visit to the hardware store where Stillen worked. Find out if any goods or cash are missing.

"Because we now have a DNA match between the sample Grendel sent and Gustaffson, we've confirmed one murder by Grendel for certain, and two others are probable. That's three bodies, possibly five, if we include the two who robbed me. Enar and Gerdi, I'd like you to work on what Grendel might have done with them."

The two looked at each other and Holm looked bemused. They had no idea how to begin a search for corpses in hundreds of square kilometers of southern Sweden.

"Is there anything else?" Ekman asked. There was no response.

"Until we locate Stillen and connect Lindfors to the missing men, the investigation is temporarily blocked. So let's take tomorrow off and start again on Monday. I plan to brief Edvardsson and Norlander this afternoon. Garth, why don't you come with me."

Rystrom nodded agreement as Ekman got up, and followed him down the hall to Rystrom's office.

"What do you propose if her car is clean and we don't come up with a computer at Lindfors's place?" Rystrom asked.

"There's got to be another computer somewhere. Unless, of course, she got rid of it before we started watching her," Ekman replied.

"If we can't connect her to the men, then our best hope seems finding Stillen and pushing him until he cracks. His taking off shows he's beginning to break. What do you think?"

"It looks that way. He seems more likely to crack than Lindfors. To me, she's the one in charge. He's the accomplice doing the actual killing."

59

Norlander's Meeting

Ekman picked up the phone and called Norlander at home. His wife answered.

"Yes, Fru Norlander, I really need to speak with him."

"It's very inconvenient to call on a Saturday morning," she replied, her voice sharp with displeasure.

"I hate to bother him, or you, but it's important."

Ekman glanced at Rystrom and rolled his eyes.

"Sorry to disturb you, Commissioner, but there are some issues in the Westberg case that need your advice. Could we meet in your office this afternoon? Two o'clock will be fine. I'm going to see if Edvardsson can join us. Rystrom also will be there. Thank you, sir."

He called Edvardsson's home.

"Malin, it's Walther. I apologize for calling on a weekend, but there's going to be a meeting this afternoon in Norlander's office and we need your guidance. Yes, at two. Thanks. See you then."

Ekman knew he could have waited until Monday to meet with them, but wanted Norlander and Edvardsson to remember he'd asked for an urgent weekend meeting. The case had reached a standstill, which he hoped was only temporary. But if it came to a permanent halt—and Westberg's disappearance, let alone the other men's—was never solved, he didn't want to be accused of not consulting them at a critical juncture. In twenty difficult years as chief superintendent, Ekman had learned to protect himself from the hazards of bureaucratic infighting.

Norlander was already in his office when Ekman and Rystrom walked in at exactly two P.M. Casually dressed in crisp black slacks and a white cashmere sweater, he came to meet them. Shaking hands with both, he led them to a seating area, and indicating the couch, settled himself in an armchair facing them. Another chair had been drawn up for Edvardsson.

She knocked on the door and came in just as they sat down. All three men rose to greet her. She shook hands with Norlander first, then Ekman and Rystrom. When they were seated, Norlander turned to her, taking charge of the meeting in his soft, smooth voice.

"Malin, thank you for coming on a Saturday. After Walther's call this morning to request a meeting, I know we're both anxious to learn what's been happening in the Westberg investigation."

Turning to Ekman, he said, "Walther, why don't you bring us up to date."

Taking out copies from a file folder of the report he'd prepared last night, Ekman handed them to the other three.

"It may save time if you would take a few moments to review the report I drafted yesterday evening. It summarizes where we are at this point."

After five minutes, the others looked up.

"The case is hanging in the balance now, isn't it Walther?" Edvardsson said.

"Yes, Malin. That's why I wanted your recommendations, and the commissioner's, about how best to proceed."

There was a knock at the door. Norlander said, "Yes, come in."

Rosengren opened the door and walked in. "Sorry to bust in like this, Commissioner Norlander, Fru Edvardsson, but I knew the chief was with you and thought you'd want to know right away what's happened."

To Edvardsson, Ekman said, "This is Inspector Rosengren."

"Yes, Rosengren?" Norlander said.

"We've found another computer hidden in a box in the back of Lindfors's basement storage locker," he replied, his voice rising with excitement. "It's got all the chess games and e-mails with Gustaffson and Henriksson."

"What about fingerprints?" asked Ekman.

"There weren't any on the computer," Rosengren replied, his voice dropping.

"It was wiped clean?" inquired Rystrom.

"Yes, sir."

"Thank you for the information, Inspector," said Norlander, going over to shake his hand. "I appreciate your getting it to us immediately. We'll discuss this and Herr Ekman will let you know what we've decided."

After Rosengren had left, Norlander turned to Ekman. "What do you make of this, Walther?"

"Finding the computer in Lindfors's storage locker with all the information tying her to the missing men should be conclusive. But with the computer wiped of fingerprints, I'm troubled. What would be the point of her wiping it down and then hiding it?"

Rystrom interjected, "Perhaps she wanted to use it in the future, but if it were found, Lindfors wanted to deny it was hers. She wants to be able to claim it was planted."

"That's exactly what her attorney would argue," said Edvardsson.

"And how do we know it wasn't planted?" asked Norlander.

"We don't," responded Ekman. "But if it was, the person who did it must have been Grendel. The question is, how did he even know we suspected Lindfors?"

"Stillen could have done it," said Rystrom. "But that doesn't really make a great deal of sense," he immediately added. "Because by implicating Lindfors, he also implicates himself, especially since he's taken off."

"If it was Stillen who was careful enough to remove fingerprints from the computer, he also should have realized by doing so, he'd raise these questions about its being planted," said Ekman, gazing at the ceiling. "The smartest course for him would have been to simply pitch it. That way there would be no connection to Lindfors or him."

"You're right, Walther," said Rystrom.

"So where does this leave us?" asked Norlander, to end this circular conversation.

"If Grendel knew enough about our suspicions to plant the computer in order to incriminate Lindfors, and through her, Stillen, it means either there's a serious leak in our investigating team . . ." Ekman paused, reluctant to go on, "or Grendel may be a member of our team."

Norlander's eyes widened in surprise. "That's an outrageous idea, Walther. You can't be serious."

"I hate to even suggest it, Commissioner, but it's a remote possibility we can't ignore."

"If it turned out to be true, it would undermine the entire police force," Norlander said quietly.

"This discussion mustn't leave this room," he said, looking at each in turn. "Walther, you should pursue this unlikely possibility only as a last recourse. You agree with me, don't you?"

"Of course, Commissioner. We still have several other avenues to follow: finding Stillen and extracting a confession; confronting Lindfors with this new evidence to see if she'll break; and trying to find who outside our team is the press leak. We've alerted our force to look for Stillen, but we may need to make the hunt public. We'd simply identify him as 'a person of interest' with no mention of a connection to the Westberg case. The problem is that the media might leap to that conclusion. What do you recommend, Commissioner?"

"If Stillen is dangerous, we need to find him quickly. Have our media officer make the request to the papers and TV. We'll risk them speculating about a tie to Westberg. It's probably unavoidable."

"We'll do that today then."

"Good," said Norlander. "What do you think, Malin? Are we handling this properly?"

"Yes, of course. But Walther, I think it's time for me to sit in on your team meetings and try to provide immediate suggestions on the investigation's direction. Are you comfortable with that?"

Ekman had been expecting Edvardsson to intervene for some time. He'd prefer to totally control the investigation, but it was her prerogative as prosecutor.

"Certainly, Malin. Any insights you have will be much appreciated."

"Excellent. I think we all have a clearer idea now of where the case is going," said Norlander. Edvardsson would shoulder some of the onus if the police investigation publicly ran off the rails. Norlander got up.

"Thank you all for coming on a Saturday," he said, as though he'd called the meeting. He shook hands with each of them as they left.

60

~~~~~~~~~~~~~~~~~~~~~~~~

Looking for Leaks

"So, who do you think is leaking information?" asked Rystrom, settling back in his chair in Ekman's office.

"I'd like to think it's no one, but I can't explain otherwise how Grendel can be following what we're doing and trying to confuse us with planted evidence. If that's actually what's going on."

"I know we agreed it would be dumb of Stillen to wipe the computer and plant it to incriminate Lindfors. But maybe he did anyway."

"Possibly, but I doubt it. He's been attached to Lindfors for years and as we heard, they're still lovers. We tried to turn them against each other, but I'm not sure we were at all successful. Besides, he didn't have an opportunity since we spoke with him and he took off. Unless he did it sometime ago. Lindfors's place has been watched around the clock," said Ekman.

"Well, until we nab him, we can interrogate Lindfors again, show her the computer and what's on it, and see what happens. The likelihood, however, is she'll deny she's ever seen it before."

"You're right. We'll have to do it anyway, but I suspect she'll have a lawyer with her this time. So that leaves us with finding the leak."

"Who's high on your list?" Rystrom asked.

"We've already questioned Alrik, and I believe he's not the one. I'd also cross off Gerdi and Enar, because I trust them implicitly. I may be wrong, but that's my judgment. I'm not as sure about Rosengren and Alenius, particularly Rosengren. He tends to run off at the mouth and may be bragging to some drinking buddy. Alenius is not the talkative type," Ekman added, laughing, "as you've seen. That leaves Bergfalk. He's a good, thorough investigator, but I'm uncertain about him."

"Where do you want to start?"

"Let's begin with Rosengren."

"Sit down, Rosengren," said Ekman. "You and Alenius did a good job finding that computer and bringing us the news quickly."

"Thanks, Chief. It's just part of the job," he said, glancing down.

"Don't be so modest. You've got bragging rights," said Rystrom.

"I guess I do, if you say so," he said, smiling.

"Maybe you've already been bragging a little about your role in the investigation? You know, at a bar with some buddies?" Ekman asked.

"What do you mean, Chief? You think I've been shooting off my mouth where I shouldn't have?"

"If you have, it's entirely understandable. Think about it. Maybe you accidentally did?"

"No way. I remember you warned everyone about leaks, Chief. I don't even mention the investigation to friends on the force, let alone outsiders."

"You're sure about that? A slip can happen. What we're trying to do is not blame anyone for letting information get out. We just want to trace it, to find out who might have overheard," said Rystrom.

"It's important, Rosengren. So don't answer too quickly," Ekman said.

Rosengren sat quietly for a moment. "No, there's nothing, Chief. I swear it."

"Okay. I accept that. Don't mention this conversation to anyone, not even Alenius."

"We're not certain there's a leak, but it's critical we find it if it exists. You can understand that," added Rystrom. Rosengren stood. His tension showed in the tight lines around his mouth.

"I really appreciate all your good work, Rosengren. Please don't feel I don't. You and Alenius have been doing an outstanding job," said Ekman, getting up and going over to shake his hand. "We just have to ask these questions."

"I understand, Chief," replied Rosengren as he left. But his voice told Ekman he really didn't.

The meetings with Alenius and Bergfalk produced the same results: no new information, but several more disgruntled inspectors. Ekman was inclined to believe their fervent denials.

"I'm afraid we've pissed off everyone," said Rystrom.

"You're right," replied Ekman. "But it had to be done. Internal inquiries are always the hardest. Now they'll be looking at each other, wondering if the person next to them is the source of the leak. We'll need to try somehow to revive the team's spirit."

61

~~~~

A Call

Bruno Haeggman was in his office at the *Sydsvenska Nyheter* that Saturday, working on a story, when the photo of Stillen and the request for information came in on the fax. Immediately, he wondered whether it was connected to the Westberg case. He hated to have to soft pedal a possible Westberg connection, much as he'd like to connect the two, but he didn't want any more flak from his boss. Could this guy possibly be Grendel, the cannibal? It would make a great story, but he had nothing to go on.

He was sitting staring out the window at the bleak day, as the wind whipped around fallen leaves on the pavement, thinking about how to play this development, when the phone rang.

"Haeggman here."

"Bruno, it's Rapp," said the muffled voice.

"Yes," said Haeggman, his voice rising in anticipation. This could be what he needed.

"You know about the hunt for Stillen?"

"Yeah. We just got a photo."

"He's Grendel."

"How do you know?"

"I can't tell you that. Just take my word for it. He's the guy."

"What else can you tell me?"

"We had him in for questioning, but let him go. Now he's skipped and we can't find him. He's dangerous and probably armed."

"Jesus, you mean you had him and didn't hang on to him?"

"Yes. We blew it. There'll be a cover-up. The public should know. That's why I'm talking to you."

"Why don't we meet so you can give me more details?"

"That's it. You run with what I've given you or I'll take it elsewhere."

"Don't do that. We'll go with the story. Just let me know what's happening."

"I'll think about it." The line went dead.

62

~~~~~~~~~~

Lindfors Again

It was five P.M. and Lindfors was sitting rigidly erect in her chair in the interview room. Next to her was her attorney, a woman in her fifties, short and stout, with dark brown bangs hanging over skeptical blue eyes. Across from them were Ekman and Rystrom. A woman constable was sitting quietly against the wall behind Lindfors.

"It's very inconvenient for my client and me to be here on a Saturday afternoon," said the lawyer, Roya Osten, as she exchanged business cards with Ekman and Rystrom.

"We wouldn't have asked, except that it's a matter of some urgency," replied Ekman. "We appreciate your cooperation."

"How cooperative my client will be remains to be seen."

"This interview is being recorded," Ekman said, naming the date, time, and participants.

"Fröken Lindfors, Stina, I assume you're aware Carl Stillen is missing?" asked Rystrom.

"Yes, I've been worried about him. He hasn't called and I can't get him on his phone. It isn't like him."

"After we interviewed him yesterday, he apparently decided to avoid further questioning and fled. We're searching for him now," said Rystrom.

"You must have frightened him badly," replied Lindfors.

"Perhaps threatened him," put in Osten.

"Not at all," said Rystrom. "But he may have feared discovery that he was involved in several men's disappearances."

"Carl wouldn't have done anything like that," said Lindfors.

"Do you know where Stillen could be?" asked Ekman.

"I have no idea. It just isn't like Carl not to call me."

"Are there any favorite places you and Stillen visited that he could have gone to?" Rystrom asked.

"There are a few spots where we've vacationed together that we both liked."

"Would you be willing to provide us with a list?" inquired Rystrom.

"Yes, of course. I want to find Carl even more than you do. If he's run away, it's because you scared him." She looked with narrowed eyes at Ekman.

"You see how cooperative my client is being about Stillen," Osten said, turning to Lindfors. Then added, "She'll give you that list later. We're leaving."

"There's one other matter your client can assist us with," said Ekman.

"What's that?"

"This," he said, bending down to take the computer they'd found out of his briefcase, and placing it on the table.

"This is your computer, isn't it, Froken Lindfors?" Ekman asked.

"I've never seen it before," she replied with a puzzled expression.

"That's quite strange, because we discovered it earlier today hidden in your apartment's basement locker."

"I assume you had a search warrant," said Osten. "I want to see it."

"Of course," said Ekman, pulling it out of his briefcase and handing it to her.

She looked it over hurriedly. "This doesn't seem specific enough to me. It's defective."

"That will be a matter you can argue to a judge after we charge your client."

"With what, exactly?" Her tone was belligerent.

"Possibly three counts of kidnapping and murder."

"That's beyond bizarre. You have no proof whatsoever of such absurd charges."

"Why don't we see," replied Ekman, opening the laptop and turning it on. Using a wireless mouse he opened the screen to a photo of Lindfors.

"This is your picture, isn't it, Froken Lindfors?"

"Yes. It looks like the photo my accounting firm has on its website. It has pictures of each of the professional staff."

"Do you play chess?"

"Yes, but what has that to do with this?"

Ekman clicked open to a game Lindfors had played.

"This is an Internet chess game you played with a man named Henriksson."

"I did no such thing," Lindfors protested, her eyes wide. "I've never played chess on the Internet and I don't know anyone named Henriksson."

Ekman clicked to a series of e-mails between Lindfors and Henriksson.

"If you read through these, you'll see that you and Henriksson were good friends. You flirted with him quite a bit."

"You've already heard my client deny any knowledge of this machine and its contents, Herr Ekman."

"Then why was it hidden in her locker? Why does it have her picture and dozens of e-mails exchanged with Henriksson and another man, Gustaffson, both of whom have disappeared? Just as Rodger Westberg, her fiancé, has disappeared."

"Are my client's fingerprints on this computer?"

"The machine was wiped clean," replied Ekman. His face said he wasn't pleased to admit this.

"Then it's obvious, Herr Ekman," replied Osten with a tight smile. "The computer was planted in an attempt to incriminate Froken Lindfors. She denies all knowledge of the computer and its contents."

"Perhaps you could let Froken Lindfors answer for herself," said Rystrom. "If someone else is responsible, do you have any idea who that could be, Stina?"

"No idea at all. Why would someone do this to me?"

"Do you have any enemies who might want to harm you in this way?" Rystrom asked. His voice was soft.

She paused. "There's only one person I can think of, but I don't want to bring him into this."

"That would be Carl Stillen," said Ekman.

Her laughter was harsh. "That's nonsense. You have no idea what you're talking about."

"Then who are you thinking of, Stina? I understand your reluctance, but you must tell us," said Rystrom.

"All right." She hesitated. "Eugen Westberg."

"Why do you think he would do this?" asked Ekman.

"It's complicated. There's a great deal of money involved, and there are personal matters too. I've already gone into this with you, and I've told Advokat Osten all about it. I don't want to say any more," she said, looking at Osten.

Ekman and Rystrom exchanged quick glances. Eugen Westberg?

"There you are, gentlemen," said Osten, getting to her feet. "You have the name of someone who has good reasons to try to implicate my client. I suggest you follow up the information she's voluntarily given you. This interview is over."

She turned to Lindfors. "We're leaving now, Stina."

Ekman and Rystrom also stood up.

"We'll probably have further questions for Froken Lindfors," said Ekman.

"We'll see about that when you have something to say less ridiculous than this," Osten said as she gestured at the computer. She and Lindfors turned and walked out of the room.

"It isn't possible, is it?" Rystrom asked.

Ekman leaned back in his office chair, his gaze fixed on the ceiling.

"I can't see how. Eugen Westberg today may want Lindfors out of the way. But the only reason he would have posed as Lindfors long ago and then murdered the two men would be if he planned all along to pin the killings on her. He's calculating, certainly not the warmest person I've ever met, but he doesn't strike me as a psychopathic killer either. And then, of course, we'd have to ask if he's Grendel and could have murdered his son, too. None of that's likely. Way too far-fetched."

"So what did we learn?"

"We got a denial that it's her computer, which we expected, and a list of places to look for Stillen. It's not much."

"Denials don't count for anything. Maybe she removed her fingerprints just to be able to claim it was planted."

"You're right, Garth. Unfortunately it gives her an argument to use in court that could be persuasive. We need considerably more to charge her. After all, what if she'd admitted it's her computer, and that she had contact with the missing men? So what? All we have is a body part and no evidence tying her to a killing. What we do have is conjecture that doesn't reach the level of circumstantial evidence."

"In other words, after all the effort we've expended, we've got shit."

"Nicely put."

"We need to find those bodies."

"Discovering just one of the three would move the case forward. Enar and Gerdi are trying to find possible places Grendel could have disposed of them. If you and I put our minds to it over Sunday, maybe we can come up with some more ideas."

63

Stillen at Rest

*G*rendel was busily at work. He'd almost finished wrapping Stillen's naked body in plastic. He hummed under his breath and chatted with the corpse as he knelt beside it, lifting it from the concrete floor to pull the heavy plastic around the stiffening body. It was difficult: rigor mortis had begun to set in. His exertions made his warm breath condense in plumes in the frigid air of the meat locker.

"They think you've run away, Carl, but you couldn't get far in your present condition could you? You agree? Good.

"There are some advantages you have over the rest of us, you know. We age and wither daily. You, on the other hand, will stay nice and fresh. At least for a few years. Now aren't you the lucky one?"

Finishing the wrapping, he stood up and stepped back to admire his handiwork before kneeling again.

Looping coarse, heavy rope around the body, he attached the hook he'd pulled down from the overhead steel rack. Using the chain pulley, he hoisted the body up and slid it along the rack until it came to rest beside the other corpses.

Grendel looked along the line of cocooned bodies. There was plenty of room for a few more, he thought.

"I'm sure you'll get along marvelously with the other boys, Carl. Now the six of you play nicely together. I have to leave for a while, but I'll soon be back with another playmate. Try not to miss me too much."

Grendel smiled to himself and whistled a Sousa march as he headed to the door.

64

$\sim\!\!\sim\!\!\sim\!\!\sim\!\!\sim\!\!\sim\!\!\sim$

News Story

Haeggman had almost completed his story for tomorrow's paper; his editor had assured him it would be frontpage news. What he needed to finish it was a response from Ekman that would put the slant he wanted on the story.

"Herr Ekman? It's Bruno Haeggman. There'll be a story in tomorrow's paper about Grendel and your search for Carl Stillen. Why did you let him go after you had him in custody?"

"Haeggman, you should be speaking with our public affairs officer, not with me."

"But you're in charge of the Grendel case, right? And Stillen is your prime suspect. You had him and now you're trying to get him back, right?"

Ekman knew Haeggman would never talk with public affairs because he'd just get a neutral "ongoing investigation" response.

"Look, Haeggman, you're wrong. We haven't identified Stillen as Grendel. And he was never in custody. He was just brought in for questioning. We want to talk to him again. There are some further questions, and that's why we asked for help in locating him. That's it."

"Ekman, I know the sound of bullshit when I hear it. Why don't you level with me and our readers? The guy's a danger to the public and you slipped up and let him get away."

"Haeggman, you can print what you like, even if it has no resemblance to the truth. You can also print my denial of your twisted story." Ekman hung up. There was no point in trying to dissuade Haeggman.

How did Haeggman make the connection between Stillen and Grendel? he asked himself. Someone inside the investigation had been talking again. Ekman didn't think it was anyone on his team, now that he'd questioned them directly about the leak. But he hadn't spoken with Holm and Vinter. Maybe I've been negligent, too trusting, he thought. But he couldn't convince himself that either of them could be speaking with Haeggman.

Who else? Rystrom? Never. The only ones left were Norlander, Malmer, and Edvardsson. The first two abhorred adverse publicity, and Edvardsson, like Rystrom, was inconceivable.

Could Malmer hate him enough to try and make him out to be incompetent? It was worth thinking about. After all, Malmer wasn't directly involved in the case, especially since Norlander had relegated him to administrative work. Maybe he held Ekman responsible for his de facto demotion and was willing to tarnish the police and Norlander to get at Ekman.

It was a possibility he couldn't dismiss. But he didn't have anything to use to confront Malmer. Perhaps he could plant a seed in Norlander's mind and see if it took root.

"Commissioner, it's Walther Ekman. Sorry to bother you at home again, but I thought you should know I just got off the phone with Bruno Haeggman. There'll be a story in tomorrow's *Sydvenska Nyheter* about the hunt for Carl Stillen that identifies him as Grendel. It will imply that we've been negligent in releasing him, and will probably put the blame on me.

"Thank you, sir. I really appreciate your support. Yes, I agree. There's a leak somewhere, or Haeggman wouldn't have been willing to stake his reputation on Stillen being Grendel. I've questioned our team and I'm confident they're not the source. I'd appreciate any suggestions you or Herr Malmer have about where else to look."

Ekman was uncertain whether Norlander had picked up on the reference to Malmer. He'd have to see what action he took.

He thought for a moment about who else to call and then phoned Edvardsson. After he alerted her to the story, he called Rystrom.

"Garth, the proverbial shit will hit the fan tomorrow, but don't worry, it looks like it will spatter mostly on me. Haeggman will be attacking us on the release of Stillen. And he's identifying him as Grendel. I just spoke with Norlander and Edvardsson, so they won't be surprised when they're asked to comment on the story, as I'm sure they will be.

"Yes, it means we haven't plugged the leak. And no, I can't think of anyone else, except perhaps Malmer. He dislikes me enough, but he'd be taking a huge risk it would eventually come out. It's a possibility, but he's always struck me as too cautious to do something like this. Actually, 'cowardly' is the word I had in mind.

"Thanks, Garth. See you Monday. Try and avoid the reporters until then."

Now Ekman had to make the most difficult call of all: he had to speak with Ingbritt.

"No, it's all right. I can take it. Don't worry about me. I knew you'd be upset if you just picked up the paper tomorrow, without any warning. Yes, I'll try and control my temper. You know me, always calm." He heard her burst of laughter.

"Yes, we'll get through this, and then you'll be home again. I love you, too."

At home, knowing what the morning would bring, Ekman decided to treat himself to a couple of glasses of French brandy before trying to sleep. The brandy was good, but it didn't help.

65

Front Page

*S*unday, *October 23.* The call woke Ekman at six thirty A.M.

"Herr Ekman? This is Hans Erlander with TV2 News. I apologize for calling you so early on Sunday, but we wanted to get your reaction for our morning program to the story in today's *Sydsvenka Nyheter*. It calls Carl Stillen your prime suspect as the cannibal Grendel. Do you have any comment? We're taping this conversation, by the way, for broadcast."

Ekman was glad he'd been told his comments were being recorded. He'd been just about to respond with a choice expletive. Instead, with every bit of self-restraint he could muster, he replied in a slow, quiet voice.

"Herr Erlander, I appreciate your asking for my reaction to this newspaper story. I can only say that there is an ongoing police investigation and Herr Stillen is simply wanted for additional questioning. Any story that leaps to a conclusion about him is simply misleading and exploitative. I have no further comment." He hung up softly.

Ekman felt proud of his self-control then. He wished he could feel that way now.

He was sitting at the kitchen table half an hour later, his teeth tearing at a slice of toast spread with apricot preserves, while he alternately sipped steaming black coffee, his face becoming a steadily deeper shade of red as he read Haeggman's front-page story.

The headline across the top blared: "POLICE SET MANIAC LOOSE." Immediately below was the photo of Carl Stillen, labeled "GRENDEL???"

Stillen was depicted as the prime suspect in the hunt for the self-proclaimed cannibal, Grendel. It described how he'd been brought in by the police, questioned and released. Then, apparently fearing arrest, Stillen had fled, and the police had to appeal to the media and the public to help recover a man they'd described as "dangerous and possibly armed." The story boiled down to a denunciation of the police as bumbling idiots.

Ekman was singled-out by name as the chief idiot. The story placed the blame indirectly on him for any killings by Grendel.

Crumpling the paper, he got up and threw it in the waste bin. I'd like to flush it down the toilet, where it really belongs, he thought.

The phone rang. The caller ID said it was another newspaper. He let it ring. This was supposed to be a day to think of the next steps. But first, he needed to try and relax a little. It was impossible. Whoever was leaking these stories was trying, fairly successfully, to destroy the reputation it'd taken him thirty years of hard work to build. Ekman had had to develop a thick skin over that time, but he'd never had to deal with a concerted effort to discredit him.

66

~~~~~~

Review

In his study he paced the length of the room and back again. If I keep this up, he thought, I'll wear out the rug. But nervous energy kept him walking as he tried to look at the case from the very beginning.

From a deranged letter threatening violence, it'd grown into at least one definite murder, with possibly as many as four others, if he included the two thieves. The sole suspects were Lindfors, and Stillen, who'd now taken off. Was the paper's story right? Was Stillen Grendel?

Although there was no hard evidence, he was linked to Lindfors, and through her to the vanished men. Lindfors was connected to Westberg, and the computer they'd found in the storage room originated the e-mails, photos and chess games tying her to the other two missing men. Without the computer they had only the evidence on the men's machines. But everything found on the computer could have been created by someone posing as Lindfors. And inspecting her car had turned up nothing.

All right, Ekman thought, back to basics. Lindfors was intimately involved with Rodger Westberg, his father, and Stillen. That'd been proven. And Grendel was not simply a crank letter writer; he existed and was a killer. That also had been proven. But what Ekman had seen of

Stillen didn't convince him he could be Grendel. Rystrom was right: he wasn't smart enough.

Let's assume for argument's sake, he thought, that Stillen was running now because he was afraid of being framed, not because he was a murderer. That meant that either Lindfors was Grendel, or there was somebody else out there. However, it couldn't be Lindfors, because DNA from the original letter had shown it was a man. The only conclusion this train of thought led to was that Grendel was an unknown person who'd tried to implicate Lindfors by planting the computer they'd uncovered, and through her, make it appear that Stillen was Grendel.

If that were true, they were both innocent of murder, even if they'd been scheming to get their hands on Westberg's money. They hadn't done anything illegal, although their ethics and morality were questionable. But that wasn't his concern.

Why had all of this been happening? Jarl had said it was aimed at him personally. But why? They'd checked for past enemies and come up empty, but they could have overlooked something. The way ahead could lie through his own past. Grendel was a trickster, Karlsson had warned, and he'd succeeded in leading them down a blind alley. If they could just find a motive, everything would become clear. He needed to run over his thinking with Rystrom to see if he agreed.

He was pleased with his analysis. Starting tomorrow, working with Rystrom and Holm, they'd go back over his old cases in depth.

67

Rook Capture

It was early afternoon, and Ekman was finishing a ham sandwich on dark brown bread, while he drank an ale. On the table beside him was a new history of Catherine the Great. He was well into the first chapter when the phone rang. He put down his sandwich and checked the caller ID. It was Disa.

She sounded frantic. Her words came tumbling out, falling over themselves. "Thank God, I found you in, Walther. Thank God."

Ekman was instantly alert. "Disa, calm down and slowly tell me what's the matter." Something has happened to the children, he thought.

"It's Erick. He's disappeared."

A hard knot formed in Ekman's stomach. This couldn't be happening. Not to his son. Take your own advice, Ekman, he thought; stay calm and don't jump to conclusions. This may be nothing. But in the back of his mind, a sickening fear had slithered into view.

"When did you last see him, Disa?"

"He went for what he said would be a short walk after breakfast and hasn't come back. That was four hours ago. He knew lunch would be waiting. It's totally unlike him. I kept calling his mobile, but there was no answer. He always answers when I call. Then I asked a neighbor to sit with the girls and went out looking for him along the route he usually took. There was no sign of him. I became so worried I called the police. They didn't seem concerned. They said it was much too soon to treat him as a missing person. Walther, what should I do?"

"Stay at home, Disa. I'm leaving now. I'll be with you in an hour. I'll talk to the Halmstad police about organizing a search. Erick may have taken a different route and become ill. We'll find him. Try not to worry." But Ekman didn't really believe what he was telling her. He was terribly afraid and had started to break into a cold sweat.

Ekman phoned the duty officer in Halmstad, identified himself, and explained the situation. They needed to organize an immediate search.

Since it was a Sunday, the sergeant said, they were short staffed. They would begin a search first thing Monday.

"Let me make myself clear, Sergeant; this is not just a personal problem. My son's disappearance may be directly related to a major investigation already underway." Ekman had a hard time keeping his voice steady. He wanted to shout at this bureaucratic imbecile who couldn't, or wouldn't, understand the dire nature of the situation.

"Perhaps you should speak with our superintendent, sir," the sergeant said. "I'll call right now and ask Super to call you back, if you'll give me the number you'll be at." Ekman gave him his home and mobile numbers as his fingers drummed a tattoo on the table.

He'd put on his coat and was heading for the garage when the phone rang. He didn't recognize the number, but picked up in the hope it was the Halmstad officer.

"Ekman."

"This is Gunnel Iversen," a woman's voice replied. "I'm superintendent in Halmstad. How can I help you, Herr Ekman?"

He carefully explained that his son had gone inexplicably missing and that his disappearance might be linked to the Grendel investigation. "We need to begin an immediate search, Fru Iversen."

"I see," she said. "All right. We'll have to call people in from home. It will take a little while, but we should be able to organize a search in the next few hours."

It wasn't soon enough for Ekman, but there was no use protesting. He realized she was doing the best she could.

"I'll be in Halmstad, at my son's home, in an hour." He gave her the address and phone number. "Please call me there when your people are ready and I'll come to your headquarters to join you."

"I'll be there myself. I look forward to meeting you, Herr Ekman. And please," she added in a sympathetic tone, "try not to worry about your son. He's probably fine."

It was the sort of thing Ekman had said many times to frantic parents when a child was missing. He didn't believe it for a minute, but it was kind of her to say it.

"Thanks, Fru Iversen. I'm leaving now."

It was a clear, cold day. On the drive to Halmstad, he looked at the speedometer and saw he was well over the speed limit on the E4, but didn't care. Ekman's mind was occupied with scenarios of what could have happened to Erick. He might have taken a different route, fallen ill, and lapsed into unconsciousness. Or he might have been assaulted, robbed of his identification, and knocked out. He could still be lying there, or someone might have found him, and taken him to a hospital.

These were the same possibilities they'd explored in the Westberg disappearance, without results. The one scenario he tried, without success, not to think about involved Grendel.

Ekman dreaded telling Ingbritt what was happening, but she wouldn't forgive him if he didn't let her know. He reached for his mobile and called her.

"Yes, I'm on my way to Halmstad now. The police there are organizing a search and I'll join them."

"Walther, does this have anything to do with that terrible case you're working on?"

"There's no reason to think so." He hoped against hope he wasn't lying to her. "Try not to worry. I'll let you know as soon as there's news."

"I'm coming down there right away to be with Disa."

"No. Please don't. It's important you stay where you are. As much as I want to have you with me, I must know you're safe so I can focus on finding Erick."

"Then your case may be involved?"

He could never fool her. "It's possible, but unlikely."

She was silent for a moment. "Walther, I'm scared." Her voice was trembling.

"So am I. I'll call you the minute I know anything."

After what seemed an interminable time, but was only fifty minutes, he pulled up in front of Erick's house. Disa had been watching for him and opened the door as he hurried up the front steps. He reached out to hug her and she clung to him for a moment.

"I'm so glad you're here. I've been going out of my mind with worry. Where could he be? Where?"

"Disa, let's go in and sit down. There are some questions I need answered. It will help with the search."

She led the way into the living room and they sat down on the couch. He turned to face her. She'd been crying and her normally ruddy face was pale and tear streaked.

~ 321 ~

"When did Erick leave for his walk?"

"It was eight forty-five exactly. I remember looking at the clock."

"How long was it before you began to worry?"

"He said it would be a short walk. I thought that meant less than an hour. When he hadn't come home by eleven, and didn't answer his mobile, I decided to go find him. I took the girls to my next-door neighbor, Fru Crabo, who looks after them sometimes when we're away. When Erick and I travel . . ." She started to cry again.

"Then you went looking for him?"

"Yes. I followed his usual route, but he wasn't anywhere. That's when I came home and first called the police. When they wouldn't help, I called you."

"That was around one." He checked his watch; it was now two twenty.

"Do you have a local street map?"

"It's here somewhere," she said, looking about as though the map might materialize in front of them. Getting up, she went to a desk in the corner and, pulling open a drawer, rummaged about. "Here it is," she said, unfolding it and spreading it out on the low coffee table in front of Ekman.

Taking out a pen and handing it to her, Ekman said, "Here, why don't you mark his route for me."

She bent over the map and carefully traced Erick's usual path. Ekman saw it ran partly along some local streets, through a small park, and then down the beach.

"This will be very helpful to the search party," he said, folding the map and putting it in his jacket pocket.

"Has Erick seemed different lately? Or have any unusual things happened recently?"

She thought for a moment. "Erick has been his usual self." She hesitated. "But a month ago something strange did happen. We'd agreed not to mention it when you and

Ingbritt visited because we didn't want to trouble you with such a minor thing. We just reported it to the local police."

Ekman's body tensed. "What happened?"

"Someone broke into the house when we were out. The back door had been pried open. That's how we noticed it."

"Was anything taken?" Ekman dreaded the answer he'd already guessed at.

"That's the strangest part: only a family photo that was on the desk."

It fit the pattern, confirming his worst fears. It was Grendel. Now he knew the search would probably prove fruitless. Erick was gone. His face had turned ashen and his hands clenched so tightly his fingernails dug into his palms.

Disa looked at him with eyes wide with concern. "Are you all right, Walther? Let me get you some water," she said, jumping up and going to the kitchen. She came back in a moment with a glass.

"Here, drink this, you'll feel better."

He took the glass with a hand they both saw was shaking, and gulped down half the water. Get control of yourself, Ekman, he thought. If there's any chance of finding Erick, it's up to you.

"Do you know how to access Erick's computer? I'd like to check it."

Disa looked at him with surprise. "Yes, of course. It's in his study." She got up and he followed her down the hall to the study that looked out on the back of the house.

Booting up the computer, she entered the password.

"This may take some time, Disa," Ekman said, and added, although he had no appetite: "Why don't you fix us a sandwich. I'm starving." He looked after her as she left. He wanted her out of the room while he found out if Erick had been playing chess and who he'd been playing against.

Erick had been playing, and for the last two months his opponent had usually been Stina Lindfors. Her picture came up beside the chessboard's image. There were also e-mails tacked alongside. She'd been flirting with Erick. But his replies had been very cool; he'd actively discouraged her. Ekman was relieved: Erick had no plans to meet her. He shut down the computer and got up as Disa came back into the room.

"Do you want to eat now, Walther? The sandwiches are ready."

"Yes, that's fine, Disa." They went across the hall to the large, sun-filled kitchen.

"Did you find anything helpful on the computer?" she asked as they sat down across from one another at a table looking out on the backyard.

"No, nothing of interest," Ekman replied, his lie masked by a small bite of the ham and cheese sandwich. He took a sip of the beer she'd put beside his plate.

"Should I go with you to the police station to help with the search?"

"That won't be necessary. I have the map you drew. Why don't you get the girls? They need to be reassured everything will be fine," he said, although he knew now all their lives would never be the same.

"I'll do that then. They were worried. Even though I didn't tell them Erick was missing, they knew something was wrong."

The phone rang. Disa jumped up and almost ran across the kitchen to the wall phone. Maybe it was Erick. She listened for a moment, turned to Ekman and said in a despondent voice, "It's for you."

Gunnel Iversen was on the phone. "We're ready to begin the search," she said.

"Give me the address of your headquarters."

"Norra Kallegatan 3. Do you know how to get here?"

"I have a map. I'll be there in five minutes."

Ekman kissed Disa on the cheek. "Try not to worry; for the girls' sakes. I'll call as soon as I know something."

"I can't stop worrying. You're right. I need to be calm for the girls."

68

Iversen's Search

Ekman pulled up in front of Halmstad police headquarters and walked quickly up the front steps. Pushing
open the heavy glass door, he went to the front desk and
asked for Iversen, showing his identification to the uniformed sergeant.

"Yes, sir. The Super is in her office down the hall, last
door on the right."

Gunnel Iversen was a tall, thin woman of fifty with
mixed blonde and gray hair cut closely around her face.
She was casually dressed in a black turtleneck and jeans
with knee-high boots. When she looked at Ekman, her
light gray eyes had a piercing intensity. This was the way
she looks at everyone, thought Ekman.

She came forward around her desk in the small office
to shake his hand.

"My officers are in our assembly room, Herr Ekman.
I've called in eight constables plus two sergeants and an
inspector. My thinking is to organize them into four two-
person teams to cover the route your son took, and have
the sergeants speak with neighbors and other people in
the area. The inspector will be checking with our local
hospital and emergency clinics to see if anyone with his
description has been brought in. Does that sound about
right to you?"

"Yes, certainly. I appreciate your quick response, Fru Iversen. I have a picture of Erick here," Ekman said, taking it out of his wallet. "And here is a map. His usual path is marked. Perhaps these could be enlarged and copied."

"Of course." She picked up the phone and called. In a moment, a uniformed constable knocked and entered. She handed her the photo and map, telling her what was needed.

Turning to Ekman, she asked, "Do you know if your son has a smartphone?"

"I assume so. Why do you want to know? He's not answering."

"The newer ones have a built-in GPS. If the phone is turned on, it could pinpoint his location."

"I'll find out," Ekman said, calling Disa. He spoke with her for a minute, and then looked at Iversen.

"His phone was a recent model Nokia from Nordisk Mobiltelefon. She doesn't know if it has GPS."

"It probably does. Let's see if we can use it. You have his number?"

Ekman gave it to her and then sat down heavily in a guest chair as Iversen consulted her computer and then began a series of calls to phone company officials.

After ten minutes of making explanations and getting home phone numbers, she said to Ekman apologetically, "It's Sunday and difficult to reach anyone with authority to try and locate the phone. This may take some time. We won't wait, but will start the search now."

Ekman pulled himself out of the chair. His mind was foggy, he couldn't focus on what was needed and was glad to leave everything in Iversen's efficient hands.

The officers in the assembly room across the hall from Iversen's office were drinking coffee and muttering about having their Sunday ruined for some unknown reason. The talking broke off abruptly as Iversen and Ekman came in.

"Thank you all for coming in so quickly on a Sunday. I apologize for keeping you waiting. This is Chief Superintendent Ekman of Weltenborg. This emergency involves his son, Erick, and the Grendel case he's been investigating that you've all been hearing about. I'll let him explain," she said, as Ekman stepped forward.

"I want to add my sincere thanks," Ekman said, looking around the room. "Briefly, what's happened is that there is substantial reason to think my son, Erick, a Halmstad physician, has been kidnapped or assaulted by the person called Grendel who's wanted in connection with one known murder, and probably at least two others. Erick has been missing since about ten this morning. His disappearance is like that in the three instances I just mentioned. My hope is that by moving quickly we may be able to pick up a trail."

Iversen explained the plan she'd outlined to Ekman and handed out copies of Erick's photo, his phone number, and the route map, assigning teams to different sections of his path.

"As soon as you find anything at all, call me. Herr Ekman and I will be waiting."

She and Ekman had settled in her office. They'd lapsed into silence as they sipped cups of freshly brewed coffee. It had been more than half an hour since the teams left and there'd been no word. Iversen's desk phone rang and she grabbed at it.

"Yes, thanks for your help," she said as she jotted down the information.

"That was the phone company. They've given us the location of your son's phone. It's in the wooded area the third team has been searching." She checked her list of the team members' phones and called.

"The phone's somewhere right near the edge of the woods at the junction of Wrangelsgatan and Enslovsgatan. Ring the number to help locate it. Call me back the moment you find anything."

Ekman desperately hoped Erick would be found with the phone; unconscious perhaps, but still alive. Five minutes passed. To Ekman it seemed like five hours.

Iversen's phone rang. "Yes, okay. Keep on with the search."

"They've found the phone, but not your son," she said to Ekman in a soft voice. He could barely bring himself to speak. He was afraid he'd lose all control.

"We haven't heard from your inspector yet," he finally brought himself to say in a husky, strained voice. Maybe Erick's been taken to a hospital, he thought, focusing on the last best alternative. As if in answer to his thought, the inspector called and Iversen listened for a minute.

"He's checked every medical facility." She paused. "No one of Erick's description has been brought in."

That's it then, thought Ekman. Unless they found him somewhere along the route, he was gone. With every passing minute, discovering Erick grew less likely. His last hope was that someone had seen something that would give them a lead.

Two hours later, the search party had gone over the entire route thoroughly, looking down alleys, and through scrub in the park. The inspector had joined the two sergeants in knocking on house doors. They'd found an elderly man who lived nearby. He'd been walking his dog that morning and saw someone who looked like Erick entering the park. It was the only sighting they'd been able to come up with.

Ekman couldn't think of what else to do. His mind refused to function properly. All he could do was sit slumped in the chair in Iversen's office, overcome by fear. Iversen, however, was not giving up.

"We'll expand the search," she said to Ekman. "Let's assume he took a somewhat different route that still leads to where his phone was found." She called the inspector, explaining what she wanted.

"It will be all right," she said quietly. Ekman just looked at her with dull eyes. She turned away and busied herself with some papers on her desk.

Another two hours passed and then the phone rang, sounding shrilly in the confines of the silent office. It was the inspector in charge of the search teams.

"Yes," said Iversen. "I understand. Thank you, and give my thanks to the team members. Everyone can go home now. I'll have Dr. Ekman's photo given to the media this evening."

She turned to Ekman. There was no need to explain; he'd been listening intently to her brief conversation.

"Is there anything else we can do, Herr Ekman?" she asked.

He shook his head. There was nothing more to be done now. With difficulty he pulled himself to his feet.

"Thank you, Fru Iversen, for all you and your people have done. Please give them my personal regards." It was an effort for him to speak. His voice was shaking.

"I must see my daughter-in-law and the grand-children." His palm was damp as he shook her hand and then stumbled out of her office as though through a dense fog.

69

~~~~~

Reaction

He couldn't remember later how he found his way back to Erick's. As he pulled up, he saw a blue Volvo parked in front. It was Ingbritt's. He was briefly angry that she hadn't listened to him, but grateful that she was there.

They'd heard him drive up. Ingbritt and Disa were standing in the doorway as he came up the steps. One look at his pale, drawn face and downcast eyes and they knew Erick hadn't been found. Ingbritt and he hugged silently for a long moment.

Seated in the living room, he explained to them what had been done. Only Erick's phone had been found. Apart from the man who saw him entering the park, they'd discovered no witnesses so far.

"But there may be others who have seen something," Ekman said. "Erick's photo is being given to the media. It should be on television tonight and in tomorrow's papers. Reporters will try to contact you, Disa. Do you want to speak with them?"

"If it will help find Erick, of course. Do you think Grendel took him?" she asked in a cracked voice.

"We don't know," he replied, although every instinct told him it was Grendel.

They all put on brave faces for the children over a late dinner the adults just picked at, but the two girls sensed something was wrong.

"Will Pappa be home soon from his business trip?" the elder asked.

"We don't know exactly when, dear," answered Ingbritt. Disa was too upset to speak. Ekman remained silent, his eyes fixed on his plate.

Lying in the guest room at Erick's, Ingbritt and Ekman held hands under the covers.

"I was angry earlier when I saw you hadn't listened to me. Now I'm glad you didn't."

"I don't know how we'll get through this, but it will be together," she answered. "You think Erick is dead, don't you?" Her voice broke and she started to cry quietly. Ekman reached out and stroked her hair.

"I don't want to say it, but that's the likelihood." He stifled a sob. "It's my fault."

"How can you believe that, Walther? No one can predict what an insane person will do."

"His victims have all been men. And somehow all of this is related to me. I should have guessed, and protected Erick by getting him out of the way."

"That's ridiculous. Walther Ekman, you're not infallible, not God. Don't take this guilt on yourself." She paused, and said with sudden insight, "It's what Grendel wants you to do."

Ekman was quiet as he mulled this over. "You're right. This is my punishment. First, my reputation, then our son. Jarl warned me it would be personal. I didn't realize how much. And the pain this has caused you, Disa and the girls. That's also been calculated. This is all about revenge. But what have I ever done to deserve this?" He couldn't believe that Carl Stillen was behind this. His friendly interview with him couldn't possibly be a reason for Erick's disappearance.

A ferocious rage was building in Ekman, pushing aside the grief, and making it somehow easier to deal with. So Grendel wants revenge. He'll discover what payback is really like when I find him.

70

~

Out

*M*onday, *October 24.* Ekman had an early breakfast and, leaving Ingbritt to look after Disa and the grandchildren, headed back to Weltenborg. Dark clouds had moved in and snow had started to fall. The first heavy storm of the season was predicted.

At six fifteen there were few headlights on the road. He was going well over the speed limit, even in the increasingly slick conditions, but didn't notice. As he came into the city, thick flakes had begun to swirl against the windshield in earnest. By the time he pulled into the garage at headquarters, snow was coming down steadily.

Holm looked up from the newspaper on his desk. Ekman could see deep sympathy in his eyes.

"Chief, I don't know what to say. I . . . we, Gerdi and I . . . were incredibly shocked when we learned on TV about your son's disappearance. I don't know whether you've seen the newspaper yet. It's on the front page," Holm said, holding up the one he'd been reading.

The headline read, "Chief Superintendent's Son Missing," directly above facing photos of Ekman and Erick. The byline was Haeggman's.

Ekman's first instinct was to grab the paper and crumple it into a ball. He steadied himself and said in a calm voice, "Thanks, Enar. If you're finished, I'd like to look at it." Holm handed the paper to him, and Ekman went into his office, closing the door behind him.

Haeggman's story was based on interviews with the Halmstad police. Gunnel Iversen was quoted, as well as unnamed "police sources." Ekman himself "could not be reached for comment." There were a few initial words of false sympathy for Ekman and his family. His request for an immediate search for his son was underscored, and readers looking for more information were referred to yesterday's story about the hunt for Carl Stillen. The implication was that Ekman's bungling had now led to his own son's kidnapping and possible murder.

He was made to seem worse than just an inept police officer. His evident stupidity had made him a dangerous risk not only to his own family, but to the public. The article was effectively a call for him to be replaced.

Maybe the bastard is right, Ekman thought. Maybe I am incompetent and should just resign. But not yet. Not until I find Grendel.

At seven forty-five, Holm knocked and put his head around the door. "The commissioner would like to see you right away."

Ekman was surprised. Norlander was never in the office before nine.

"I may be late for the eight o'clock. I'll be down as soon as I can. No doubt Norlander has been reading this trash, too," he said, pointing at the paper on his desk.

Norlander was standing, talking with Garth Rystrom, when Ekman knocked and entered. They both stopped speaking and turned to face him. Norlander came forward with his hand extended.

"Walther, Garth and I were just saying how horrified we were to learn what happened yesterday. Words seem meaningless. Please know that our thoughts are with you and your family."

Rystrom didn't say anything. He just went up to Ekman and, looking into his anguished eyes and tight-lipped face, clasped his hand in both of his.

"Let's sit down," said Norlander, leading the way to the seating area. He took an armchair, while they sat together on the leather couch.

"Walther, what I have to say has nothing to do with the articles in *Sydsvenska Nyheter*. Please believe that. But yesterday's events have to change the way the Grendel investigation is conducted. I've spoken with Superintendent Iversen and she agrees that your son's disappearance is part of our original investigation.

"You're too emotionally involved now to continue to lead, or participate, in the case. This is the time for you to be with your family. They need you. I've asked Garth to take over the investigation and he's kindly consented, even though I know he's longing to get back to his family in Stockholm." Norlander looked at the expressionless Rystrom as he said this.

Ekman had been expecting something like this. When an officer became personally involved in a case, it was standard procedure to relieve him. But he resented it anyway. It would look to the outside world as if Haeggman were right and he'd been removed for incompetence. It was hard to bear.

"I understand, Commissioner." He turned to Rystrom. "And you've picked the best possible man to head the team. I'd like to meet briefly with them . . . they're waiting for us now . . . to explain the change."

"Certainly, Walther. Starting right after that, I want you to take thirty days of administrative leave . . . more if you need it . . . so you can help your family through this awful time."

Ekman appreciated Norlander's doing this, but couldn't help feeling anyway that he was being diplomatically shunted aside.

"Thank you, Commissioner. I appreciate your consideration," he said with effort, accepting the inevitable.

Norlander rose and walked with them to the door. "Oh, Walther. Olov asked that you see him."

Outside, Ekman said, "Garth, this won't take long, and then we'll get to the meeting."

Ekman went down the hall, knocked on Malmer's door, and went in.

"You wanted to see me?" The bastard wants to give me paperwork to fill out for this leave, he thought.

To his astonishment, Malmer got up and came around his desk toward him. He stood in front of Ekman, and looking up at his face, took his hand.

"Walther, I know we haven't gotten along well, but this goes far beyond any differences we've had. I just want to tell you how profoundly sorry I am for your terrible loss. I have a son, too, and if anything happened to him, I don't know what I'd do . . . Be brave. I'll be praying for you and your family."

Ekman was speechless. He just looked down at Malmer, amazed. My God, he thought, he's a real human being after all. I didn't even know he had a son. I've misjudged him.

"Thank you, Olov," he finally got out.

"Don't think about the paperwork. I'll take care of everything," Malmer said. "Just go home."

Ekman nodded and went out. Sometimes, he thought, people can totally surprise you. I've become too damned sure I'm always right about them.

When Ekman and Rystrom came into the conference room, the others were seated, waiting for them. Rystrom sat down, and Ekman took his usual place at the head of the table.

Before he could say anything, Holm stood up.

"Chief, the others have asked me to speak for them, as well as myself. What has happened is horrible. We want you to know how much we all feel for you and your family. We'll never rest until Grendel is found. None of us will take a day off until we bring him in. This is our personal commitment to you." He sat down.

"Thank you, Enar, and thank all of you, everyone," Ekman said, his lips trembling. He was overcome by emotion and couldn't say any more for a long moment.

"This is my last meeting with you. Because I've now become personally involved, I mustn't be part of the investigation. The commissioner has asked Garth Rystrom to take over. I know each of you will do your best for him, as you have for me."

Turning to Rystrom, he said, "My only suggestion is that since it's now clear how focused on me the case has become, there may be a motive buried in my old cases. Enar, I know you already did this, but I think the others should also take a look at them. I'm going on leave and won't be back for at least a month. Good luck to each of you."

He got up and went around the table; silently shaking hands with Holm first, he held onto his hand, looking him in the eyes, and then did the same with each of the others. When he got to Gerdi Vinter, she reached up and gave him a long hug. There were tears streaming down her cheeks, which she didn't bother to brush away.

Ekman had spent an hour clearing out his in-box. Now he looked around his office for a last time before putting on his hat and coat and taking the elevator to the garage. He felt that a chapter of his life had closed forever. There was a hollowness inside him where Erick had been that was filled with grief at his unalterable absence. And there was a deepening rage at the person who had taken Erick away.

71

~~~~~~

Check

The snow had gotten much heavier by the time he got home and was forecast to get worse. The silence in the house was oppressive. He couldn't sit down and paced from room to room. I've got to get hold of myself, he thought, or I'll be useless to Ingbritt and everyone else. They're counting on me to bear up. He reached for the phone and called her.

"Yes, I'm home now for a good month. How long will you be with Disa? I understand. This storm is supposed to clear out by tomorrow. I want to come down and be with you. There's no point in my being here. I'll close up the house and we'll stay with her as long as she needs us. Okay, I'll see you tomorrow morning. I love you, too."

He'd slapped some cheese on a piece of bread for lunch and had just finished it when the doorbell rang. Who the hell can that be in this weather? he thought. A package delivery, perhaps? Maybe Ingbritt ordered something.

He went to the front door, and opening it, was astonished to see Froken Sundquist from Edvardsson's office. The snow-laden wind was whipping around her, blowing her long brown hair about her face.

She brushed the hair away and said, "Herr Ekman, Fru Edvardsson wants to see you right away. She heard that you were at home. Because the weather is so bad, and she knew I have a four-wheel drive, she asked me to come and get you." Backed into the driveway was a white van facing the street.

Ekman wondered what on earth Malin was thinking. Perhaps she felt the need to offer her condolences personally, or maybe it was something about the case she wanted to talk about.

"Please come in, Froken Sundquist. I appreciate your coming to get me, but it really wasn't necessary. I could have managed." He closed the door behind her.

"I'll just get my coat and hat," he said, turning his back on her, and going to the hall closet to get his suit jacket and overcoat.

When he'd put them on, he turned around, and stared with bewilderment at the pistol in her hand aimed at him.

"Surprise, surprise," she said with a crooked smile.

He immediately understood. "You're Grendel's accomplice. You delivered the briefcase. And you're the source of the leaks."

"You've finally figured it out. You've been rather slow. It's been a bit of a disappointment."

"What are you going to do?"

"Why, I'm going to take you to see your son, of course. But first you're going to reach very slowly into your jacket, and with your thumb and forefinger take out your gun and give it to me. If you try anything, I'll shoot you right here. Then you won't discover what this is all about, or see your son. And your wife will come home to find you dead in the hall. We don't want her to get a nasty shock like that, do we?"

Ekman believed her. She'd said exactly the things that persuaded him not to simply lunge at her. He reached into his jacket, carefully with two fingers took out his gun from the holster on his belt, and dropped it into her outstretched hand. She slipped it into her coat pocket.

"That was smart. Now take out your mobile and give it to me."

Ekman took it out and held it out to her. She pocketed it, and backed away from him.

"Good. I think we're ready to begin our little journey. Open the door and go ahead of me."

Ekman did as she wanted, and when they were outside, with a blustery wind swirling the snow around them, saw her shut the door.

"Go to the van. You'll ride in the back," she said activating the van's sliding side door with a remote.

Ekman got in the back of the van and sat on the bench seat as she closed the door with the remote. Looking around, he saw the van had been customized. There were no inside door handles, side or rear windows, only metal walls. Between the rear bench and the front seats was a heavy steel grille running from roof to floor and riveted to the side walls. He was in a prison.

∞ ∞ ∞

A block away, Holm watched through binoculars as the van slowly pulled into the street. He and Vinter had been sitting there in an unmarked car since Ekman came home.

At that morning's meeting, Rystrom had followed Ekman's suggestion and assigned the others to a page-by-page search through Ekman's old cases, going back twenty years. Then he'd asked Holm and Vinter to stay behind.

"The pace of abductions has speeded up and become increasingly personal. With his son's disappearance, the killer's focus now has to be on Ekman himself. I think he's in real danger. I want the two of you to stake out his house. Be very careful. He mustn't see you. We're going to keep a twenty-four-hour watch on him."

Vinter protested, "Shouldn't we get him to a safe house instead? Forgive me for saying it, Super, but if he's in such danger, it feels like we're using him as bait for Grendel."

Rystrom's expression had become fixed as he stared at her. "Walther Ekman is an old and dear friend. How can you think I would do such a thing? Listen to me, knowing him, he would never agree to go into hiding, especially from someone who has no doubt just killed his son. That's not the man I know. And he also would never agree to be kept under constant surveillance. So all we can do is quietly protect him. That's your assignment. After six hours, you'll be relieved and two of the others will take over."

As they stood up, Rystrom said, "If anything suspicious happens, anything at all, you're to call for backup immediately. There's no place for personal heroics. Is that understood?" He looked grim, then smiled at them. "I care about you, too."

They'd watched as the van pulled up and a woman had gone to Ekman's door. "It's probably a friend offering condolences," said Vinter.

But when Ekman came out a few minutes later, trailed by the woman, and climbed into the back of the van while she got in the driver's seat, they'd become alarmed.

Holm picked up his phone and called Rystrom. "It looked really strange to us, Super. Because of the snow I can't be sure, but she had something in her hand. It could have been a gun. We need backup right away. We're going to follow the van and will let you know where we are."

"For God's sake be careful not to let her see you. If she's Grendel's accomplice, she might just kill Ekman in the van."

"Understood. We're heading south on Brunnvagen."

"I've got a SWAT team standing by. They should catch up with you in less than thirty minutes."

∽ ∽ ∽

Ekman leaned forward and spoke to Sundquist through the grille.

"Why are you helping Grendel? Don't you know he's deranged, a serial killer?"

"Of course, I know," she replied, not looking back at him, keeping her eyes on the road.

"Are you in love with him?" Ekman was desperately trying to establish some sort of rapport with her.

"Now you're getting personal. But yes, I'm madly in love with him." Looking at her expression in profile, Ekman saw she was grinning broadly.

"When did you first meet him?"

"Years ago," she replied. "You'll learn everything when we get there."

"Where are you taking me?"

"To see your son."

"Is it far?"

"Not at all. We'll be there in fifteen minutes. Why don't you shut up, sit back, and enjoy the ride."

Ekman had been watching the turns. Right on Brigadgatan, and after what seemed like four kilometers, left on Alvsborgatan for five minutes, then right on Laroverksgatan.

∽ ∽ ∽

Holm was having trouble following the white van in the blinding snow. The wind had picked up. The wipers were going furiously, but the windshield was smearing and ice was forming at the corners.

"She's getting too far ahead of us, Enar," Vinter said.

"I'm losing traction in this damn snow. I'm going as fast as I dare."

The white van seemed about to disappear in the storm.

Vinter called Rystrom. "We've losing them. We're at Stampgatan and Eskilsgatan."

"The SWAT team will be with you in twenty minutes. If his phone is on, I'll see if we can get a GPS fix on their location."

∞ ∞ ∞

Her last turn was onto Strombergs Vag. She's heading for the industrial park, Ekman thought. Once in the park, with its row after row of identical warehouses, Ekman lost track in the storm of how many turns she'd made.

72

Grendel's Gambit

The van pulled up in front of a tall, steel door that she opened with a remote. Driving into the brightly lit garage, she parked beside a silver Volvo sedan, and using the remote again, closed the garage door. Getting out of the van she went to concrete steps leading up to a loading platform that ran the length of the semitruck-sized garage. At the top of the stairs was a wide metal roll-down door she unlocked and pulled up, reaching inside to turn on overhead fluorescents.

Going back down to the van, she took Ekman's gun out of the left pocket of her raincoat and put her own gun in the right. She flicked off the safety on his gun, and pulling back the slide, chambered a round. Stepping away from the van and using the remote, she opened its side door.

"You can come out now, but don't even think about trying anything. As you can see, I have an excellent weapon here: your own gun."

Ekman got down with cautious movements. He didn't want to alarm her and get shot.

"Go up the steps, slowly, ahead of me, and stop."

He did exactly as she'd told him, pausing at the top of the short flight of steps, to look back at her. She was three steps behind. Maybe I can knock her down now, he thought.

She stopped two steps below him and the muzzle of the gun came up. "You're deciding whether to jump me. If you do you'll die right here, although I won't welcome having to drag your fat body inside. Keep four feet in front of me and go through the door."

As he came into the freezing cold of the meat locker, Ekman shivered. His breath came out in a cloud. Five feet from the front wall, a red cloth curtain had been hung across the width of the room from ceiling to floor. On the far side of the room was a curtain pull.

Sundquist was in the meat locker now, leveling the gun at his heart.

"Where is Grendel?" Ekman asked.

"Right in front of you, Walther," she said, with a triumphant smile.

"But Grendel is a man," he said, astonishment written on his face. "DNA confirmed that."

"You still don't get it," Grendel said, feigning frustration.

And then suddenly, Ekman understood. Grendel was transsexual. It was so complete a transformation, he guessed it had to be surgical.

"I do now. But why did you become a cannibal?"

"I've never been a cannibal. The letter certainly got your attention though, didn't it?"

"Then why these killings?"

"Partly, to leave you a trail, which you certainly took a long time to find. Very disappointing."

"And the other part?"

"It's all about you, Walther. You've finally figured that out, haven't you?"

"But I've never done you any harm," he protested.

"That's where you couldn't be more wrong," Grendel said in a shrill, rising voice. "You killed my father and ruined my life. What I've done is retribution."

"I don't understand. I've never killed anyone."

"You convicted my father and destroyed my family. You sent Bo Anderberg to prison, where he died. Before he was killed, he swore he'd get revenge and I swore I'd carry it out. After he was in prison, my mother divorced him, and married a monster.

"I was only twelve, when he first raped me. My mother knew, but did nothing. She was deathly afraid of him; he beat her mercilessly. He abused me every day for five years, until I finally worked up the courage to run away. The bastard died before I could kill him. But I have you."

"That's horrible, but I had nothing to do with any of that."

"If it weren't for you," Grendel screamed, white-faced with rage, "none of it would have happened. It was your fault. All of it, and everything else that happened. You turned me into a whore. I started with sailors on the Malmö waterfront and ended up with a few rich customers. Then I met Carl. We were together until he left me to go back to that bitch, Lindfors. That was when I decided to get even with all of you at the same time.

"And my plan worked: Stillen and Lindfors became your prime suspects, while I destroyed your reputation."

"What's happened to my son? Where is he?" asked Ekman, trembling from fear, as much as the penetrating cold.

"You want to know where he is? I promised you I'd take you to him, didn't I? Why don't you open the curtain?"

Ekman went to the curtain pull and Grendel followed him.

"Go ahead, do it." He stared at Ekman, watching terror flit across his face as Ekman grasped the pull and opened the curtain with one strong tug.

Seven frozen, cocooned corpses hung in a row in front of him. Their eyes were open and the plastic had been pulled back from their gray faces, revealing the small, dark holes on their foreheads.

The body nearest Ekman was Erick's. Next to him was Carl Stillen, Rodger Westberg, two young boys . . . the thieves . . . then Gustaffson, and Henriksson. The look of horror on Ekman's face at the sight started Grendel laughing in a terrible, high-pitched cackle.

"Satisfied?" Grendel asked.

With a quick movement, Ekman stepped behind Erick's body and with all his might swung it at Grendel. It knocked him down, and the gun skittered across the floor toward Ekman. He scooped it up and stepped around Erick's swaying corpse.

Grendel's own gun had fallen from his coat pocket and his hand seemed to be groping for it.

"Don't move," said Ekman, "or I'll kill you." His voice came out in a harsh rasp.

Pounding began on the garage door and a bullhorn-amplified voice said, "Grendel, the building is surrounded. You can't escape. Let Ekman go and come out with your hands up."

"The cavalry has arrived," said Grendel with a smirk. "I was wondering when they'd get here."

"You expected them?" said Ekman, disbelief etched on his face.

"Oh, yes," replied Grendel. "It's part of my plan, Walther. I never intended to kill you. Why do you think I didn't turn off your phone? I knew they could trace us. Now you can't kill me, as I know you want to, with your friends just outside.

"You'll be a hero, bringing in the 'cannibal killer.' It will help restore your shattered reputation. But why should I want that? You see, Walther, your punishment isn't over. No, not by many years. You have to suffer much more. I'll end up in Karsuddens Hospital for the criminally insane. After ten or twenty years, I'll be released; I'll have 'recovered,' or else I'll escape.

"I don't mind waiting, but you will. I know you have a grandson . . . Johan, right? When I get out he'll end up like these. You'll be old and won't be able to stop me. You've got years to think about what's coming, Walther. That's your final punishment. And after it's all over, I'll just be sent back to the hospital," Grendel said, with a triumphant smile.

"No, not Johan, too," Ekman whispered, and aiming the gun, shot Grendel between the eyes.

Ekman put his gun on the floor. Then he turned to Erick's body. Lifting it with difficulty off the hook, he lowered it slowly to the cold concrete. Ripping away the remaining plastic around Erick's head, he raised him and cradled him in his arms. Ekman's tears fell down his cheeks onto Erick's frozen face as he leaned over and kissed him on the forehead. "Rest in peace, Erick," he murmured, as he gently placed him on the floor. "Rest in peace, my son."

The pounding had increased, and the demands of the voice outside had become more insistent. Ekman went over to Grendel's body and, reaching into the coat pocket, took out his phone. He called Rystrom.

"It's over, Garth. Grendel is dead. I'm coming out. Tell your people not to shoot."

Ekman walked with halting steps out of the meat locker and staggered down the stairs to the garage. Beside the door was a control switch. As the door rose, he stood motionless, arms raised over his head, his figure illuminated in the spotlights' blinding glare.

73

Resignation

Tuesday, October 25. The storm had left a deep blanket of snow covering Stortorget square. It was eleven A.M. and brilliant sunshine was streaming through the windows of the commissioner's office. Ekman was standing in front of Norlander's desk. He'd just handed him his resignation.

He'd made his statement and been released late the previous night, and as soon as the sun rose, Ingbritt had driven home to be with him. He met her at the side door to the garage and clasped her tightly in his arms. Both their faces were wet with tears.

"I almost lost you, too," she said, looking up at him.

"No, Grendel never intended to kill me. He wanted me to suffer. That's why he killed Erick," he said, leading her into the kitchen. She threw her coat over a chair and they sat facing each other as he told her everything that had happened.

"You didn't have a choice, Walther."

"Yes, I did. But I couldn't put Johan at risk. I chose to break my oath as a police officer. I had no right to execute him. He was a human being."

"He was a monster, a mass murderer. And our Erick was one of his victims. I have no pity, no sympathy. And don't you dare have any for that creature." Ingbritt's face had gone white and her eyes had again filled with tears. Ekman had never seen her so ferociously angry.

"Justice was done and another murder prevented, because that's what would have happened. You knew it, and acted the only way you could.

"I'd never forgive you if you hadn't," she said in a whisper.

Ekman took her in his arms and brushed the tears off her cheeks. "I did what I felt I had to. But Ingbritt, please try and understand I can't go on as a police officer. I'm resigning this morning 'for personal reasons.' There's no need for me to bring more grief on this family by telling what actually happened. It will be investigated, but the decision will be justifiable homicide, self-defense."

"Walther, the police have been your entire life. Don't just walk away."

"There you're wrong. You and our family have been my life, and that will go on. It's all I want."

"It's your decision, but I know you, Walther Ekman, you need that work," she said, her voice pleading as she smoothed back his hair.

"My mind's made up. I'm meeting with Norlander this morning."

"Walther, I refuse to accept this resignation," Norlander said, tearing the sheet of paper in half and throwing it in the wastebasket.

"You're obviously terribly depressed about your son, and having to kill Grendel. This is not the time for you to make such a decision. You're still on administrative leave, and will be until the board of inquiry makes its finding. After that I want you to go on vacation for at least a few weeks. Go to some place warm, far away, and recover from all this horror. Then come back here and we'll talk about you resigning."

"Commissioner, I won't change my mind."

"Maybe you won't. We'll see. But you should know I think you're the finest officer we have, and everyone on the force thinks the same. We can't afford to lose you. No, don't say anything, just think about it."

Norlander got up and, coming over to Ekman, took his hand. "Go home, Walther, and rest."

74

Rystrom Explains

In the afternoon, three days after Ekman's parents had hurriedly flown home for Erick's private, family funeral, Garth Rystrom appeared on Ekman's doorstep. It was bitter cold outside and the sky was overcast as Ekman let him in.

Rystrom was shocked by his appearance. Ekman's pallid face was drawn and lines had suddenly appeared that aged him years. Instead of his usual impeccable clothes, he was wearing an old robe over pajamas.

They shook hands without saying anything as they stood in the front hall for a moment. "Ingbritt is asleep . . . finally," Ekman said. "She's had to take pills to rest. It's been absolute hell for her . . . and all of us. My parents could barely stand during the funeral service."

He led Rystrom down the hall to his study.

Ekman wanted to talk about what had happened, but knew he couldn't tell even his friend the entire truth. It would just burden Rystrom. He did want to go over the case, however.

"Please sit down, Garth. Can I get you something?"

"No thanks, I'm fine. The entire team wanted to come with me, but I told them it would be too soon. They'll come by individually later this week, if you feel up to it."

"I'm not an invalid, Garth. Tell them I'd be really pleased to see them."

"You should know I'm heading back to Stockholm at the end of the month. Norlander has decided to take your recommendation. Rapp is being promoted to chief inspector and he'll be handling things after I leave."

"Good. You'll be missed, but he'll be okay."

They sat in silence for a few minutes.

"Have you learned anything more?" asked Ekman.

"A few things. We found a kind of shrine in Grendel's apartment. He'd set up the stolen photos of the victims and their families, and some jewelry, in a corner of his bedroom. We also found bank statements. He was rich. They added up to five million kronor."

"Grendel told me he'd had some wealthy customers when he worked as a prostitute; they must have been very generous. That's how he paid for the van and the . . . warehouse." Ekman couldn't say meat locker. It brought up an image of Erick and those other frozen bodies suspended on hooks. It was seared into his brain and kept coming back, much as he tried to shut it out.

"Those wealthy clients included several well-known politicians he was blackmailing; that's where most of the money came from. We found DVDs he'd made hidden behind a cabinet. They were taken in another apartment we haven't located yet, but I'm betting was in Stockholm.

"We also wondered how he'd gotten the job in Edvardsson's office. By the way, Walther, she'd also very much like to see you. She's beyond shocked, finding out Grendel was sitting in her outer office the whole time, reading your confidential reports. Malin did the usual checks before hiring Grendel, but his forged ID and background story held up.

"We traced Malin's previous receptionist in Malmö. After we applied some pressure, she admitted she'd been deeply in debt and desperate. Grendel, as Sundquist, bribed her to quit and recommend him for the job. He paid her two hundred thousand kronor. She was lucky his obsession was with men and he didn't kill her to make certain she stayed silent."

"He only killed men who must have had a resemblance to the stepfather he hated," Ekman said. "I don't think it was coincidence they looked similar. The two thieves were incidental victims. Perhaps they wouldn't agree to leave town after he paid them off. That was their fatal mistake."

Rystrom nodded agreement. "We went to the bar where Stillen vanished. The bartender noticed a woman who'd come in through the rear entrance and went over to Stillen. They spoke for a few minutes and then left together out the back. And that was Stillen's fatal mistake."

"Grendel must have been tracking Stillen, just as we were," Ekman said. "He decided to revenge himself for being dumped years before, and at the same time, keep us running around searching for Stillen. It fit his game plan to make us think Stillen was Grendel. Just as the special knot he used was intended to add to our suspicions when we learned Stillen had worked in a naval supply store."

"Yes," said Rystrom, "and by making Lindfors appear an accomplice, he revenged himself on her, too. He must have thought it was an absolute gift when she got involved with the Westbergs. It gave her and Stillen the perfect motive for murdering Rodger. He knew this would keep us focused on them."

"Well, Garth, I guess that wraps it up. There will never be another case like this."

"Grendel was a one off, thank God. And thank God you escaped, Walther. It was a close thing. We almost didn't find you. Holm caught a glimpse of the van just as it went into the garage before the GPS was blocked.

When I read in your statement what Grendel said to you, that all the killings were about taking revenge on you for his father, I thought only your quick action saved you from becoming his last victim."

"Yes," said Ekman, "I was lucky." But he knew this was only part of the truth.

75

~~~~~~~~

Endgame

After his conversation with Rystrom, Ekman decided he had to talk with someone besides Ingbritt about what had really happened. The burden of keeping it to himself had become too much.

The next afternoon, he was sitting in Jarl Karlsson's study, with a glass of Renat in his hand. A steady rain was beating against the windows.

He'd told Karlsson the entire story, omitting nothing. Jarl was looking at him with compassion.

"Well, what do you think? Don't spare my feelings."

"It's clear you acted outside the law. There was no charge, no trial, and no sentence. You were Grendel's judge and executioner in a country that has no death penalty. Grendel would no doubt have been found insane and committed to an institution."

"So I set myself above the law I've spent my life trying to uphold."

"Yes. But you should realize that when you did you were playing Grendel's game, and you're still playing it."

"What do you mean?" Ekman asked, his eyebrows raised in surprise.

"Simply that. As Grendel said, he never intended to kill you, but he did want you to kill him. It's part of the pathology of many serial killers that they want to be caught and punished. The rate of killing had speeded up and reached a crescendo. Grendel guessed accurately what would provoke you most: seeing Erick's body and his promise to kill your grandson. He threatened to cut off your posterity, just as his was cut off. He knew this would bring you to the point where you would kill him. He let you knock him down.

"Grendel satisfied his need for punishment, and at the same time, makes you like himself, a killer. In doing so, he also forces you to punish yourself. He makes you suffer from overwhelming guilt, which leads you to destroy your own career and the work that gives you satisfaction.

"As long as you do this, even in death, he wins. This is Grendel's final gambit in his elaborate game: check and mate."

"My God, Jarl, he planned all this to come out the way it has?"

"Yes. I think so. In his own twisted way, Grendel was brilliant. As I said when all this began, what a terrible waste of human life and ability.

"Walther, you have to stop punishing yourself. You have to forgive yourself. Don't let Grendel win."

Two months later, Ekman was again in Norlander's office. They were seated in armchairs facing each other.

"How are you feeling, Walther?"

"Better. I'm not over the grief of losing Erick: I never will be. But the guilt of killing Grendel has lessened."

"It was self-defense. That's what the board found. You have nothing to reproach yourself about."

"It's something I have to deal with."

"But you can deal with it, and will stay on the force," Norlander said. It was a statement, not a question.

"Yes," replied Ekman. "I need to get back to work. Retirement isn't all it's made out to be."

Acknowledgments

Many people's kindnesses and efforts have come together to make this book a reality. My sincere gratitude and thanks are owed: To my friend, Howard Owen, for taking time from his own prizewinning fiction and distinguished journalism career to read the manuscript, suggest changes, and recommend it to his publishers; to Martin and Judith Shepard, copublishers of The Permanent Press, who enthusiastically endorsed this late career effort and improved it with their thoughtful suggestions; to Chris Knopf, their associate publisher, for his perceptive comments; to Barbara Anderson, the most understanding of copy editors, for gently pointing out where improvements were needed; to Lon Kirschner, for his striking cover that conveys Grendel's murderous cruelty with graphic immediacy; and to all the others at The Permanent Press, and its literary agents, who have worked diligently to bring the book before the public; lastly, with affection, to my sister, Barbara, my daughter, Alicia, and my wife, Suzanne, who read the book in early drafts and offered many helpful insights.

And finally, my thanks to you, kind reader, for traveling with Walther Ekman on his troubled quest.

Erik Mauritzson